Ray Brown is a writer and broadcaster. Born in the West Riding he now lives in Leeds. He has broadcast around one hundred features, plays, talks and short stories, all on BBC Radio 4. His short stories have won prizes and his stage plays have toured from Hackney Empire to Nafferton Village Hall, by way of Wetwang, Scarborough and Soho.

For stage:
...is normal!
'...is terrific...'
Trevor Griffiths
'...compelling mixture of understated outrage and pity...'
Arnold Wesker

Living Pretty
'...touching...stirring...powerful...affectingly human...'
The Times

Vacant Possession
'A delightful play, rich in humour and language.'
David Nobbs
also
The Iffy Codex of Nag Hammadi
Nobody Feels Any Pain Numbers 3, 7, 9, and 18
The Yerney Project

Plays for Radio:
In the Absence of Loving
Barnes and Molly
Steinbeck in Avalon

Also, with Alfred Williams, the print biography,
To Live it is to Know it
'Obviously a little classic...'
Colin Wilson
'A spellbinding and confident book...'
Ailsa Cox, The Artful Reporter

For Ros who lived through it
and Marlais and Billy Casper
so they know about it.

I wrote this novel twenty five years ago. In respect for the person I then was I have changed only a few words. However, I think he would appreciate my structural changes. And I am sure he would be pleased that my values are unchanged. He would also recognize that beneath the tinsel and froth of the free market the conditions of today are as dire as those of 1984.

As the old Labour Party charged off to the Right, I stayed put. One day, discussing party politics with novelist Stan Barstow, he said, 'Listen lad, there's plenty of folk can do politics. Get on with writing.' One way or another I've been doing it ever since. Thanks Stan.

Those who helped with this book, directly or indirectly,
are too numerous to mention.
They know who they are.

In All Beginnings

Ray Brown

For Kevin
from Breda

Ray Brown

Published by Armley Press 2015

Cover Design: Ros Marsden

Layout: Ian Dobson

Contact: <info@armleypress.com>

ISBN 0-9554699-6-1

1

The din of police cars and ambulances scratched the night. Simon looked into the mirror above the mantelpiece.   Dusty surfaces caught firelight and undulated.

'Kitchen looks bigger this way.'

Returning from her thoughts, Lindy said nothing. Ghosts moved.

'Like the early days.' He nudged a log with his foot, settled into a wicker chair.

Lindy watched sparks flower and curl upwards leaving amber tracks. She wanted to say her father called them soldiers going to heaven, but firelight and the slow unfolding of time held her silent.

This fire and the fires at Greenham were of the same substance. Fire was the only link between the two worlds in which she lived; fire, and the knowledge, when that knowledge was sought, that she no longer felt at ease in other places. The smell of a classroom would make her sick. All too often, in all too many places, she was frozen by anxiety.

May 3rd, 1984: the city's official May Day. The march was late in starting, they always are. A crowd of lefties, loonies, Labourites, punks and trades unionists swollen by a flood of striking miners and their families. National Union of Mineworkers and pit support group banners were unfurled by men who looked older than their city counterparts and displayed unselfconscious love for kids who darted and clustered like small fish.

For the kids these were special days. Fathers and big brothers no longer came home grey with fatigue. Parents who once snarled in family argument now raised their voices in unison against a common enemy.

At one end of the square was a war memorial, paid for by public subscription after World War I. It had been topped by a finely balanced figure of... Victory or Liberty? Simon couldn't remember. Whichever it was, the authorities had deemed her dangerous (she stood on one foot and might fall, they said). Victory, or Liberty, was banished to a suburban cemetery.

Perhaps her new constituents would be as fired by her message as had been the population of Leeds who, by and large, scurried through their city without even a vestigial recognition that Victory, or Liberty, could be theirs. And that triumphant, romantic figure (brought by sea and canal from Belgium) daringly balanced on the point of one foot, high on the grey cenotaph, was replaced by a Henry Moore reclining woman. Smooth and featureless, she guarded the entrance to the City Art Gallery.

Simon flipped the lens cap and began to take pictures.

SNAP. A stocky man in dark suit and grey pullover, tightly curled white hair, open-mouthed grin. He is making parallel hand movements: fingers curled, elbows jutting, one knee raised. This is an N.U.M. steward pretending to ride a pony. Why? He is stark against a rippling scarlet banner which carries in black letters the name SAVILE COLLIERY.

In less than two years Simon will see a pile of brick and concrete by a canal side, weeds growing among the coal-dusted rubble. He will ask what it was and be told by the man who steers the barge: 'Savile Colliery.' And a sharp blade turns in his guts.

SNAP. Five bandsmen in pale blue blazers and grey flannels, shining black shoes. One bends forward, his hands cupping the light offered by another. A third stands with his arms tight by his side, fists clenched, looking to heaven as a ginger haired bandsman probes the corner of his eye with a handkerchief screwed into a point. About their feet are silver instruments, each standing on its bell: cornet, trombone, euphonium. A young policeman looks on, like a schoolboy in autumn without a conker to his name.

SNAP. SOCIALIST WORKER seller and NEXT STEP seller in classic stance of confrontation. Toe to toe, heads thrust forward, swell of muscles in necks and cheeks, lips drawn back to show teeth. Young MILITANT sellers, short hair and clean shirts, display mocking smiles.

SNAP. Black mongrel, some whippet in him, head poking between owner's pink dungareed legs; small C.N.D. sticker between raised chestnut eyebrows.

SNAP. A line of police, three abreast, swing round the corner from their station under the Town Hall. Stopped traffic. Green double decker bus; passengers, faces turned from tabloids, stare at the demonstration.

SNAP. Lindy with Derek Blythe. Lindy pats a red, yellow and black COAL NOT DOLE sticker to the lapel of the old soldier's belted car-coat. Derek smiles, at his feet his large plastic shopping bag, zipped tight, covered in stickers for one libertarian cause after another, dominated by an image of a snapped missile: *Refuse Cruise*.

The police halt by the war memorial where banners flap in the wind. Waiting for the off. Order is being found. The police stand shoulder to shoulder, unsmiling, darkening the previously colourful scene. A chant goes up: Seig Heil! Seig Heil! Seig Heil! The crowd scats a theme from a TV police series.

The big Yorkshire Region N.U.M. banner jerks forward, carrying its richly coloured images of past presidents, smooth on a rubber wheeled trolley. Kids sit on the metal bogey, waving, trailing their feet.

The colliery band strikes up, drowning derisory chants and songs. And then the miners' singing, drowning the bands.

Here we go! Here we go! Here we go!

The march snakes onto the Headrow and begins its procession round the town.

Simon finds Lindy and Derek as they approach Dortmund Square, where the fascists hang out. Today they are in force: tight faces, tight trousers, high boots; their shaven heads sport NF tattoos and Union Jacks. Today they are sullen, silenced by the miners' physicality.

Boar Lane, the band plays 'Ilkley Moor Bah T'at'. The carnival atmosphere animates the faces of onlookers. Young people, like outrageous flowers with their stickers and badges, rattle multi-coloured buckets as they run crowded pavements. Buckets fill with coin and crumpled notes. Leeds's ever present, bulky, heavy coated women raise their plastic carriers and shout, 'God bless you, lads.' And the miners' wives call back: 'And lasses!'

A hundred yards behind the band, young socialists gambol, singing their song of the moment: '... he's a forelock tugging, arsehole licking, right wing Tory SHIT... Yes he's a dedicated follower of Thatcher!' They are silenced by the threat of arrest. And from yet further back comes another chant, a conga: 'Maggie Thatcher's got one, Ian MacGregor is one... La-la la la! La-la la la!'

The march stops beside the Corn Exchange to allow a build-up of traffic to flow. Lindy runs ahead and lifts her camera.

SNAP. Black leather stretched tight across the enormous buttocks of a motor cycle policeman. Tanned Superintendent rises above the stooped bulk of the cyclist; the crash-helmeted head appears to be buried in the Superintendent's groin. The Superintendent has a dazed look on his face, a young woman wearing the baggy rainbow suit of a clown offers him a bunch of artificial roses.

Simon and Lindy take a short-cut to stand opposite the Town Hall and watch the march retrace its path down the Headrow. The gentle slope foreshortens and compresses. The banners, some large and proud, others waved on sticks. Red balloons jig above the marchers. Sun glistens on silver instruments belting out The Red Flag. COAL NOT DOLE stickers are everywhere.

Beside Simon stands a crumpled man, five foot nothing, flat cap, white silk muffler, no collar on his shirt, waistcoat and jacket undone in the May sunshine. His right leg is twisted and he leans heavily on a thick walking stick. His face is dark and deeply creased, freckled with blue scars. Tears run down the lines of his cheeks and fall to the pavement.

'Simon,' Lindy said, her voice descending in a plea for understanding and support. He turned to her.

'It's the onions.' He pointed the tip of his knife at his watering eyes. Then he dropped the knife and took her in his arms. They clung to each other in silence, neither knowing who was comforter, who comforted.

Lindy's return to Greenham was a source of pain and anxiety to them. Simon knew there was more for Lindy to tell him, but he also knew that she would only tell him when she was ready. Attempts to drag things from her ended in disaster.

At last he said, 'Why won't you talk about it?'

She pulled away from him. 'Do you mean talk about going back or being there?' she asked, not looking at him, a new formality in her voice.

'I don't know. Both. Either. It's the same really. No it's not; one's general, the other's particular.' He slid finely sliced onion into the pan.

10

'Listen, I know that if you feel the need to go back, then you must go back. But you said you were home for a few weeks, and now you're going after a few days. And you've changed, it feels as if part of you stayed there and—'

'That's right. Part of me stayed.'

'Is there someone else?'

'Don't be bloody daft!' She emptied the sink, squeezed the shirt she was washing.

She ran more water. He sliced another onion.

'There are women who've given up everything. There are women who've left jobs and husbands and kids.' She turned off the tap and began to rinse her shirt. 'It's home for some.'

'What about you?'

'I don't know. Something is happening to me. When I'm there I feel I should be here. I miss you. I tell myself I don't fit in there. I don't have a worked through political perspective, I'm not a four square feminist. But when I look at the faces singing in the firelight, red-eyed, mucky some of us... Nobody fits in really, it's just where we have to be. I mean, it's Greenham. I can't turn my back on it.' She began to cry. Simon tried to hold her but she shrugged him off.

'Last week they came and cleaned us out. It's routine.' She wiped her eyes with the back of her hand. 'We saved a few bits and pieces, most went into the dust-carts. Chewed up in front of us. Some women lay down under the lorries. The police were dragging them off. There were soldiers watching from behind the fence. Paratroopers. Somebody started singing.

'A young soldier went off on his own. Walked along the perimeter. I don't know why, I followed him. I think I thought he'd had enough, that he understood.

'He walked until he was out of sight of everybody but me... then he undid his trousers and started to masturbate. I was about twenty yards away. He was watching me.'

Her arms hung loosely, her shoulders hunched. She took a deep breath and straightened her body, ran a hand through her spiky hair. Her face was drained, she stared at Simon as if she was straining to see him. He waited for her to continue.

'I didn't know what to do. He just stood there, laughing at me, his hand jerking. Then he started talking. I couldn't hear what he said. It frightened me.'

Simon stood very still, only his hand moved, tapping the point of his knife against the cutting block.

'I couldn't tell anybody. Only you. Don't ask me if there's anyone else, Simon. Don't ask.' She began to sob and he held her, feeling her body heaving, seeing his tears in her short brown hair.

Later, on the flock mattress which took up one corner of their bedroom, neither felt like sleep. A gibbous moon poured light through the windows and turned the room silver and black. They had shared this room for five years, but now its contents and dimensions were unfamiliar.

'You brought something back with you, I don't know what it is. It clings like smoke.'

'Perhaps that's all it is: smoke. Two weeks in a bender'.

'No. That's not it. I sensed it there.'

'I know. Don't try to put it into words.'

'Don't think I can. Our language doesn't reach into the area we're experiencing.' He rolled onto his side and put his head on her shoulder. 'Do you remember the first time we went? Car packed with blankets, all those thick polystyrene sheets we'd got from somewhere.'

'Eiderdowns, sweaters. And about thirty quid. Don't forget that. They can't take money.'

'All that stuff was given by good people. No matter what else, our people mean well. Where is it now Lindy? Chewed up by the bin vans, landfill.'

'I know, but they, we, they have to have warmth, protection from the weather –'

'I don't mean that. It's fundamentally wrong to destroy a person's shelter... It shouldn't be happening. What does it do to the people who do it? What does it do to the country that allows it?'

They looked at each other in the moonlight. This was how they used to wake, morning after morning after morning, eyes opening simultaneously, inspecting the other's face, kissing...

'That first time, with the car down on its springs, we were excited, remember?' He waited for her to smile in answer. 'We didn't know what to expect. We felt good. We drove into lush lanes full of dappled green light from overhanging branches. We stopped in the end, remember, just to see what the light tasted like, what it sounded like –'

'And it tasted of wild garlic, and it smelled green and dappled. It was so clean and soothing, like England is supposed to be.'

'We had our sandwiches and wondered how much further we had to go. We talked about the women...' Simon's voice trailed off. He remembered the light.

'I think I know what it is now,' he said, suddenly a hard edge to his voice. 'We got back in the car and in a few minutes we were there. No more country, just muddy roadsides and that fence. Police, soldiers, smoking camp fires, women in dirty clothes. Mud-spattered tents and piles of rubbish covered with polythene that turned out to be benders. It was like a fairground or a gipsy encampment – alien but exciting and inviting. Then those squat buildings, black in the sun. Like dead whales, squat black humps on a desolate plain. They were sucking something out of the light. That's what Greenham did to me, that's what clings to you, Lindy.   The denial of light, of innocence. That's what Reagan and his fucking missiles have done for England.'

She could feel the tension in him and smoothed the furrows on his brow with her thumb, then said, 'There are sections of perimeter where you go cold. It's like walking through clay and... and you're enveloped by a sense of evil. So we sing songs, chant chants, we light candles and humanise the fence with pictures of kids and multicoloured webs. We try to cancel out whatever it is that's there.'

They were silent. Lindy closed her eyes. Simon rolled onto his back and then sat up, holding his knees to his chest and looking down at her. After a while he unlaced his fingers and stroked her hair.

'In the end, you know, it's that,' he said, 'that sense of evil and all its implications and consequences... it's that I'm opposed to. The weapons themselves are nothing compared to their effect on our values, our mentality.' He stretched in the bed, feeling slightly better for coming close to expressing his thoughts.

Lindy said, 'No country that has them has much worth defending.'

Simon hugged her to him. 'That's one reason I love you, Lindy. You say in a few words what I ramble on about. Let's finish the bottle.'

She rolled cigarettes and he collected the unfinished Spanish red from the kitchen table.

'Keep still,' she said, as he came back in. 'You look like a statue.' He was naked, marbled by moonlight.

The implications of the strike were settling into the consciousness of people in the peace movement. For Simon and Lindy the May Day March had been a revelation. It wasn't just a case of my enemy's enemy. There were simple arguments to link the destruction of the coal industry with nuclear weapons. But more than this, there was the invigorating discovery of a working class body in open revolt against the exploitation of power. And whilst some of the songs and attitudes had been Neanderthal, it was obvious that the miners and the peace movement could learn from each other to their mutual advantage, not to mention the advantage of the country.

'Not to mention the fucking Northern Hemisphere,' Simon said.

Lindy laughed, put on her 'Simon' persona and gruffly slurred, 'Not to fucking mention the fucking globe and not to mention the fucking Milky fucking Way and the whole fucking universe.'

Bottle empty, they agreed that this particular red was the worst they had ever tasted ('Which is saying something,' said Simon. 'Which is most certainly saying something without a shadow of a doubt,' said Lindy), and was a disgusting approximation to Siamese cat piss ('If that isn't being racist and speciesist'). But, having taken these things into consideration, they were able to agree that, without yet another shadow of doubt, they wished they had bought three bottles.

'Yea, though we walk through the valley of the shadow of death,' he held the empty bottle to the milky moon, 'may we frequently be legless.'

Lindy lay awake until dawn. Simon slept silently, head on her shoulder and an arm across her stomach. When she closed her eyes she saw faces in the firelight, or the dead lights which shone around the perimeter wire. Sometimes she found a helicopter hovering above her, downdraft stinging her eyes, its searchlight burning her, leaving her charred and flattened as her shadow. There had to be somewhere she would feel whole again. Not

Greenham: she couldn't share in full the sisterliness that abounded; not Leeds, where her involvement in the peace movement felt inconsequential since her lengthening stays at the peace camp.

She didn't know how or why or even what love was, but she knew she loved Simon. He was part of her. Greenham didn't damage that, it strengthened it. But what was Greenham doing to Simon? She experienced a too familiar shifting dismay.

As she drifted into the deep blackness of sleep she found herself on the outskirts of Manchester, re-experiencing an indestructible moment of rightness.

It was the last day of the Leeds-Manchester March. As they approached a right-angled bend through greened wasteland, everything came together in a moment of perfection. The sky was deep spring blue. Summer heat in April. A van went by, painted with rainbows and flowers, its back doors open, speakers booming John Lennon's 'Give Peace a Chance'. Ahead, round the corner but still in view, a group of Hare Krishnas chanted and danced to cymbals and drums and bells. Dogs barked, children shrieked, C.N.D. kites swooped. It was a moving, brightly coloured celebration of love. Lindy and Simon held hands. Lindy wept. It was then they committed themselves to the peace movement and nothing but the peace movement.

But, of course, it hadn't been as simple as that.

Simon shifted in his sleep, rolling onto his back, 'What?' he murmured.

'It's not as easy as we thought,' she said, momentarily wakened by his movement.

The city clattered into another working day. They slept.

At Greenham Common Peace Camp two men in civilian clothes poured petrol over the blind side of a bender. It had taken the women two days to make this structure where a Croatian woman would give birth to a son and name him Mir.

At Daws Hill Peace Camp an American airman, stoned on home grown marijuana, directed his piss onto the food supply and, even though he seemed to piss for an hour, it wasn't long enough because gooks should drown in piss. Across the road a young woman sentry watched and smiled and dreamed of home,

15

where the snow was so deep that cars flew flags on their aerials, and that was what you saw as you they drove through the flat, whited country.

And at Orgreave, police and pickets began to take their positions as the sun slowly swung into a clear, clean, English sky.

II

Lindy took a creased postcard from her inside pocket. TAKE A RISK FOR PEACE NOW in red script on a yellow background and the C.N.D. symbol. She was alone, sitting in morning sun by a cooking fire. She licked her stub of pencil and wrote, *Dear Simon*, then stared at the card on her knee. Lost in thought, she began to play with loose threads which fringed a hole in her denims. She tucked most of the threads under the material where it stretched on her knee, leaving enough strands, strategically placed, to make a C.N.D. sign.

Once she had cycled through a Highland village where pavements were covered by a distinctive hop-scotch design. She watched a four year old carefully draw the design in miniature on the step of a cottage. Greenham was like that, the sign turned up everywhere: austere, baroque, sophisticated; here woven into the wire in multicoloured wools, and there traced with a finger nail in morning dew.

"Can't kill the spirit, eh?' Mary walked up and tousled Lindy's hair.

Lindy, who sat on a pink bentwood chair, was dwarfed by Mary, who squatted on her heels. Mary was over six feet tall. She had broad shoulders and strong, muscular legs. Her dirty fawn raincoat was tied at the waist with ribbon which had once been sky blue. On her head she wore a red and black knitted cap to cover half-inch dirty blonde stubble. There wasn't an angle to her, every line was rounded, from her ankles to the tip of her nose. Even the corners of her mouth followed a smooth hairpin bend. And her exposed flesh had a patina of shiny dirt.

The thought crossed Lindy's mind that in marble or oils, Mary would be an embodiment of the gentle, powerful, humane aspect of womanhood.

'The miners' struggle is our struggle,' Mary said, taking up where they had left off, her Geordie accent rich with emphasis.

'Well, I suppose any fight for... fairness and decency is our struggle.' Lindy put the postcard back in her inner pocket and kicked the fire. White ash eddied in the heat.

'It's not just that,' Mary began dropping twigs onto the embers; flames crackled. 'There's a lot of links. They're getting all that shit from the media same as us. And they're getting even more stick than we do from the cops – but more liberties they take with them, the more they'll take with us, you know. It's politics and economics unite us.

'Thatcher wants to cut back on coal to push forward with nuclear energy. That means breaking U.N. resolutions and importing uranium from Namibia, and that means supporting slave labour. Not to mention cancer. And it means a constant supply of so-called waste products they use to manufacture nuclear weapons. Waste products my arse.'

She paused to grimace at two soldiers who walked the corridor between link fencing and razor wire: 'Away, lads,' she shouted, waving her hand in a dismissive manner, 'you might be bony, but your far too small for a woman such as I.'

Lindy laughed, the soldiers stopped and stared for a while, but the two women ignored them. Lindy said, 'One of those women from Sweden said it's an attempt to atomise the working classes.'

'Well if she means smash communities and beat us into submission, she's right. But, I tell you Lindy, there'll be one hell of a fight. You don't push miners about. I should know, I was married to one, me.'

'You!' Lindy looked up in astonishment.

'Did you think I was too big or something? Three years, man. Nasty little runt, he were.'

'I thought you were too kind, too knowing, too gentle... well, yeah, too big.' She shoved Mary's arm so that Mary rocked on her heels and had to steady herself with a hand on the ground.

'Bloody classic case, me. Head case! Our Tommy were only five foot four. I could pick him up and stand him on the table! He still used to smack us though.'

'He didn't.'

'He bloody did. What's more, I let him. Started a year after we were wed. It were two year before I landed him one back. I mean, I thought it were my place to get knocked about. You do if it's all you've known. Where I come from the chaps are the bosses and there's no two ways. But he went too far, did little Tommy. Got what was coming to him.'

'What happened?'

'He came home addled and woke me up to make a cup of

tea. So I did and was on my way to my bed when he calls me back. What you want now, Tommy? I said. Sit down while I finish, pet, he says. I might think to have another cup. So I say: You might have another think coming, Tommy lad, 'cos I'm off to my bed. Anyway, he starts shouting and cursing and then he punches me in the bread basket. I went cold all over and said, Don't you ever do that again, Tommy Birn. He laughs and calls me a big soft cow. You can call me as much as you want, I said, but you don't lift another finger to me or I'll fell you. He were shocked, I could see that. So I stared him down then went up and left him with the wind out of his sails.'

It was clear to Lindy there was more to come. She handed Mary a roll-up and began making another.

'Anyway, I went to bed and started thinking.' Mary accepted a glowing twig, lit up and drew deeply. 'Seeing my life through somebody else's eyes, like. It was ridiculous.

'I could hear him downstairs, shuffling about. He kept playing with the fire. Then I heard the cupboard go and I knew he were at the whisky.

'I was glad, but I didn't know why. I was willing him to get a bit of Dutch courage and come and land me one. I'd been simmering for two years and I was just about ready to boil over and put that little bugger's fire out. Next off everything goes quiet; the sod's gone to sleep. Me, I'm wide eyed and that little sod's snoring.'

'I'm enjoying this,' Lindy said, lighting her roll-up with the twig.

'I know, it's good. Anyway, I get worked up and start shouting. I didn't get out of bed, mind, just shouted. Tommy Birn! I shouted, Tommy Birn, you short-arsed little sod. That did it, he came up them stairs like a dog at a rabbit, shush-shushing me, telling me the Jacksons would hear. The Jacksons'd hear! I mean it's...' She searched for a word, her round face shining in the sun, back-lit by laughter. 'It's extra-terrestrial! That little sod used to leather me and I'd to keep quiet so the Jacksons didn't hear. God, can you believe it? I thought it had slipped by at the service when I were busy looking at my ring and hoping sun would come out for the pictures: ... to honour and obey and to keep quiet when he cracks you one so the Jacksons wont cotton on. I'd have agreed to it, that's how we were raised. Anyway, he's trying to quieten me and asking us what's up and I tell him to go get us a cup of tea. He's taken aback at first, then he says he thinks there'll be one left in the pot. I want fresh, Tommy, I say, and I sit up in bed so I'm bigger than him.

'Well, it's anything for a quiet life now. Off he trots and next to no time he's back with a pot of tea and a doily on the tray. Just like Christmas morning. Here yer are then, petal, he says. Move up and I'll be with you. And he starts getting undressed. You're not coming in this bed, Tommy lad, I say. What's that, pet? he says. I say, You've had your last night in this bed 'til you start making it. I can see he's riled now. In his vest and pants and quivering, bless him. Anyway I start to drink me tea and after a couple of right ladylike sips I say: Go get them chocolate-bottom biscuits out of cupboard. That lit his blue touch paper for him. He goes off like a squib.

'He were fast. I've seen him fell men twice his size, he were so fast. Psychological advantage, you see. He had me by the hair, both fists in it, and he dragged me out of bed. I had long straight hair then. Cut it off after Grunwick, a copper took hold of it and belted me in the gob. Last time any chap used my hair to get a hand-hold. Anyway, that's another story.

'He'd got about three in before I knew what was happening. For a second or two he was in control again, you see. I'm telling you, it was like drowning in reverse, I saw all my life ahead of me. That did it. I hadn't hit anybody since I were seven, but it came from somewhere. I landed him an almighty biff on the side of his head and he goes sprawling. Then I pick him up with his arms pressed in his side and prop him against the wall while I open the built in wardrobe. He were as white as a sheet. Hadn't a word to say for himself. I could almost see stars for him.

'That wardrobe were Jackson's side, mind. Sex is alright, and he were good at it, but locking that door were like an orgasm and a fortnight in Spain.'

'You're a marvel, Mary. A bloody marvel.'

'Aye, and I play the tin whistle.'

Simon found Leeds increasingly alien. It seemed without charm; a harsh, crass place where the best of shops catered for the worst of taste, where brute commercialism had always taken precedent over all else, including architectural grace.

20

In the mid-seventies, scrambling out of crisis, seeking Lindy, his *life-kit* on the back seat of a mini-van, he arrived in Leeds and the city delighted him: the thoughtless, cack-handedness of its developers, the way its people lacked edge. But now he saw a Thatcherite settlement where pensioners died of hypothermia and the business establishment feared that cranking up the Welfare State would encourage slothful dependence amongst the 'feckless'. To him the city teemed with the human consequences of domination by the New Right.

What Leeds now manufactured was greed, bitterness and despair. Greed and bitterness draped in tawdry, synthetic 'designer' clothes. Despair declared itself on the faces of the unemployed and aged.

As the eighties got into their stride, the city came into its own. A cheap, dirty Victorian town suited to the cheap, dirty Victorian values so dear to the Government. Sweat shops and the outworking system flourished; essential if little crooks were to make big profits in the clothing industry. A whole new pool of dispossessed immigrant workers, easily identified by skin colour, were available for special exploitation. Factory work waned and the inner city estates, and those who lived in them, were left to decay.

'All in all, this is a shit house,' Simon thought, as he drove slowly past a queue of uniformly grey flotsam (those in work who would have been scarcely worse off on Social Security).

And then he reached that part of Burley Road which affords a view over the city to flats and cooling towers beyond (a view now obliterated by a brick-built office block). The low morning sun, lazering mist from between the mish-mash of buildings, created a muted palette with the columns of smoke on the horizon.

His spirits rose. He had a short and lucrative commission to create a photographic folio of the Leeds-Liverpool canal. The light was good. The sky was good. His eye felt good. The commission put him ahead for a couple of months: time to share with Lindy.

It was a spring day, the light had the golden quality of early October and the air was clean and cold. Simon left the car in the canal basin and hitched a lift on a working barge. The bargee was in his late fifties and this was his last run before taking over as a lock-keeper in South Yorkshire. He was taciturn, a pipe-smoking man with red face and callused hands. And he was happy to wait while Simon stepped to the bank and took pictures. Before leaving, some five miles on, Simon made portraits of the bargee, blue enamel mug in hand, pipe in mouth, flat cap pushed back to show mottled scalp and tufts of salt and pepper hair.

Walking through deep countryside he caught the sound of motorway traffic, but the canal belonged to another more silent age. After a couple of miles he crossed the canal at a lock and sat among dandelion and gorse, eating egg sandwiches, thinking of nothing. Mountainous white clouds drifted, their shadows patterning the landscape. In the end an Indian family were pleased to take him on the long boat they had hired for the week.

The grandmother sat with him at the prow. He couldn't have imagined a better way to find the heart of Leeds. The smell of spices drowned that of urban fumes, music from a different time and a different culture came from the cabin. The old lady rested her dry, slim fingers on his forearm to say 'It's nice, love?' and 'You happy, love?'

It was! He was! The boat chugged between dusty Victorian brickwork and then the canal broadened, its surface mottled by oil and keyed by breezes channelled between old warehouses.

As he reloaded the camera, he tried to express guilt for what England had done to the woman's culture; to express shame that she and her family were not always welcome in Britain. She made a delicate gesture with her hands, moving them outward from the wrist and said, 'Never mind, love.'

The woman's son, a broad-faced, fawn-skinned man in transparent framed spectacles, his white hair cropped short, said, 'This is enterprise society, we are working very hard and succeeding in business venture. Please do not apologise, no peoples are faultless. Many English are lost and unable to cope with changing times.'

Mother and son spoke together, then the son said, 'My mother wishes you to know her belief that you are a good young man, taking your pictures and harming no-one. She says not to feel guilt for the actions of others but to seek virtue in all people. She says to learn from past experience without accumulation of guilt, which is heavy burden of no value.'   Simon said he wished he had her wisdom.

22

'Thank you, love,' she said, smiling and touching his sleeve.

III

In the Seventies Simon was a Market Research Executive, hair in transition between razor-cut and fashionably long and curly. He shared a small flat in Crouch End with memories of a disastrous marriage. He was letting the dust settle, drifting and drinking through a life with no friends but a lot of acquaintances.

Each year he received an invitation to Nigel's party. Nigel used to be a friend, but was now an acquaintance who himself had no friends but an expanding universe of acquaintances. Nigel informed every acquaintance that he or she was a very special friend. He worked hard at it. It paid. One day he hoped to see his party recorded in the colour supplements or honoured by a mention in Private Eye. He sent invitations of variable creativity to *Private Eye* and four gossip columnists. To date the invitations remained unacknowledged.

But the gathering expanded: part battlefield, part market hall, part bordello. With so many acquaintances, and no moral scruples ('I'm a man of the times'), Nigel could more or less guarantee to fix anyone with useful sexual or business contacts. ('I see it as a social service.')

Simon no longer enjoyed Nigel's parties, but he still went. I am a witness, he told himself. He was no longer depressed, but he wasn't happy either.

If he'd been happy he wouldn't have driven to Nottingham straight from a discussion on the target market for a new crunchy breakfast cereal. He would have had a home to go to. If he had still been married and not particularly happy – which was how he remembered being married to Anne – he wouldn't have gone to Nigel's party because Anne despised Nigel. Most women despised Nigel, he used them as oil to smooth the wheels of his business machinations. But Nigel had a way with him.

Simon was getting by on alcohol, music, cigarettes, alcohol, sycophantic young research executives, alcohol, acquaintances, and alcohol. He drank a lot. I am a sort of witness, he told himself.

The first stage of the party was on the ground floor of Nigel's large Victorian house ('Cost peanuts. Wogs, God bless 'em.'). During this stage Nigel moved amongst his assembling guests oozing variations on *X meet Y, I simply must put you two together because you are both my absolutely special friends.* As the rooms filled, small groups stood around talking about Nigel.

The important guests were invited to arrive at the peak of stage one – they were all men with more money and status than Nigel. They were taken straight into Nigel's study, simpered at, larded with good drink and compliments, then into the body of the party to be *fixed-up* with whatever they cared for. Nigel had yet to discover where to draw the line – 'Most want sure-fire cunt with no complications!'

As Nigel's special friend of longest duration, Simon (who didn't rate as a particularly useful business contact, though, as a junior director of a research agency he had his uses and could always be passed off as a character) didn't cause Nigel to expend much energy. 'Manpower Planning now, old boy. This means I select and oversee the training of young female shoe operatives. They tell me about their periods and sexual spasms with greasy Notts yobbos. Which means, old boy that the crème de la quim comes to – and usually at – my parties. Norma is just dying to bare it to you… her soul I mean, eh!'

I am a sort of witness.

Nigel took the crumpled teardrop lapels of Simon's denim jacket and turned him about. 'Norma's the blonde in the corner. The bald chap, you can safely ignore. She has a very big mouth and you know what they say, Simon old lad: big mouth… big cunt. Believe me, believe it. I can heartily recommend either orifice. Off you go, she's expecting you!' He laughed like a Jack Russell barks, then moved off.

I am a sort of witness.

Here are some of the things Simon said in the first stage of Nigel's party the year he met Lindy… is he?… oh yes… sometimes… not everyone, no… over there I think… are you… really… no, Crouch End as a matter of fact… yes, Statistics mainly… is he… oh, years… are you… over there I think… is he… yes, at university… he is, isn't he… are you… over there I think.

'I suppose I'm a sort of witness,. Everybody's got to be something.'

The first stage of Nigel's party had Simon wishing he'd stayed at home and tackled the backlog of work.

He took possession of a half pint of soft and fruity Italian goat piss, found an armchair in the darkest corner of the darkest room and assumed the appearance of one in a drunken stupor.

He watched Nigel cuddling Norma, the attractive (though sadly marred by her presence in this hell hole) shoe operative. The girl was leaning into Nigel's side; Nigel waved towards Simon; his arm circled Norma's shoulder, the hand tucked under her arm, the fingers gently kneading the sideswell of her breast.

As the glass emptied Simon's spirits lightened. He recognized Nigel's combined coup and error of the night. The coup was the arrival of what would almost certainly be Nige's new Managing Director, or Chairman, or whatever. The error was that he should never have been invited. And the consequences of the error were multiplied because the MD (say) had brought his wife!

I am a sort of witness.

Simon sat up and took notice. The man was fifty, plump, and outrageously out of place. His wife displayed contempt and disgust with minimal gestures. Nigel bobbed and writhed in an eruption of smarm.

Fired by goat piss, with a smoothness and cunning which impressed him (and later would flood him with retrospective self-loathing) Simon glided into the trio at exactly the right moment to collect himself a third of a pint of Nigel's single malt.

'Smashin' party, Nige you old zoophiliac.' Then as he returned to his den, he offered, to the MD and wife, 'Sort of witness.'

He had regained his chair, downed the single malt and re-filled with goat piss, when Nigel fired a starting pistol three times. The party entered its second phase in stunned, ear-ringing silence.

'Grub's for grabs in library!'

Party-goers wriggled off the hook of Nigel-centred conversation and crushed to the door. Simon watched through half closed eyes. Someone was battling against the stream. It was the Managing Director's wife, early middle age, French pleat, flowing silk suit, whisky grin.

She took Simon's arm, swayed against him and breathed

single malt.

'Listen, darling,' she said; an arid, aggressive surface on her voice threatened to crack and reveal... Simon had no idea what. 'Shitty Nige, or whatever he calls himself, tells me you are quite a character. Escort me to the nosh, darling. George is simply encrusted with arse-licking management.' She swung a bottle of Glen Fiddich into view.

'Hide that!'

'Oh! You are too a character.' She squeezed his arm and gave a peaty gurgle; Simon forgave her everything. She took his glass and emptied goat piss onto Nigel's carpet. With the concentration of a lush she shook the glass, held it to the light, then gave it back almost filled to the top with Scotch. 'Now,' she said, 'let us find somewhere to secrete this dwindling treasure.'

Simon nodded and took a large swig from his glass.

'Nectorino, dear lady.' He felt a slappy smile spread across his face without his even thinking it, let alone forcing it. 'Oh, that's nice.' It opened like a flower in his chest and abdomen – just like in the books, he thought.

Hilary was her name. George's firm was, she said, a shitty nut on a teeny twig of a multinational. George was a shrew who wanted to be a squirrel and swing in the shite-dripping branches.

She delighted in her scathing judgements, she amused herself. The core was self-satire. Relating the cause of her latest skirmish with George (to whom she would be absolutely sweet after a binge like this), she said, of Blather, one of his King Charles spaniels, 'The shitty little shite shat on the sofa.' Then she grinned, pushed Simon's arm with her drink-laden fist and added, 'Bet you can't say that without mixing your ss-s and sh-s.' She cracked a laugh as effective as Nigel's pistol.

'Glad you're such a scruffy oik, Simon,' she said, as they crossed a hall and he slid the lovely green bottle into a wellington boot.

They were soon pressed into a corner of the library, healthy glasses resting beside them, forking down an assortment of salads, quiches and cold meats. Someone squealed as a dress caught fire. 'God, how dreary, how dire, how dreadful, how disastrous, how disillusioning, how... shitty.'

'Just be a witness.'

A circular library table and three trestles carried two large turkeys, a leg of pork, an assortment of cheeses, trifles and fresh fruit. French sticks curved from chamber pots. Dips dripped, butter and Flora were adulterated by bread crumbs, rice and ash. Noise more fitting to a shipyard came from tacky, chewing, look-at-me-I'm-worth-knowing, food-littered, flapping mouths. Hilary swivelled her eyes and focused firmly on the rows of books.

'Does he actually read?' she asked, stabbing at them with her fork, splattering a very special friend's striped three-piecer with rice and mayonnaise. (The young man turns, his costly shag cut flops, he recognizes status and simpers). Simon explained that the calf-bound Victorian jobs were strictly for display, bought from a very special friend in the book trade. 'Bit like employing an interior design consultant, but also an asset which appreciates and may be liquefied. '

They concentrated on eating for a few moments, then Hilary asked, 'Do you have positive thoughts on our mutual friend?'

'On the more positive side you could say that he will utilise anything to expand the consciousness of your George's young female shoe operatives.'

'You mean he fucks them!'

'Fucks them. Trades them. He hands them round like Christmas gifts, sales promos, business cards. It's a timeless activity, you know. I speak as a sort of witness.'

'God, what an obscene world.' Her face twisted and creases showed through the make-up round her mouth.

She straightened her back and raised her chin. 'Let's explore. Pry. Is he really a very special friend? Am I being an awfully, unforgivably shitty thing?'

'Seems to me you're fighting a tide of spiritual pain. He's a very special friend of everybody. A man at home in a tiny environment. The real world isn't like this and never will be.'

They squeezed between bodies. The hall was empty. Hilary collected the bottle.

'In London,' Simon said, holding out his glass, 'there'd be fewer dark suits and Pathé News accents.'

'You are far too young to remember Pathé News. Anyway, darling boy, I want you to know that I do know that I am a shit myself and –'

'I know, there's –'

'Let me finish. I'm an awful shit. I make a cocktail of bitterness, disgust and naughtiness. Unless I do, darling, I just absolutely go into total internal collapse...'

'I know that, silly sod.' Simon put his arm round her shoulder and squeezed.

'I thought you did.' She gave him a dry kiss on the cheek. 'I felt I must say it, even so.'

'Come on then, let's go be slime evil upstairs.' He felt her stiffen against him.

'You don't mean sex?'

'Nope. Just giggles.'

She hugged him. He saw it as an image that would last forever, the pair of them, clasped together at the foot of a broad, curving staircase, streaks of golden light on the polished mahogany.

Disentangled, hand in hand, tip-toeing, they climbed the stairs.

'I feel the giggles coming,' she whispered, then she snorted in her glass.

The exploration was systematic and increasingly hysterical. Nigel's soft porn was on display in a small bedside book-case.

They read postcards on his mantelpiece and sniffed his collection of male cosmetics.

'Can you remember the last time you smelled sweat?' Hilary asked, turning up her nose at a stick deodorant called Sexy.

'Yes.'

'I suppose you do. George is so desiccated, he doesn't even pee anymore.'

In the walk-in wardrobe, tutting and humming at the wide range of personae their host kept well hidden, Simon said, 'Shall I ask the inevitable question?'

'If you want. If you must.'

'Why do you stay with him?'

She leaned back against the wall, holding a sulphurous yellow kaftan to her chin. Her face was serious, her eyes locked on his like a child who fears something is to attack from behind. 'I can't remember anything else. I'm forty-three and he's fifty-five. It's been over twenty years. We never had children. Once upon a time we both wanted them, desperately. And... And what else? No talent, no training, no prospects, no desire to be an identikit divorcee running antique, jewellery or flower shop on alimony. No nothing, darling. Absolutely shit awful, isn't it? Absence of anything at all.'

'Fear of the unknown then.'

'Oh Christ! And I thought you showed signs of originality. Shall we join the herd?'

The mood swung, mist crept in through a thousand cracks. Outside someone was trying bedroom doors, handle-rattling. It was George, his voice dripping anxiety like a sponge raised from a cold bath drips thin water: 'Hilary! Hilary!' Half imploring whisper, half open razor.

Simon said that this was where they got the giggles, remember! And she remembered, but it was too late. She was drowning. She pushed the kaftan at him and said, 'I must go, darling boy. Stay in here a few moments. I'm afraid it's the only gift I have for you.'

She pressed her lips against his cheek, they were cold and moistureless, then she pushed him gently amongst the dangling shirts and stepped out of the wardrobe, silently closing the door and leaving him in the dark.

'I'm in here, Georgie darling.'

'Where the hell have you been, Hilary?' The anxiety was gone, the razor open.

'I just wanted to be on my own for a few moments, darling. And you were so busy enjoying yourself.'

'Get your wrap. We're going. Where is the lout?'

She inhaled rapidly. 'Let go, George. My wrap is downstairs and your little boys will see the marks. Thank you, darling. His name is Simon, he's the nicest person I've ever met at one of your functions and this is the shittiest one of your functions to which I have ever been. 'And he is in there, frantically buttoning up his trousers, I should imagine. Don't! I shall ask him to step out and hit you. Now, darling. Shall we go downstairs, or would you like to open the box?'

George said that she was mad, that she needed psychiatric care, that she was a drunk.   Simon exhaled, slowly, then sunk onto his haunches in the darkness. He felt sick.

He was too drunk to drive back to London. Too unhappy to contemplate re-entering the party. Nigel would fix him up with a room, and a companion. Not something he wanted, not after the moments of closeness with Hilary. Norma's body would excite him, he would stiffen, perform, spurt into her, feel the blanket of despondency settle over him. Despise himself, despise the woman.

He drained the bottle into his tumbler and tossed the empty on Nigel's pillow. Taking a book at random from the cheap and nasty book-shelves (what kind of life would he and Hilary have shared?), he set out in search of a quiet spot in the attic where he might sleep off the booze and allow the experience of Hilary to settle into his life.

The door to the attic staircase closed behind him and the wild synthetic music dropped away. At the far end of the landing was a small door, narrow and low, made from pine planking. It stood open and revealed a narrow staircase, uncarpeted and inviting. He sipped his drink and accepted the invitation.

It was a small room, its panelled walls faded and crazed. There was an empty, glass-fronted cupboard, two cane chairs, a three-quarter bed with heavy grey blankets, a desk thick with dust, and an armchair. Dominating this silent, undisturbed room was a long brass telescope pointing to a dirty skylight. A full moon flooded the room with milky light. Simon was entranced, he stood in the doorway on one leg for a few moments, not daring to unsettle the image.

Had he thought about it he would have known this was a room where something special would happen. But he wasn't thinking. It was just now. He was just alive... living. All the things the trendy sub-culture told you to be, but you never could be when you were trying to be.

So he would remember the room and describe it, many times, over the years. How often he relived the moment, drunk, in some snug bender, numerous degrees of frost outside, M.O.D. police poking about and muttering to their radios. Smashed round the table in the big kitchen, Lindy laughing and waiting to chip in on some detail she liked to hear from her own lips.

IV

'Oh, listen, congratulations, your names were passed for the Party last night.' Derek Blythe nudged Simon and settled himself in the passenger seat, big plastic shopping bag on his knees.

'Which party?'

'Which party? Labour Party, you daft ha'porth. You applied, didn't you?'

'Before the last election. When Foot got the leadership. I thought we'd failed our entrance exam. Why'd it take so long?'

'Oh, you'll learn. It was King John sitting on your application, he's been Mem. Sec. for years. Tells folk like you it's full.'

'Who's King John?'

'Who's King John? Really, Simon, call yourself a socialist. Councillor John Harmer, the man without who Leeds would grind to a halt.'

'I'm not sure we want to join now. It was Foot. He seemed like a man of principle.'

Derek patted Simon on the shoulder, then said, 'Neil the Kid's not all that bad, you know. If we keep us hands round his throat. Anyroad, you see, Simon, when you've been in as long as I have, you learn to live with disappointment.' He nodded, then added, 'And despair.'

Simon told him about the Indian woman. 'Oh, they are,' Derek replied, full of his usual enthusiasm, 'theirs is an old culture, do you see. Had things well organized when we were running round in wolf skins and woad, no better than Mrs Thatcher's men. Anyway, there's only one place to criticise the Party from, and that's in it. No more daft talk. You're in it now. Only honourable way out is expulsion. It shouldn't be too difficult for you and your mucky lady friend. You've both enough off.'

Derek made one of his familiar jumps in conversation. 'Thatcher's not playing games, you know. Don't underestimate her, I'll not.'

'You don't think there's anything in it then, when she says she has nothing to do with the strike?'

'You what! And here's me thinking you had some nous! I

mean, she meddles every day, and she's scarcely neutral in her pronouncements, is she, I ask you. Macgregor's just her front man.

'I've seen this all before, Simon, you'd best remember that. We'll probably have a decade of this lot and believe you me, you won't recognize this country in a few years' time. She's rewriting the book. If she breaks the miners she breaks the working class, it's as simple as that. And if she breaks the working class, well...'

Simon had never known the normally hyperactive Derek to be so still, so leaden-voiced. Face set in unfamiliar lines, the old man stared into the future; even the wave of blue-grey hair seemed sapped of vitality.

'Come on Derek. Everything passes.'

'Does it? I haven't got that long left, not that that's of any consequence. But what've we got these things on for?' He tapped the black and white C.N.D. badge on his lapel and indicated Simon's with a nod of his head. 'It's all unravelling like in the twenties and thirties. Only thing is, Simon, there'll be no victory election this time round.'

For a few moments they drove in silence through heavy traffic, then Simon asked Derek if he would like to eat with him. Derek effervesced: 'Ooh, vegetarian muck, no thank you. Now you could come and share mine if you want, that'd be more like it. A couple of nice pork chops with spring cabbage, new potatoes and thick onion gravy. Then sponge pudding to follow. With custard. That's what I call tea. I'll be gardening tonight so I need my nourishment.'

For a while they discussed the plan to blockade Grosvenor Square. Seven or eight members of their C.N.D. group had attended a meeting and expressed interest in civil disobedience, but, as Derek put it, 'Half of them are silly beggars, you know.'

Simon turned into the council estate where Derek lived. 'We work with what we've got, Derek. You know what they say, "Together we can stop the bomb". We've got to open our arms to everybody. We'll win in the end.'

'We'd better. If we don't nobody will.' Derek slapped the dashboard to emphasize his point. 'I've talked our Jed into coming on the demo, by the by. Well, I think the Communist Party of Great Britain have given him his orders, daft begger. They'll all be there in force. Right wing shirkers, eh! Just look at the leaf on that tree, isn't it lovely? If you've got time, Simon, I'll show you my apple trees. I've never seen them looking so lovely. It'll be a grand summer for weather if I'm a judge.'

When he got home Simon found a crumpled postcard on the mat. *Dear Simon, I've got such a lot to tell you, but I don't know how to write. I'm well, hope you are, Love Lindy.*

He went upstairs, filled a half pint glass with homebrew and found a clip-board and ball-point. Then he sat by the window and tapped the side of his nose with the pen.

Dear Lindy, another day another thirty bob!   *It's been a smasherooney of a day. Guess what. We're now members of the Labour Party. It seems Councillor Harmer sat on our application but since he's been ousted from the position Derek calls Mem. Sec., we've been duly processed and accepted. According to Derek, Harmer tried to keep the party clean of anyone with left wing views. You can imagine it: 'We don't want politically motivated infiltrators in La Bore Party.'*

I took Derek home and went in for a cup of tea. He's an amazing old lad. I mean, he was amazing enough already, but you should see the inside of his house. I got the conducted tour. It's like a perfectly constructed machine with everything exactly where it's needed. But it's grown like that over the years, so it's quirky to say the least. Crammed full with flowers and plants as well. Anyway, add this to your stock of Blythe knowledge: he makes his own caps and blazers; he's a stamp collector; a cyclist with a fabulous lightweight tourer (kept in the bedroom since he topped seventy); he's got a collection of mandolins and recorders and a violin – all of which he can play; and he paints and draws in pastel.

Would the world was full of Derek Blythes.

After refilling his glass he found himself hanging back from continuing the letter. He really wanted to describe the work, the Indian family, the stolid bargee... but he knew that he should develop and print the pictures first. To talk about them, or write about them, was to risk impeding the creation of the images he knew were locked in limbo, caught between the exposed film and his experience.

Lindy understood. That was why he loved her. Yesterday, well, yesteryear, belonged to someone else. He hardly ever thought about London anymore, about the agency, about his marriage, about the others...

The sun was going down. It flooded the valley with pink light. For Leeds it was quite a view, incorporating a little of almost everything urban, including woodland, the canal, an old brewery, high rise flats and a railway line which carried radioactive waste.

You'll love his garden. He's tended it for thirty or more years and it shows. Nothing spick and span about it, not like his clothes, it's his alter-ego, the laid-back, casual bit that you know is in there, like a slow current under his well-channelled surface (Christ, that's the canal bubbling up – and one with a slow flow at that! Oh, well, we can't answer for our sub-consciousness can we, eh, see what I mean do you, mucky Lindylugs). So, anyway, Derek's garden: scruffy, lived-in, loved. Fabulous dignity. A very big apple tree spreading shade the full width and absolutely laden with apples, or it will be by the look of it. Then a few small trees. A peach tree he's grown from a stone, and a smaller one that he says we can have because he has no room for it. The remains of bulbs thick on the ground, there's been massive clumps of snowdrops, daffs, tulips. Areas where he's broken out small vegetable plots. And a dingy little shed that smells like every garden shed should. Should I shay should shed? I need a drink!

He stole the apple tree from some country house where he was billeted... anyway, I won't go on with that, but I can hardly wait to tell you some of the stuff that came out when he was talking.

I can hardly wait anyway, Lindy. Truth is I'm feeling low at the moment. Derek was depressing about the state of the country, or, to be more accurate, the direction we're heading in... but that's not it. I'm just missing you a lot. You'd think we'd grow out of it, but here I am feeling like a lovesick kid again...

I know he's probably right about what's happening, but I can't help being optimistic. I mean, when you think of the October March last year: half a million of us in the streets of London. That spirit won't be subdued, it can't be, it would be like stopping spring following winter. No matter what else we stand for, we stand for a positive attitude to life....

He put the clip-file, pad and ball-point on the floor by his chair and stared out of the window again. Losing was unimaginable, unthinkable. It was just a matter of letting ordinary decent people know what was being done in their names, the implications of what was being done. Once the general public knew what was going on – the weapons, the American bases, the political use of the police force, the empty hospitals, mothballed for use in the war – once everybody knew, surely they would end it.

Simon realized that his optimism was being adulterated by some other emotion with its source in his feelings about Lindy. Two things, he told himself, they are two separate things: don't run them together.

But there was a dark struggle inside him, drawing colour from his impression of where the forces of progression and peace were heading; it was rooted in something other than national or international politics...

His mind flinched away from a head-on approach to his feelings about Lindy's increasingly lengthy stays at Greenham. Instead he began to wonder how well-informed the police were about C.N.D. and its activists. About the Left in general. Stories were already coming out of the strike about the role of *agents provocateurs* and soldiers in police uniforms doing picket line duty. He'd been told of a miner pushed up against his brother on the picket line – and the brother was in the Guards. 'Shurrup our kid, I'm not here!'

Whatever else, it was clear that the wind of militarisation was blowing through the force. Bobby was no longer an appropriate tag for the stone-faced sods. He remembered a Czech psychologist at a meeting of statisticians: 'You have saying – *some person step over grave!* We have saying – *policeman just born!*'

V

'So who we waiting for now, girls?' Paul Ridding, burley in middle age, wore a maroon sweater, ill-fitting jeans and scuffed pink trainers. He lowered the tailgate of his rusting estate car.

'Less of your lip, buster. She's Lindy, and she's thirty-five, and I'm Mary, and I'm thirty-three. In my book that makes us women, not girls.'

'Come on, lass. It's only us way of talking. We mean no harm, do we David?' Paul was visibly upset by Mary's assertive reaction. David, (yellow T-shirt: 'Come home to a real fire, burn MacGregor') said, 'That we don't. It's difficult for folk like us. I mean, to me, woman... it's a bit of an insulting term, like. I mean, a woman, to me, is what you'd call a sex object. A lady is a posh... woman.'

'Careful.' Lindy said, then felt mixed pleasure and remorse as David's open face coloured up.

'Yeah, well, I'm not used to it. But what I'm saying is this, where we come from, girl is alright. It means pal or comrade. Do you see?'

'And where we're coming from, comrade, it's a put-down. So what are you going to do about that?' Lindy smiled, trying to take the sting out of what she had to say.

'We won't call you girls, then,' David said.

Mary, who stood six inches taller than him, ruffled his hair. 'Away! Yer a bonny lad,' she said. David coloured more as the other three laughed.

Paul pushed the sleeves of the acrylic sweater above his elbows and leaned back against the car to let the sun see his face. 'It's a damned sight better than being underground, I tell you that.' He turned to Lindy. 'What do I say if I want to tell you about the person who I'm married to? What's form for that, pray?'

'What do you usually call her?'

'Our Lass.'

'Oh aye,' Mary said, 'what breed is she then? Border Collie, Terrier? What's her name, man?'

'Penny.'

'Well call her Penny then.'

'I tell thee, it means nowt. Just us way of talking.'

'I know that, you daft beggar. But it does mean something to them as you call lasses. And if it doesn't, it should.' Mary's rounded, dirty face scowled, then, pointing towards a bender, she grinned and said, 'Here's a lady. Sarah's vair vair powsh, so watch your tongues, lads.'

Sarah Cotes wore a muddy lime-green ski suit, unzipped to reveal a yellow Greenham Women Are Everywhere T-shirt. She was small, slim, and tight bodied with a crop of tawny hair that would have done justice to a lion. Her green eyes mesmerised David as soon as he saw them.

Introductions were made. Sarah's travel bag was stowed in the back of Paul's car along with other luggage and food and money collected by the two miners. They had just spent three days as guests of the South London Branch Labour Party. The Party had collected for the miners and for Greenham. And since lifts were needed...

Sarah was returning to Richmond in North Yorkshire, because her mother had been taken ill. Lindy was going home.

Mary had taken kindly to the idea of a trip up North. It would be her first time away from the camp since the big 30,000 demonstration a year earlier.

'Hang on,' Sarah said. She ran across to the wire where two squaddies were looking on, one making notes, the other speaking into a radio. After a brief exchange, Sarah came back. 'Just checking that they had all their details correct,' she said.

'They'll have us logged, you reckon?' Paul screwed his eyes against the sun.

'They'll do that anyroad,' David said. 'It's a bloody crime to step out of us houses.'

'I get nowt, Sarah.' David looked across Lindy to the younger woman. 'Not a bloody sausage from DHSS, and we're not on any strike pay, tha knows. Arthur reckons we'll go soft if we get strike pay. A couple of quid a week for picketing, and what the support group can hand out. Mind, I'm not complaining. I never knew people could be so kind. It's an education, this strike.'

Sun streamed through the makeshift blind of Coal Not Dole stickers covering the top four inches of the windscreen.

The journey was a period of intensive education. Gradually

they dropped their personal defences and opened up. Challenges were made and accepted, arguments stated, opinions changed, and opinions held. The result was a feeling of mutual respect rarely experienced in such diverse company.

Sarah, whose childhood had been spent in a country vicarage and a boarding school, said she had never even sat next to a working man before.

'A striker, not a working man,' Dave corrected her. The pair of them were pleased as kids with new toys. They teased, making fun of each other's accents and, even within the confines of a back seat shared with Lindy, found space to land playful punches.

To their delight, the women discovered that Paul, who gave the impression of being rather stolidly masculine, was easily reduced to eye-streaming hysteria. He was a natural comedian, telling stories in flat, dead-pan voice, punch-lines carefully concealed, then signalled by his heaving shoulders. Part of the pleasure was in his own obvious enjoyment and infectious laughter, part in the dawning of understanding.

Once Paul stopped the car on the hard shoulder to get over the squall of high-pitched giggles that racked his meaty body. He was describing how Dave had been delighted to find N.U.M. slogans all over the walls of a particular street.

'Look,' he said. 'Look, it's all over t' place... oh. Lord help us...' Paul took calming breaths and wiped tears from his face with the back of his hand. 'And it were! Pillar boxes, doors, shop fronts: support TOTNUM. It were local kids' phonetic spelling.' Then he'd swung the car back onto the motorway and they whooped like kids on a switchback. Time passed quickly.

Kirkfield Chance is a company village. Built at the turn of the century by the Hollingwell Coal, Chalk and Gravel Company. Chance had changed little in eighty years. At one end of the hundred-yard street was a small church and schoolroom, at the other end a miners' Welfare-cum-Community centre. As they drove up the short street, the old pit-head lifting gear was black against a violet sky.

Paul parked his Vauxhall by the Welfare. The brick and concrete of the contemporary pit-head buildings formed a hard-edged, shadowless bulk, a colourless, geometrical monster. Lindy slid from the car and took a few steps into the darkening evening, the old lifting gear came back into view. It was friendly and familiar. Why? Perhaps the monochrome illustrations in history and geography text books at grammar school, maybe she'd copied a picture of it. She shuddered as a few remnants of cultural deceit perpetrated by her school slid from her.

Paul and David had learned their history outside the system. Different history. Paul had been astonished: *You did history till you were eighteen and you never heard of Invergordon Mutiny!* She had some reading to do. Some accounts to settle with those nicely spoken teachers who, supportive and stimulating, guided her through her teenage years…

'This is it, then,' Paul said, splaying his arms to indicate the shadowy street with its fifty terraced houses, the church, six management 'villas' and a dozen old people's bungalows. 'That's mine over there, twenty six. Red door and windows. I was born in number three.' The women, stretching to relieve cramped limbs, nodded and murmured acknowledgement; twilight had all the doors monochrome.

'He gets about, does Paul, don't you, Skipper?'

'Seen life from both sides of road.'

Lindy noticed how the miners breathed deeply of the evening air. She did the same and caught the distinctive smell of coal fires.

They walked in single file along an earthen path between a privet hedge and garden fences ranging from store-bought 'ranch style' to bed-ends and rusting sheets of corrugated iron. Twilight softened and unified the gardens, giving them the appearance of wood-cuts. Some were neatly turned and trenched, others were long since converted into flower gardens or children's play areas.

'Chuck, chuck, chuck a lai cock! Them's mine.' Dave indicated a creosoted shed and wire-netting run where shadowy birds scratted and pecked. Even as they were watched the hens took a last look round, then jerkily hopped into the shed and began a contented chucking and chortling.

'I didn't think anybody your age kept hens,' Lindy said.

'You're in the country now, pet,' Mary said. 'I bet you're glad of the eggs, eh, Dave?'

'I am that. And there'll be chicken on the table come Christmas, even if we still out.'

40

They reached a road which ran between high, ragged thorn hedges. Lindy saw dancing firelight twenty yards off. It was the picket.

'Ey up, lads!' Dave called. 'We're back.'

Three miners sat outside a rough lean-to, built against the pit fencing. They were close by a low tubular iron gate which led into the pit yard. Slogans were painted on the lean-to; Lindy made out 'Scargill Country'. The men were in their late twenties. Two lounged on a battered sofa, the other sat on a kitchen chair, hunched over a brazier made from an oil drum.

'What've you got for us, Paul? How were it?'

'Ey up, who's this then?'

Dave made introductions as Paul handed out cans. 'They gave us these in an Indian shop. He said they were for the Yorkshire picketing men, still, he won't mind you young 'uns having them. How's it been?'

'Nowt much. We've had a few paper sellers. Oh, ay, and we've got a bloody big load of cabbage, about six sacks of it. Lasses say we're in for three months of cabbage soup.'

'Like Russia!'

Dave was standing at the gate with Sarah, pointing out scarcely visible buildings. Mary shared a can with one of the pickets, taking turns to swig, wiping her mouth with the back of her hand, to the manner born. Lindy felt ill at ease. Part of her would have liked to draw up a crate, stare into the flames and feel the cold, wet tin against her lips. Endure the chatter and silences until she felt the same familiarity with the pickets she now felt with Paul and Dave. But another part was itchy to be away, to get back to the flat, to have a bath. To see Simon.

'Sit yourself down and get warm, love,' one of the pickets said, dragging a chair from the side of the shed and settling it by the fire.

'I think we're going to see the support group,' her words felt unnecessarily formal and brittle.

Paul said, 'Ay, we got brass – over three hundred quid and endless tinned goods. Other stuff an' all. We'd best be off before they're all gone home.'

'We'll come again,' Lindy said, smiling in the dark.

'Drop in any time. We're here for the duration.'

'We not off through them gates till we do so with us heads

held high.'

'I will. I'll be back. I promise.'

Maybe it was outdoor fires, battered furniture, the companionship of Paul and Dave.... She cared intensely. She wanted to express her caring.

Dave walked them round to the village church where the Support Group had its headquarters. Lindy was surprised and pleased to find Jed Blyth, sleeves rolled above his elbows, peeling potatoes. He was at home, swapping catchphrases and snatches of song.

All activity stopped as they entered, then volunteers relieved them of the cartons of tinned food.

As introductions were made, Jed acknowledged Lindy with a characteristic, 'Now here's one comrade with whom I am not unfamiliar since she is regarded by many as the Rosa Luxembourg of Church Hill, is that not indeed the case, Linda?'

It was months since Lindy decided to accept that Jed would call her Linda for ever. Doubtless he thought Lindy a bourgeois affectation.

'I am putting into practice the tenets of my political philosophy, Linda, and proud to be so doing amongst such fine folk...'

The fine folk in question were clearly used to what Jed called his 'oratorical hyperbole'. Men and women were happy enough to leave him centre stage and, whilst throwing in words and titters of approval, drift back to their individual activities. Luckily for Lindy, Jed was aware of a larger than usual audience. For once he neglected his conversational practice of standing close and skewering his listener with unblinking eyes. Lindy slumped into a chair and accepted with gratitude a cup of tea offered by a denim-clad miner introduced as Gozzer.

The church hall had a simple altar and lectern at one end, divided from the rest of the room by a partition of ranch fencing. The body of the hall was big enough to house twenty or so small tables and three large trestle tables where Jed, the miners and their wives and children prepared vegetables. In one corner of the room was a pile of clothing which obviously waited to be either sorted and allocated to families, or sold as jumble. In another corner were collecting-tins and buckets, each covered with the familiar orange/red and black stickers, but also carrying some new versions and a few C.N.D. logos.

Five women were stitching coloured cloth onto a double sheet which was stretched between them on the floor. This was the new banner, it carried the legend *KIRKFIELD PIT WOMEN'S SUPPORT GROUP* across an outline drawing of Kirkfield Street with the old pit-head rising behind it.

Penny Riding, Paul's wife, rose from the floor, rubbed her knees and draped an arm across Lindy's shoulder. 'Where you planning on stopping the night, love? You're welcome to the spare room. It gets more use now than when our Barry were still here.' As Lindy explained that she hoped to get a lift back to Leeds with Jed there was an outburst of communal laughter.

Jed and Gozzer were duelling with potato peelers. Jed held his left arm in a curve high above his head; his cap dangled from the hand and was being used to obliterate Gozzer's view. Gozzer flicked his head backwards and forwards, miming the action from which his name derived. Cries of 'Drown him, Gozzer!' and 'That's the stuff, Jed, lad. Cut his whistle off!' ended when the pair of them wrapped arms about each other and shuffled a few steps of a dance. As they returned to their potato peeling, Jed swung his cap low in a courtly bow.

'He's a comic, your Jed,' Penny said, accepting Lindy's makings and beginning to roll a fag.

'He's got a brother. Derek. They're as daft as each other. Lovely couple, but they do go on at each other. Half the time I don't think they even know if they're serious. Jed's CP and Derek's Labour.'

'Oh God!' Penny accepted a light. 'There's nowt worse than mixing politics in families. Our two are at it like hammer and tongs.'

Paul had outlined the problem. Barry had been a bright boy at school and ended up going to University to read politics. Now in his late twenties, he worked as a researcher for a couple of Labour MPs. He was 'keeping his nose clean' with the intention of entering parliament. Gary was a miner. 'I tell you, Lindy: bad blood between CP and Labour is nowt. Try Labour with Labour!'

Lindy felt an immediate warmth coming from Penny. She had no edge. Where Paul was big and broad with a gentle open face, Penny was tall and skinny, her face an arid delta with deeply gouged valleys of laughter and pain. Country-rose beauty was battered into a form which exuded beauty of spirit. The grey-blue eyes glittered with intelligence, and the sparse blonde hair, which floated down to her shoulders in loose curls, showed signs of a prolonged affair with the peroxide bottle.

'Are you in the Party?' Lindy asked.

'Not I, marry. But I always use my vote and never ought but Labour. My father voted Labour, and my granddad.' She rested her chin on her hand and exhaled a plume of smoke. 'Granddad helped sink this pit when he were thirteen, in 1906. Worked it all his life. It took my Dad and a brother in one night. Dad and brother. Paul and Gary work alternate shifts now – I can't have it any other way.' She paused for a moment, then said, 'And that bitch talks about economics. Worthless, loveless, soul-less sod!' She dragged hard on the cigarette then laughed and shouted, 'Eh, Denise, what's knew one from Worsbrough?'

Two young women looked up from their work and, after a quick conference, knelt side by side, as if at the front of a stage: 'A is for Arthur Scargill, who's leading the N.U.M. fight, and B's for that bastard MacGregor, who's full of conservative shite...'

Penny put her arm round Lindy. 'What you think, love?'

She thought for a while, then inclined her head to the older woman. 'I almost feel sorry for Thatcher. You're right, a loveless sod. She knows nothing of this. I feel at home.'

VI

The telescope was disappointing at first. Just a fuzzy glare. He fiddled with various focussing devices. Suddenly the moon was there as he had never seen it. There were huge craters, craters within craters, mountains with ragged peaks, stark, hard-edged shadows, dunes, massive splashes of silver as if a giant had spilled boiling lead. It was breathtaking. Suddenly he was self-conscious, he corrected the cliché: *breath-stilling*. He exhaled.

Something called him back to himself (or was it away from himself), his mind was racing, full of fleeting images of potential change. He must change things. This isn't life.

Then the door opened and she was there.

'What's your name?' he asked.

'It doesn't matter.' She was scruffy in denim, holding a pint of beer, turning to leave. 'I'm sorry, I –'

'I'm Simon. Don't go, I've just seen the moon through this. It's amazing.'

'I know. It's Lindy. My name.' Her voice was sinewy, classless, as exciting as her sudden appearance.

Simon returned his eye to the telescope, to make sure it was still there, the moon, 270 thousand miles away, timeless, waiting all this time…

As she came to his side he pulled back to let her take a turn and her glass caught his shoulder. Most of the beer splashed over him. Some trickled down his spine. He heard laughter and recognized it for his own.

'God, I'm sorry,' Lindy said. She slid his denim jacket off his shoulders and down his arms. 'I'm so bloody clumsy at times.'

Simon stood, turned, knocked over the chair. With indecent dexterity she flicked open the buttons of his shirt. He felt like a large child with a small mother, a cuckoo, beak gaping, the dancing reed warbler vibrant with puzzled energy. His guts were liquefied by her. His legs shook.

She had a narrow, heart-shaped face, wide-set, wide open, sky-blue eyes, a small, tight, grinning mouth, and a roughly slashed haircut which, in years to come, would be fashionable and expensive.

'Lindy,' he said, trying it out, then again, more breathily,

'Lindy!'

'Don't worry, I almost trained to be a nurse.' She was tugging his shirt out of his jeans. She was like a conjurer, the shirt was gone and he felt the chill of night air on his damp skin. She screwed the shirt into a ball and rubbed him down, telling him he'd got a nice chest for his age. Then she stood back and looked at her handiwork.

'So, again then. Sorry.'

'It's okay, you know. I was just looking at the moon.' He was dazed.

'I know.' She dragged a blanket off the bed (leaving two others strewn across the floor) and wrapped it round him. She replaced the tumbled chair and said, 'Start looking again. I'll do something about this.' They both looked at the crumpled ball of pale pink shirt. It had been his best white one, which he loved. He washed it with new red underpants – someone had told him that new underclothes were the first requirement of separated couples – and the shirt went pink. He loved it. Now it was a mess of bile-yellow beer stains.

He loved it.

He pulled the blanket under his chin and sat at the telescope. But he couldn't take his eyes off her, even when he shut one and peered into the telescope, he could still see her, so he turned and looked at her again. She climbed onto a chair and gently dusted the final lens with a dry corner of shirt. Simon was fascinated by her movements. She twisted about and he could feel the tight cords and muscles, the springs, strings and pulleys of her body as if they were in him.

As he watched she used his much loved shirt to rub the skylight streaky clean. His shirt now had a flat, black surface. He could have eaten it, to amuse her, to gain her attention.

'Get your eye on the moon, it'll be twice as good now.' It was as if the room had strobe lights, he experienced tachistoscopic images. Her twisting body, her two-footed jump from chair to the floor, her laughing face. Her mouth.

'Back in a tick!' – the door closing behind her.

He made a deposit in his memory bank. Seventeen years later he gives her *The Old Gringo* by Carlos Fuentes and says, 'This has a special significance for us.' It takes her three guesses: 'The chair in Nigel's attic!' 'That's love,' he says, and they hug away pain and conflict and a little more of Nigel's poison is drained off.

She shut the door. A knot unravelled. He felt tears in his eyes. He was awash with good feeling. He put his eye to the telescope, pulled the blanket over his head. She had been right, it was twice as good now. It was cool and timeless, a source of silent ecstasy.

He jumped when she jabbed a finger in his side and said, her voice muffled by the blanket, 'How about this then?'

She held a crumpled but clean blue and red plaid shirt. Between her knees she gripped a carrier which contained his pink, yellow and black shirt.

'Where's it from?'

'One of mine. It's clean and should fit, I think, bit tight maybe. When I say it's clean, I mean I've only worn it once... or twice maybe.'

He put it on. It was brushed cotton, warm and soft. It had a smell that stretched forward in time. 'We must be more or less the same size.'

'Hm, slightly different shape...'

'The difference is nice, in shape...'

People were supposed to have exchanges like this, it was vaguely connected with *liberation*, medical aid to the Viet Cong, Che posters and so on. It was called being swinging and was the harvest of the sixties. The object was to be easy, to achieve personal growth, political awareness, to have deeply meaningful sexual experience. For Simon, being a swinger was a cause of tight self-consciousness. He had already learned that being a swinger ensured endless casual sex, mutual admiration and expenditure on clothes. It also appeared to require frequent periods of desolate loneliness and self-doubt. The philosophy or *lifestyle* was flawed, but he couldn't put his finger on its failing. For this reason the exchange about body shapes sent a small dark cloud scudding across a brilliant blue sky. Enough to have him thinking who he was, who she was, what he wanted, what he should do and say to get what he wanted. And then to wish he wasn't thinking any of it. And to wonder what he should be thinking. Best to speak.

'Sometimes I wish I'd just woken up having slept since birth.'

'You mean you want to exist in the here and now, right?'

Cloud threatened to block out the sun, he felt drunk and bloated.

'Maybe living in the here and now misses something out.'

But they were trapped in the conventions of the day, as Lindy said (oh, that innocent Lindy, trying so hard to make something of her life...), 'Yes but look, I mean, take now for instance. If two people are attracted to each other, and I think we are, I'm confident enough to say that we are, right, then it's ridiculous to allow convention in the way.' It had been an effort, her face pinkened.

'I know, I know' – brittle throated by internal torment, *oh god, bring that feeling back* – 'but I sometimes find that new conventions can get in the way as well.'

Two furrows crinkled her forehead and the corners of her mouth tightened and fell. 'Okay, yes, okay, you're right, natch. I mean, you don't fancy me. That's okay by me, right! I mean, there's no law saying we have to get it together, right?'

He couldn't bear it, he pulled her tight to him and said, 'God, god, I fancy you. I fancy you something rotten. I've never felt like this.' She wrapped her arms round him and pressed her rigid body against his. He could hardly breath, she was making throaty noises and biting his neck.

'For fuck sake,' he pushed her away, he was shivering, anguished. 'I'm trying to tell you something important.'

She was shocked and stood, held at arm's length. There was a silence while they looked at each other, eyes glistening.

'Tell me then for Christ sake, or are you being telepathic or something?'

The pause was short and tense, then he blurted a string of words: 'I want two dogs and some chickens and a small-holding, and a lot of kids and us living and working together. No car, we won't pay fucking taxes to murderers. Grow our own food, make our own bread... You know. That sort of thing. Me and you...'

He hadn't expected all that to come out. He didn't know what to expect, she had narrowed her eyes and was standing very still. He took his hands off her shoulders and let them fall to his side.

Suddenly she grinned and her forehead cleared. 'I know all that, you clown.' She stepped forward and rested her head on his shoulder. 'Why d'you think I followed you up here?'

'I don't know, why?'

'Cos you're a scruff and I want all those things as well. Don't know how to get 'em. Making do with all sorts of crap until I do. Know I won't get 'em downstairs, just tight suits and dirty weekends. So I followed you. You didn't even see me. You were flying high with that very beautiful, sophisticated lady. I can't believe we're here, that we've done and said what we've done and said. But we can't run before we walk can we, so shall we go to bed?' Then, standing back, she puffed out a breath – *huh!* – and shook the tension out of her arms and shoulders.

'I think I might have fallen in love with you,' he said.

'Never mind that,' she was tugging at her boots, 'just get out of my shirt.'

The moon was leaving the skylight. In deep shadow they got into the bed. The blankets were rough and prickly. For a few moments they lay side by side, not touching, looking at the sloping ceiling, then with, a thrill that made them tremble, they found each other for the first time.

And the snug fit.

Simon drifted into an increasingly joyful and exciting awakening. As the previous night came back to him he lay still and breathless. A movement might break the chain of remembered sensation and show it all to be an illusion.

But it was real!

He was flat on his back, no pillow, sun on his eyelids. Gradually he inched his hand across the mattress until his knuckles brushed against her smooth tight skin. He held it there, savouring the sensation, feeling an unfamiliar smile on his face. It had been a long, long time since he had known this feeling. There had been times of awakening in strange beds since Anne, and whilst he was still with her... but not like this awakening. On earlier occasions he found himself uneasy, smelly, his mind trying to escape down narrow tunnels obscene with the slime of the night's deceits, or abrasive with the broken glass and rusty wire of brutal honesty.

Mostly he tried not to sleep after sex, he made an excuse and left as soon as he came.

Now he built a picture of her face, and all the time his body rode waves of ecstatic memory.

'You're chilly,' he said, his voice soft and scarcely more than a whisper. She didn't answer. He raised his fingers to increase his contact with her skin. It was the outside of her thigh, smooth, hard, round... unbelievably cold. He turned his head and slowly opened one eye.

He sat up. The blanket fell from him. Beside him, jutting over the end of the bed, was the telescope.

VII

They were late in leaving the Chance. Lindy sprawled across the back seat of Jed's carefully maintained Triumph Herald Saloon (vintage 1964, real leather trim and walnut facia!), Mary sat beside Jed, who hung from the window and offered parting quips to the miners and their families. But at last they pulled away and began a stately cruise towards Leeds.

There were physical resemblances between Derek and his younger brother Jed, but each attempted to conceal them. They shared the same dove-grey hair, but chose styles which emphasized their political allegiances. Derek favoured the Michael Foot look which he described as *bohemian*: two loose wings running backwards and sideways. Jed's was a severe crew cut. An unflinching commitment to International Communism inhibited all thought of the American military, he was a nineteen thirties commissar.

'The *blitzkrieg* of time,' Jed said, not concealing pleasure caused by Mary's enthusiastic 'Well, I hope I look as good when I'm your age, pet' but keeping his eyes very steadily on the empty road ahead. 'Yes, the blitzkrieg of time, even in this capitalistic society which, as Linda will affirm, I intensely abhor, has not succeeded, to date, in destroying in totality the youthful charm of my exterior appearance, this is true. But anyone can stay young, it is a matter of achieving inner calm which is itself only accessible to those who embrace the doctrine of Marx, who was more than the world's greatest philosopher, for, as I am sure you know full well, Mary, he was also a beautician and exponent of the alternative medicine. Hah!' He finished his elaborate joke with a short explosive laugh.

Removing a hand from the wheel, he pushed his checked cap to the back of his head and vigorously rubbed his stubbled scalp with the knuckles of his clenched fist. As a consequence of decades of Party meetings, Jed had developed a habit of speaking in long sentences which inhibited all but the most politically practised interrupter. But it was also a conversational ploy which went well with his understated Yorkshire humour.

'I never knew that, Jed. I'd better get stuck in and see what he can do for my wrinkles. What about you Lindy?'

Lindy snorted, then felt that, nodding off as she was, a snort was still insufficient response to her friend's question. 'I think he's just giving us sales talk. I bet you have to sell *The Morning Star* at weekends and attend Branch meetings if you want to stay as young looking as Jed.'

'I cannot deny that increased political activity does have its benefits... beauty-wise.' It was a reasonable impersonation of W. C. Fields. 'I'd rather be in Philadelphia,' he went on, getting into his stride, 'after all, they say that Delhi's filthier!' He explained that whilst the first was what Fields had wanted on his tombstone, the rather nifty inversion of Philadelphia to Delhi filthier was his own contribution to the stockpile of Western humour.

*

Terry Skinnow was nineteen, an inactive member of Church Hill C.N.D. who put his energies into the Labour Party and its youth section, the Young Socialists. Simon remembered Terry's contribution to a public meeting called to assess Church Hill's attitudes to nuclear weapons. Allowing for his tendency to tail off into silence, Terry had delivered an emotional plea for limiting C.N.D. membership to recognized socialists. Simon came to the conclusion that Terry was yet another member of the Communist Party. There had been several party members, led, as always, by Jed Blythe. It was Jed who, later, in the pub, referred Terry as 'the young Militant lad, good at heart but victim of muddled analysis...'

'No, listen. Listen.' Terry was about to have another go. 'It's like I say, Simon. Where C.N.D. goes wrong is in having posh people in. You can't be a middle class socialist, it doesn't make sense. I mean, it can't can it? Make sense.'

Simon reached across the table and refilled Terry's glass.

'Take that vicar for instance, how can he want to get rid of nuclear weapons? He's a Tory, so it doesn't make sense. The Tories need the bomb to repress the working class.'

'I don't see it in such simple terms, Terry. I'm looking for progress, not just a reversal.'

'That's where you're wrong then... Unless the working class rule this country there'll never be fairness.'

Terry had arrived half an hour earlier, a smartly dressed young man, short hair, white shirt, red tie, pressed blue jeans. When Simon opened the door he found him clutching a plastic carrier bag to his chest, blurting that he had called on Labour Party business. It was a sort of welcoming visit, providing an opportunity for the new member to ask questions, be put at ease, pay membership money and, if possible, be given a run-down on the goodies and baddies in the Branch. So far, it would seem, the baddies far outnumbered the goodies, the latter being two Young Socialists: Terry and his sidekick, Pat. There were, Terry conceded, one or two other left wingers, words pronounced with a slight lowering of the voice and a powerful injection of reverence. Unfortunately, they were all over twenty-five and therefore not much use.

Simon filled the glasses again and asked Terry what he did. An old habit of speech – few young people in the North 'did' anything anymore. For all his fiery revolutionary rejection of the capitalist state, Terry was ill at ease in admitting that he was unemployed.

'If you're political, Terry, and you obviously are –'

'No, listen, listen,' Terry interrupted, 'I am political, that's what I'm telling you. I'm in a secret society.' He laughed.

'Right, well, as a politically committed member of a secret society, it is absolutely honourable to be drawing SS. Taking Thatcher's money to work as a political activist.'

Terry drank deeply. Simon got up and put on the lights.

'When I left school,' Terry said, speaking very slowly, as if thinking about each individual word, 'I did get a job. I did. I worked at a hairdresser's. They said you got training. That's why the pay was bad, same as dole, less after your bus fares. But you were supposed to be earning good money in next to no time. Anyway, all I did was sweep up and wash mucky sinks. Then they sacked me... sacked me. It's what they do. They underpay you for a year, then, when they should be giving you employment rights and holiday pay and that, they sack you... They bloody sack you...'

Terry had both hands wrapped round his glass and was looking at something beyond Simon, looking to a rosy future which would rise from the confusion of his recent past. Even as Simon watched, the young man's face re-enacted the replacement of youthful enthusiasms by deep hurt and puzzlement, then anger and, finally, his present mask of steady, humourless, determination to bring about a better world where such injustices were banned for ever.

'What did they sack you for?'

'Said I'd been stealing. Shampoo and combs and things.'

'Had you?'

'No, I bloody didn't. I bloody didn't.' Simon was shocked by the intensity of Terry's words.

'My dad nearly killed me. We've never been thieves in our family, never...' The young socialist was near to tears. 'I worked hard at that place. I believed them. I bloody fell for it. Thought I was going to have a career. Then they did that. They always do it. It's slave labour. After a year they say you've stolen things or you don't come on time, or you're rude to the customers, anything. It's just an excuse for sacking you. What chance have you then? It's hard enough without being called a thief.'

He was no longer the seasoned class warrior but a distressed boy carrying a massive load of pain.

'Was there nothing you could do? What about Industrial Tribunals, wrongful dismissal?'

'That's for the ruling classes. There's no justice for us. They need the unemployed to keep wages down. My dad went to see them, but they just said I was lucky they weren't pressing charges. I wouldn't mind but the woman who owns that shop has three others and a garage. You should see her, all tanned and fancy blonde hair and a Porsche. She doesn't care about anything but her bloody money. She wouldn't even talk to him.'

'He believed them?'

'No. He's beaten. He just said if we took it up, we'd come off worse. I might end up inside.'

'So what now?'

'I'm in Young Socialists and I sell *Militant*.'

'The secret society?'

'Yeah. *Militant*. We have meetings of *Militant* readers, sort things out. I was nearly crackers when I lost my job. But I understand now. I'm doing something about it. That's the thing about *Militant*, it teaches you the things they try to keep hidden. I'm in the Party so nobody goes through what I went through. So people like my dad aren't scared to stand up anymore. So I've got chance of a job and a future, and the other millions they've chucked on the scrap heap. We'll get Labour in at next election, then we'll start to see socialism coming. It'll be another world... when we see socialism coming.'

Simon stuck the carefully folded *Militant* in his back pocket and closed the front door. For a few seconds he rested his forehead on the cold stained glass of the door panel and thought of nothing. Then he noticed how some colours were lost in the light from the sodium street lamp. Then William Wray, a retired railway worker, Jamaican, a neighbour and friend knocked and opened. As ever, he had a pipe in his mouth and a mug of tea in his hand. Colours reflected on the lightened skin over his high cheek bones.

'Visitor he gone now, Simon? '

Simon took a couple of steps to one of the chairs which flanked the narrow hall table and flopped onto it.

'It must be nearly midnight. Too late for me to drink tea.' He rolled a cigarette as he spoke.

William sat in the other chair and they looked at each other over the scatter of leaflets and freesheets. 'Can drink tea day or night, man. Tea is good.'

'Rots your guts.'

'Sound to me like you done a week work for a day pay, man.'

'I did a day's work.'

'Taking picture? That not what I call work, but if it make you tired, then must be.'

'Well, I've just joined the Labour Party. Maybe that's it.' He put the roll-up in his mouth and leaned across the table as William held out his lighter and snapped it into flame.   They relaxed back onto their chairs; William said, 'I don't understand. Why you join politic, man? You not have enough problem with bomb and drinking wine and taking picture till your finger tired?'

'It's part of the same thing, William. Only the Labour Party offers a chance of us getting rid of the bombs. Then there's unemployment, education, National Health. We've got to do anything we can to get rid of this Government.   Look what they're doing to the miners.'

'Excuse me,' William said, pointing with the stem of his

pipe. 'Excuse me, I think you right: get rid of Margaret Fletcher, soon as you can. But why join party? You think Kinnock going do better. You think Kinnock he give miner what miner want. I tell you, Kinnock and Owen and Fletcher... they all cut from same cloth. When that cloth get to Ten Darling Street it not long afore it make same jacket. See what I mean? I did see this in West Indies and I did see this in England. Some politician get rich robbing poor man, some get rich saying they helping poor man. What the difference, Simon? Politician get rich and poor them stay poor.'

'You are a cynic, William Wray.' Simon was smiling, but uncomfortable. William wasn't smiling, his brow was creased and his lips drawn tight; red and orange and blue streaked his face and he was ageless.

'Don't know what is cynic as you call it, but if it thinking politician is lying bogger then you bloody right – I cynic. I cynic because... cut it short – all politician I ever heard of is lying bogger and put own skin afore others, be that skin black, brown or white. Better you trust scorpion. Leave scorpion alone, he leave you alone. Leave politician alone he come sting you!'

Simon stretched his foot across the hall and flipped the pedal of Lindy's bicycle. The pedal spun and the orange reflectors flashed. He stopped the spinning pedal, then flicked it into action again. William coughed, then said, 'You think Kinnock any different?'

'No. No, I don't. But I think the Party is different. And I think that joining the Party I can be one more trying to keep him in line, one more trying to get a decent government. I think with Labour there's a chance of some kind of decency in politics. It's a democratic party – the others aren't.'

William stood up and stretched his arms above his head. 'You believe that, man?'

'I think so. Anyway, I'm giving it a try. But, I know what you mean, William. It's just that I can't stand aside anymore. It feels like this is the time to start meddling in party politics. Shit, course you're right, but what else can we do?'

'I know I right, but maybe you right as well. Maybe we both right. Give it a few month, you still say it right to be in Labour Party then maybe I join. Somebody got to do something about Margaret Fletcher. She drink from spring and poison stream.' He turned and made to open the door. 'I going bed. You young man, able sit and play with bike pedal all night.'

Simon sat and watched the pedal turning and thought about what William had said. Of course he was right. Power corrupts – no two ways about that. On the other hand, the country, the world, was wobbling towards disaster like a riderless bike.

He was dozing in the hall, one foot on the bike crossbar when the door opened and Lindy bent to pick up her bag before coming in. Outside a car drove off. Simon stood and stumbled towards Lindy. They hugged. Cramp in Simon's thighs and back dissolved, as if Lindy were a source of therapeutic heat. Over her shoulder he saw a giant in bobble cap and raincoat.

Late as it was, and dead beat as she was, Lindy decided to take a bath. 'I've been waiting for this,' she said, taking a half pint of home-made red, leaving Simon and Mary to their own devices.

Simon turned on an electric fire and drew up two painted wicker chairs. 'I've heard about you, Simon. But I didn't expect to find you on guard at the door.' They smiled, Mary raised her glass and Simon returned the salute.

'How's Greenham?'

'It's Greenham. I'm itchy, me, what with the strike and all. Mining stock, you see. And we've had women come from support groups. I mean there's lasses on their feet now who've spent forty year on their bellies. Mining's not exactly famous for its position at the forefront of feminism.'

'I suppose not. Where do you live anyway? I mean apart from Greenham.'

'I have no apart from Greenham. Had rented accommodation in Peckham before. Haven't been back to the North East for yonks. Just thought I ought to come and see what's what. Don't mind me staying a few days do you, till I get my bearings, like?' She swung the bottle round from the table, topped up her own glass, then held it out to Simon, her rounded face a picture of eagerness and anxiety.

'Stay as long as you like, longer if it keeps Lindy around for a bit. I miss her.'

'Greenham widower. There's women there who talk about their chaps, and the longer they're off from them, the more they wonder what they saw in them. Now Lindy's different. She pines for you. My heart bleeds. "Come on you silly cow," I say, "pull yourself together. He's only a subspecies like the rest."'

She paused, a concerned frown settled on her shiny, dirty face, then she confided, 'I think she's worried you'll drink all the home brew and there'll be nothing left for her.'

Simon spluttered into his glass, then stood up and took the bottle by its neck. 'You've got her number then,' he said, going to the door, 'I'd better go and fill her up or she'll be at our throats.'

Lindy was asleep, her thin arms rested along the sides of the bath, her head on one side, her breasts slightly raised by the soapy grey water. Simon noticed, with satisfaction, that her fingers curved round the empty glass and held it steady. He poured wine as slowly as possible, maximising the trickling sound. She reacted with a slight wrinkling of the pointed nose, a pursing of her lips. He was overcome with love for her. She opened her eyes and seeing him, smiled a slow, sleepy smile.

'It's you,' she said.

'Yes,' he said, topping off her glass with a professional turn of the wrist, 'Mrs Smith, isn't it?' He lowered himself until he was kneeling, his hands on the side of the bath, his face close to hers.

'Ms Smith, smatterfact.' She dropped her hand into the water and flicked her fingers at him. He dodged, then licked his lips.

'Love you,' he said. She smiled and flicked water again, her body still relaxed. He kissed her shoulder, then said, 'I like Mary.'

'Said you would. She's got a stealthy sense of humour.'

'I know, I just fell in it.' He stood up. 'Look, you drink that and wash your mucky bits, I'll warm the towel then come and get you before you fall asleep again. Nice to have you back.'

"'Snice to be back.' She took his hand, which he had placed on her shoulder, and kissed it. 'I've got a lot to tell you.'

*

'So you're Lindy and Simon. I've heard good things of you two. Very good things indeed. Big in our local peace group, I've been led to believe. Well, I can't get to the meetings myself, but I'm a keen supporter, got my original Aldermaston badge on the mantelpiece. Lifelong campaigner, that's John Harmer. Am I right, Chris?'

King John swung his great bulk to face Chris Rowntree,

stooping six foot three with flaking grey skin and a mottled scalp sparsely covered by transparent fawn fuzz. Simon noticed that Rowntree had the habit of clipping and unclipping the ball point pens he carried in his breast pocket.

Councillor Harmer himself was a looming figure in a shiny black suit. Dandruff was just one of his problems. His inflated neck gave him the appearance of a vintage nineteen seventies Tory on a bad day.

The pair of them had greeted Lindy and Simon in Rowntree's corner shop. When Harmer held out his hand, Simon shook it, carefully giving a masonic handshake by applying pressure with his thumb on the knuckle of Harmer's forefinger. Harmer withdrew his hand and scrutinized Simon's face. 'You're not one of them, are you?'

'I thought you were,' Simon said.

'You'll hear all sorts of tales about me, lad. And some of them could be true, but just remember one thing and you won't go far wrong: if you want a straight answer from King John, ask a straight question. I'm a Socialist born and bred and proud of it.'

'Right,' Lindy said, recognising that Harmer had no intention of shaking her hand. 'Why did it take so long for our membership to be passed?'

'Now I can't help you there, love. You'd better ask Miss Travers, she's responsible, you see. She's Membership Secretary.' He reached into Rowntree's child-proof display unit and took a Kit Kat.

'But,' Simon said, coming in before Lindy rose to the red herring of being called 'love', 'I understand that you were Membership Secretary a year ago, when we applied.'

'Ah, I see. Well that puts a different complexion on matters. How did you apply? It sounds to me as if you might have been recruited by certain elements. Which party were you with before you joined?' He poked the last bit of chocolate biscuit into his mouth, like a novice sword swallower.

'We weren't,' Lindy said.

'There you go then. You fell victim to our extremists. We're infiltrated by an International Marxist cell. You'll have been checked out and found wanting, of moderate persuasion or, like myself, to the left of the Party but with some sense in your damned head.' He turned to Rowntree and shook his head, his neck swung after it. 'Devils. It's too bad.' He took an Aero and turned back to Lindy and Simon.

'Never mind, you're in now and very welcome. If you have any problems, just let me know. It can be confusing. There'll be some as'll woo you. Watch out for Elaine Spencer and Charlie Yates, they'll stab you in the back as soon as look at you. They'll be all over you now mind. Give 'em a wide berth! Honest John's advice. They're out to destroy the Party. Over my dead body though, eh Chris. Over Honest John's dead body.'

Somewhere deep in the flab of Harmer's face were muscles used to create displays of integrity, good humour, and other expressions necessary to the professional politician. The present configuration of hillocks and ridges displayed passionate concern for the Party and a wish to present a fair case to two new members. In case this was not clearly understood, Rowntree now explained exactly why Harmer was speaking to Lindy and Simon in this way.

'You see, Mr and Mrs Smith,' Rowntree, who arranged the late delivery of Simon and Lindy's Sunday paper, insisted on having them married, 'What John means is –'

'Aye. Call me John,' Harmer interrupted, his small mouth brown with chocolate. 'No need for this Councillor nonsense. I'm plain John Harmer to my colleagues in the Party. Honest John. Go to it, Chris, have your say, lad.'

'What John here means is that one or two positions of authority –'

'Membership Secretary. He who holds the branch records holds the key to the selection process. Never mind, never mind, it will return to the hands of the righteous.' Harmer seemed to find his intervention deeply amusing; his belly shook, his neck wobbled, laughter spilled from the small, chocolate-froth hole.

Rowntree pumped his shoulders up and down. For good measure he wiped his eye with one hand, and adjusted his ball points with the other. Simon found himself offering a few dry *ha! has!* Lindy stood her ground. Stony faced, she counted out change for Golden Virginia and green Rizlas.

Honest John terminated the display by ripping open a Mars Bar, biting off half and, red faced and wet eyed, offering the other half to Lindy's mouth like a carrot to a donkey.

'Oh, dear,' Rowntree said, sadly watching the remainder of

the Mars Bar, refused by Lindy, restoring symmetry to Honest John's cheeks, 'you'll be the death of me, John. What a comic. You should be on the telly. Don't you think so, Mrs Smith, comic? On telly! I've said it before.' He fiddled with his pens then, pleadingly, 'I'm always saying it, John, you should have been on telly.'

'There's a lot of things I should have been, Chris.' He took a Fry's Cream Bar, unwrapped it, broke off a piece and popped it in his mouth. 'And there's a lot of things I could have been.' Two more pieces joined their liquefied peers. 'There's even things I think I ought to have been and might not have been able to be.' The remaining pieces disappeared; he squeezed the wrapper in his fist before dropping it into a litter basket. 'But I'll tell you this, and I'll tell it you straight, my friends, when you're in service to Socialism and the electorate, you do as you are bid. And John Harmer always has been, and always will be...' he paused, one hand gripping his lapel, the other momentarily straying to the chocolate display, then, in slow, sonorous tones: '...a servant to Socialism.'

'Well said, John.' Rowntree smiled sadly, catching the eyes of first Simon and then Lindy, sharing with them a historic moment.

'Ask not for whom the Labour Party toileth,' Simon said, his face grave, 'rather give freely of thy toil for the Labour Party.'

A liminal flicker of confusion marked Harmer's response, then he stretched out his long arms and gripped Simon by the shoulders. 'You'll do, lad. By God, you'll do. Won't he do, Chris? Won't he just do, though?' Removing one hand, he turned Simon towards a red faced Lindy and jabbed him in the chest with a thick forefinger.

'This lad of yours will do very nicely. Stick with Uncle John, eh? You'll do. Now, me, I'm off. No rest for the weary, eh? Function to attend, Dortmund dignitaries! Mein Heirs, eh?' He placed a finger horizontally beneath his nose and raised his right arm in the Nazi salute. Then, pausing only to stuff chocolate in his pockets, Honest John was gone.

'That man lives and breathes Labour Party,' the newsagent said, counting his stock.

Outside, Lindy said, 'I don't know whether to laugh or cry. I am so sodding angry. Honest John! And he's a Labour

Councillor!'

Simon took her arm and they moved off. 'Look what the electorate put into Downing Street! Come on, ask not whom wisheth to go to the toileth.'

They hurried along the litter-strewn street; a shared desire to urinate had them leaning forward, like Lowry figures on a windy day.

Simon swayed by the open lavatory door, hunched forward, hands clasping his genitals.

Lindy, who sat bolt upright, a good Catholic girl entering her second minute of controlled urination with a sweet smile on her lips and her arms folded. 'Stop trickling, you sadistic prat.' Simon said, banging the side of his head against the door, 'And another thing, your knees are dirty and you had a bath last night.'

'It was a resting bath, not a washing one.' she said. 'I might have a washing one later on, or I might not. It depends on how I am moved.'

Simon began to laugh. 'If you don't move quickly I'll do it between your legs.'

'Promises, promises. Have you thought about becoming a politician? Who's that?'

Mary called, 'I'll get it!' and they listened as she ran downstairs to answer the door. There was a brief exchange, then she shouted, 'It's a Pissy Wood for you, Simon.' She made full use of her Geordie accent. 'Says you'll want him to enter and have a cup of your lovely coffee.'

Lindy pushed past Simon, zipping her jeans. 'Go on,' she said, 'and don't take all day or I'll grass on you.'

PC Colin Woods, Church Hill's community constable, was, according to Lindy, the only man with less between his ears than a stick insect.

VIII

'The fucking Americans shouldn't be in Vietnam,' he said, and savagely switched off the radio news bulletin he had turned on only a minute earlier. 'They should keep their fucking, imperialistic, neo-fascist, fucking noses out of other people's business.'

He looked around Nigel's kitchen: a cube of white and yellow plastic work-surface, white and yellow tiles, white and yellow appliances and modern pine furniture. Light filtered through pale green curtains which matched rugs scattered over a cork tiled floor. 'This is like being inside a boiled egg,' he said, 'or a fucking plastic daffodil.' He flicked open both sets of curtains and winced as sun hit his whisky-pink eyes.

'Sit down, old chap. Sit down and have some coffee. My head's bad enough. Angry young men are years out of date, you know. Terribly outré.' Nigel was wearing an ankle-length, Paisley dressing gown. He poured coffee into a china mug and with his red-slippered foot manoeuvred a pine-and-rush seat away from the table. The slight scratching this action created was enough to make him wince. He held one hand to his head and waved Simon to the table with the other.

Simon sat in silence and drank his coffee. Norma turned from the work surface and put four slices of toast on the table. He grinned at her and said thanks. From her less than friendly response he decided that his grin had been mangled, or some such fucking expression.

'Don't sit down yet, ducky,' Nigel said, sliding his hand up Norma's leg, under the white and yellow dressing gown which, Simon assumed, came with the job. 'Four slices won't go very far, will they? And you'll find some Gentleman's Relish in that wall cupboard. Simon? Gentleman's Relish for you, you rascal. You turned it down last night!'

'Don't mistake me for a fucking gentleman, smart-arse.' Simon picked up a piece of dry toast, tore off its corner and began to chew. Nigel gave the left cheek of Norma's buttocks a couple of strokes, strayed his fingertips over her anus and vagina, then withdrew his hand. 'Chop, chop, then, Norma, dear heart. Two or three more slices, then entertain Simon-bear-with-a-sore-head with your witty stories about soles and heels and what you can do with your simply lovely little tongue.'

Norma coloured slightly and turned with a flashy swirl of dressing gown. Simon couldn't tell whether Nigel's attentions pleased or disgusted her. He couldn't tell and he absofuckinglutely couldn't give a fuck. He stuffed more dry toast into his mouth and washed it down, after a rudimentary chewing, with the last of his unsweetened black coffee. Nigel watched him with a display of silent amusement, or could it be fucking contempt?

'You know mate,' Nigel said, raising a slice of toast to his mouth and holding it at the point of entry, 'you know, I've just been sitting here for the last few minutes, observing you with what I can only call silent amusement. Ignore fair Norma here, and tell Big Brother Nigel all about it. You are suffering more than the A1 hangover which is our shared desert.' He bit into the toast; little pop eyes settled on Simon's face, the bags beneath them glistening as his vigorous chewing tightened and slackened greasy skin. Simon noticed that the toast had its crusts removed. There they were on Nigel's plate, nicely crisp with hints of charring, and liberally smeared with butter and Gentleman's Relish.

It was a moment of decision.

He stretched across and scooped the crusts from Nigel's white and yellow plate. He folded a couple and popped them in his mouth. They were perfect, or, as he put it, his mouth still half filled, 'Delifuckingliscious, man.'

And then he lapsed into silence, because he still couldn't raise the topic of Lindy.

Norma dropped two more slices onto the plate and sat down. She eyed first one then the other over the rim of her white and yellow striped mug. 'What've you got against the Americans anyway?' she asked, her eyes having lighted on Simon.

'Nothing against the Yanks as such. It's the fucking administration, brutalising a whole fucking generation. Using advanced technology weapons to commit genocide on a nation of peasant farmers. I mean, if they'd taken all the money they've invested in this war and bought food and given it to Vietnam… do you think there'd be anything to fight about? Do you think Dr Spock would be under arrest and thousands of young Americans classed as criminals looking for political asylum all over the fucking world. Jesus, I'm just glad I'm fucking English and we haven't got messed up in this lot, that's fucking all, man.'

Nigel had his hand under the table and was leaning forward in order to stroke the inside of Norma's thigh. Without faltering in this movement, and with his eyes on the young woman's face, he took another small bite of toast then said, 'He fancies himself as some sort of rebel, but it doesn't go very deep.'

Norma took Nigel's hand and pushed it away. Nigel moved it back and began stroking again, his eyes fixed on hers. She tried to move his hand again and a little tussle went on under the table. The contenders went pink with effort, or perhaps, in Norma's case, embarrassment. The conflict terminated when Norma stood and walked across to the stainless steel sink with her mug. Nigel leaned towards Simon and made a slurping noise. Then he said, 'Now that is delifuckingliscious, man. You should have taken what was on offer. And you shouldn't have mucked about with Georgie Porgie's raddled bint. That was very naughty. Could have damaged Nigel's promotion prospects. Unforgivable, especially for the sake of dehydrated cunt.'

From his pocket he took a packet of Benson and Hedges and a silver and black cigarette holder. Simon watched as he fitted the fag into his holder and lit up.

'Heh, Norma,' Simon said, raising his voice as if to allow it to pass over Nigel's balding head, 'how long has he been doing this fucking Noel Coward bit?'

Norma was leaning the base of her spine against the sink, one hand holding her mug near her mouth, the other cupping her elbow, as if to support it. Sunlight made her hair shine like a halo. As he spoke, Simon saw her as a person for the first time. Last night, and then during the preceding exchanges in the kitchen, she had been part of the laid-on entertainment.

She put her mug down with care and respect, turned and walked past them. Hers was a calm dignity but with the white and yellow stripes of her borrowed gown she wore layers of sorrow and dismay which flowed from the sad eyes and the downward fall of her mouth. As she passed Simon she said, 'I don't know who Noel Coward is, but I have heard of him.'

And then she was gone, the door softly closed behind her.

'A moody cow,' Nigel said, with the steady syllable by

syllable enunciation of a wine taster passing judgement, 'with a moist but firmly capacious cunt and fine, big thrusting titties.' He grinned and took Simon's forearm in his buttery fingers. 'She is also the best knob-gobbler in the Midlands, as I know to my recent delight since she had just eaten me up and sucked me dry a few moments before you made your rude entrance. Why didn't you have her last night? And where did you get to? You disappeared before things warmed up. This is for you.'

He pulled an envelope from his pocket and handed it to Simon. It was addressed to Simon Brown OIK.

'Found it on the mantelpiece, mate. Go on, open it.'

'I'll wait.'

'What a retiring prune.' Nigel stubbed his cigarette on Simon's plate and ejected the tip. 'Never mind, I'm going to use the facilities again before she packs her little bag and runs. I'd let you have a go, but your such an evil-tempered bastard.'

Nigel's kitchen window looked over a walled garden. Someone had thrown rice salad and bread onto the patio and pigeons flicked their heads, feeding or regurgitating.

The garden was a hundred feet by sixty; a froth of cherry trees concealed the Nottingham skyline. Beds of undernourished perennials and weeds curved around the foot of the wall, which provided support for several espaliered fruit trees and climbing roses. Set into the wall, at a point where its crumbling mossed brickwork shone with dark-green and custard ivy, was a small door faced with a herringbone of split rustic poles.

As Simon looked on, coffee in hand, a black kitten squeezed under the garden door and flowed like oil to the side of the lawn. Its eyes were steady on the puffed-up pigeons; its tail extended parallel to the ground, tip-whipping, its haunches, now the highest points of its body, rose and fell like pistons as it padded the soil beneath its back paws, seeking a secure footing for the next sprint forward.

Simon lit a cigarette and dropped the match into the sink. The outrageous thing about Nigel was that without any of the natural grace of this kitten, with, indeed, what should have been the enormous encumbrance of his clumsy, pretentious and transparent ploys, he still managed to screw almost anything he fancied. Certainly gave that impression. Simon decided pity must play a part, his unscrupulousness, their pity. He used to regard it as a joke, a seventh wonder of the world when Nige turned up wearing his latest bit like others wore black 35mm cameras with flaccid zoom lenses resting on their beer guts. Wasn't funny anymore.

The shite awful thing about Nigel was that his attitude to women blocked the kind of companionship Simon most sought. To see him sporting his hold over Norma was like watching a slow motion close-up of male masturbation – a treat provided for a chosen few at a previous party.

The kitten flowed forward, a push of ten feet. It wrapped itself around the base of a stone urn which held a dehydrated shrub. The black tail curved and rippled, the sooty head moved slowly forward and watched the unsuspecting pigeons. Perched on the rotted guttering of the conservatory, sparrows watched the scene with interest, putting their heads together as if to exchange observations. A shadow flooded the garden as a puff of cloud moved over the sun's face.

Simon watched the kitten move out and along a shallow trough which edged the lawn; he felt a tightness in his chest. In its new position the young cat was well concealed. The trough took it to within a foot of the pigeons.

Everything he believed in told him that Lindy could not just step into his life and then out of it, leaving no traces other than this state of agitation. He was neither hippy nor diabolist, but he had little faith in the limits of conventional reality. As a statistician he loved the soft ambiguities of nonparametric analysis.

'I was   just   an   ordinary   statistician   until I   met Kolmorogov-Smirnov. It's an in-joke.'

'So far   in,' she licks his naked shoulder, 'the skin's healed over it.'

There was more to life than swinging. There was magic! A concealed flow of meaning, forming an obscure, organic pattern, an invisible platform. A foundation for the non-rational certainty that Lindy could not go, never to be seen again.

But he could only contact her through Nigel.

The kitten made its run, and much to Simon's surprise, perhaps the kitten's, and certainly the chestnut and white pigeon's, found its teeth and front claws sunk deep into the pigeon's neck.

Simon's knowledge of literary criticism rose above that of the next person's in one respect only: on a train journey to Edinburgh, a Chinese poet had patiently (and extensively) explained the meaning and literary deployment of the term *objective correlative*. As the cat dragged the struggling and blood-pelleted pigeon into a dense flower bed, and Simon faced the fact that if Nigel knew Lindy, then he had almost certainly had his nasty, slimy little prick in her, it was this literary term he suggested should be fucked.

IX

Crossing to the top of the stairs, Lindy called down, 'Fetch him up,' then, to the constable, who was half way up the stairs, 'Sorry, Colin, that makes you sound a bit like sick, doesn't it?' Mary followed, blank faced.

Lindy held out an arm to direct the visitor into the kitchen. As Mary passed her, she took her hand and squeezed it. For a moment she was lost in a confusion of screaming, shouts and the clatter of a low-flying helicopter. Mary was limp as three policemen carried her away from a group of women who blockaded the road. She was face down, suspended three feet from the road, hair streaked with wet mud. A sergeant held her by the shoulders, a constable by the legs, a second constable had one hand between her legs, grasping her vulva, the other fondling her breast.

'I'll put the kettle on, shall I, pet? Thirsty work walking about under them big helmets, I shouldn't wonder.' Mary smiled at Lindy.

'And where's the man of the house? It's him I've come to see really. Not that the company of two charming females isn't always welcome.' He put his helmet on the kitchen table and ran his hand through his ginger hair before taking a slow and careful look around the room.

'He's in the lav, 'smatterfact.' Lindy took the helmet and put it on the floor. 'Sit down, he won't be a minute.'

'Ah! Attending to the call of nature.'

'What's that, petal?' Mary asked, spooning tea into the teapot.

"The call of nature, attending to it. It's what people say in polite company, I'm given to understand.' He undid the button of his breast pocket and took out his notebook. Opening the book to a clean page, he placed it on the table and ran a hand over it.

Simon entered and grinned over the policeman's head. 'Now then, Colin, what can I do for you that won't get me into serious trouble with the vice squad?'

The young policeman sat a little straighter in his chair and pulled back his shoulders. 'I'll ignore that remark, seeing I don't understand it. I've come because I think I can put a little bit of money in your direction, and I understand that that wouldn't go amiss.'

Mary handed round mugs of tea without milk or sugar. Simon saw the compassion on Lindy's face, looked towards Mary and noticed that her hand trembled as she put the mug before Woods.

'Breaking and entering?' He asked, taking a milk bottle from the sink and putting it at the policeman's elbow.

'It's your skills as a photographer.'

'Go on,' Simon said, stirring his tea.

'Well, I've been working with some of the local kids. We've cleared an area of land down by the canal, with the owner's permission. They'll be building there in a year or so, anyway, meantime we've laid out a little football pitch. Thought you might come and take pictures of the lads playing football.' He drank his tea and stared at the notebook. Mary left the kitchen. Lindy sat at the table with her face in neutral.

Simon lit a roll-up and pushed the makings across the table to Lindy, who took them without comment.

'It's a bit difficult at the moment,' Simon said, squinting through smoke whitened by the afternoon sun. 'You see, night after night we see you lot knocking the shit out of miners,' he raised his voice to quieten the first interruptions, 'and, because of our experience in the peace movement, we're fairly certain that the reality is much worse than we're shown. I'm not saying, Colin, that you take pleasure in cracking skulls with your standard issue cosh –'

'You've got –'

'Let me finish, right! You can have your say, but let me finish. I'm not blaming you personally, but, community cop or not, the sight of that uniform is nauseating to more and more of the people you're supposed to be serving.' He opened his hands in front of him, like a conjurer: 'Your turn.'

'Strike's got nothing to do with me.' His round face was red with anger. 'Far as I can see it's par for course, life as usual. We're caught between the Government and a set of bloody animals. They've gone too far. As per bloody usual, we're having to do everybody's dirty work for them. But, anyway, I'm talking about football and local kids, not Mr Scargill and his thugs.'

'Would you like to reconsider "animals" and "thugs"?' Lindy's voice trembled. 'Or would you like to piss off?'

'You don't talk to me like that.' Woods pressed the edge of his clenched fist into the kitchen table. Simon stood behind Lindy, rested a hand on her shoulder.

'Why not? What makes you different?'

'This does. This uniform does. You respect this uniform like everybody else does. If you don't you take the consequences. That's the law of this land and that's what the miners are being taught. You can't flout it. If some of the lads get out of hand, what the hell do you expect? Nobody's perfect. Nobody! Anyway, I didn't come here to argue about something that's nothing to do with you or me. I came to ask you about photographs.'

Simon took the mug from the policeman's hand. 'You've got your answer.' He picked up the helmet and gave it to Woods, who was now standing.

'We'll say no more about it then.' Woods took a last look round the room, tried to make eye contact with Lindy and failed, then added, 'You'll likely regret it.'

Simon opened the kitchen door.

'This is the way out.'

Lindy was white and shaking. Woods hesitated then moved across the landing. They heard his boots descend to the hall, then the front door slammed. Mary came into the kitchen and sat down without speaking.

'I can't stand it,' Simon broke the silence. 'I can't stand the sight of them. I can't stand the tight-skinned, shirt-sleeved superintendents saying their men have acted with restraint under intense pressure. I can't stand their smug fat faces with tashes like turds…'

Lindy and Mary sat in silence, their faces blank, hands immobile, fingers curled like dead things on the scrubbed table. Slowly Mary's hand moved and settled over Lindy's. Simon said, 'Don't exclude me. Don't let them take what we share.'

X

He had been separated from Anne for over a year. The brief flowering of their relationship was well behind him. She lived with an estate agent in Harrow Weald. When, on sleepless nights, he looked back to his married days he saw a desolate country.

After the party, after Lindy, he felt a need to tidy and organize his existence. To make himself clean. He reduced his drinking and bought a new suit in fawn brushed denim; he threw himself into his work as company statistician with Opinion and Attitude Research; he accepted invitations to dine with the directors of the firm. He was promoted.

In the pub housed beneath the O.A.R. offices Simon drank Campari with double soda, ice and lemon. He allowed himself one at lunch time, one before leaving at night. In drinking schools he stuck to Perrier.

But as bland months slid by, he frequently lapsed: dramatic episodes of scotch and bitterness followed by hangovers which left him anxious and confused for days.

'I'm the only director to wear a safari suit with teardrop lapels and flared trousers,' he joked. And the young research executives stood around and flattered him. He played squash. All but one of the young research executives allowed him to win. He refused to play golf with the MD, but wondered how long he could hold out. He refused to dine with married executives, lest they offered their wives; worse still, their wives might offer themselves. Even worse, he might accept one. Worst of all, he might try to take one not on offer.

Something inside him wanted to break things.

As the only director to wear a denim safari suit and chiffon scarf he was, within the confines of O.A.R. Ltd, in danger of becoming a target, a culture hero, and an embarrassment.

'Do what you've got to do! Be what you've got to be!' REs glanced at their watches. Casseroles were drying, babies were crying, women in herby kitchens were looking at electric clocks with sweep second hands set in shiny pine surrounds. Twenty feet above their razored heads, beyond the revealed plastic beams, the O.A.R. switchboard was falling asleep. After a couple of Camparis to wash the day down he found himself on his third or fourth, or was it fifth Glen Fiddich? The pink embroidered roses on his blue silk tie were decorated with ash. A teardrop of spilt whisky darkened the deep purple of his shirt.

It was months since it had happened. Lindy!

'I think I'd better be off, actually, Sime.' The young man took a pig-skin briefcase from between his well-polished boots and patted the pockets of his double-breasted tan suit. 'Sharon's due to drop the first sprog any time now. Be just like the bitch to go off early.'

Simon watched him wait nervously for a group reaction. A round of laughter. He'd said the right thing. A blond executive in a dark blue suit and pink shirt slapped the father-to-be on the back. The leave-taker brought his eyes to meet Simon's, searching for the final accolade, seeking permission to leave. Simon felt something heavy, like a section of girder, settling in his stomach.

'Do what you've got to do, Jimmy. Like I said, be what you've got to be. In your case, I assume you have an uncontrollable desire to wash nappies and flood the offices of O.A.R. with the smell of sour milk and puke.' He turned about, to avoid seeing the consequence of his cruelty. 'Same again for everyone but Jimmy, who has to run off and hand-deliver a sprog.'

The barman rubbed his nostril with a crooked finger as he held Simon's glass to the optic. He started the double, then, over his shoulder, 'They never know what's coming until it's too late.'

'Wouldn't know, Barney. Never had any myself. Always seemed a mug's game to me, know what I mean?' The girder settled, its edges dragging and tearing down his left side.

At half past one the next morning he was being sick. His eyes streamed as he gripped the side of the lavatory bowl and his throat and nostrils burned as his stomach pumped undigested chicken bhuna.

He'd ended up taking three of the executives to a local Indian place, putting food and pints of iced lager on his new credit card. There had been much laughter and swearing of eternal friendship and preferment in O.A.R. as they helped him into a taxi.

Simon was a swinger again.

He sat back on his heels, tried to steady his breathing. The lemon geranium needed watering. And the paint work was thick with dust. Perhaps he should get a cleaner. Perhaps she would be young and fuckable. Perhaps she would be old and fuckable. He flushed the lavatory and splashed cold water in his face. The sink was disgusting.

Slumped across the small settee, drinking well-watered whisky, a Benson's hanging from his mouth, he inspected his grey buffalo hide boots, twisting his ankle this way and that. He ran through the exchange with Jimmy in the pub. He wondered if the baby had come. 'Mr In-between, why's your face gone green?' he murmured.

The girder in his stomach was moving again. He could taste the blue steel of it. He thought about Lindy. Remembered their bodies fitting like hands in prayer. But she jumped away from his control and stamped mercilessly on the girder. He drank from the whisky bottle, mumbling, 'Not my fault. I mean, what's it all about? That's fucking all! What's it all about?'

The room was spinning and swaying. He knelt by the coffee table, gripping the Glen Fiddich bottle. Promotion present? No, that was weeks ago. Half empty anyway. Half fucking full, man! He held it with both hands just to steady the label, which seemed to be slipping about on the wet, green glass. He'd kept her letter, the boss's wife. 'I'll ring her,' he said. 'I'll ring whatsername... I'll ring whatsername. She'll care about me maybe.'

His elbow slipped from under him and he slid forward onto the table. Slowly and clumsily he stood, swayed, then fell across the bed.

They met in the restaurant on the top floor of Fortnum's. Her choice. When Simon arrived he was feeling queasy from the previous night's drinking. He hadn't expected her to say 'Yes, today!'

'Who is it?' she asked, after he had given her his name and mentioned Nigel's party.

'Simon,' he said, beginning to feel like a spare. 'Remember, the oik from the party last year. You left me a letter saying to call.'

'Ah! That Simon. How are you?'

'I thought we should meet. I mean, I'd like to see you. What do you say?'

'Yes, today!'

She sat in the alcove, just as she said she would. Tea and buns for two on the small table. Her brown hair shone and fell down over a silver-grey silk jacket. She wore pearls and a grey silk shirt. Her face was thinner than he recalled. It was as if she had been ill and then spread a veneer of health over the signs of distress.

'But you are so... trendy,' she said as he sat beside her. 'Where has the scruff gone?'

'These are my work clothes. My uniform.'

'And, at the party you were in your casual clothes, another uniform?' She poured tea for him and smiled a gentle, artificial smile.

'I didn't expect to see you so soon.'

'I'm sorry. Have I rushed you?' Now a look of concern. 'George is away for two weeks. He's in Hong Kong... I'm sorry, Simon. I've disappointed you...'

'No, no you haven't. It's good to see you. And no you haven't rushed me.' He drank his tea. She offered him cakes, he shook his head. 'Couldn't,' he said. 'Had to eat with a client.'

'And what did you have? Tell me.' She opened a snakeskin handbag and searched it as she spoke. Simon watched with interest, wondering whether to tell her the truth. He decided he would.

'Boiled potatoes, green salad, no dressing, bread, and water.'

'Good gracious. Do you work in the prison service now?'

'Ulcer. Very fashionable in my line. Increases your chance of promotion.'

'My line of country! A George expression...' As she spoke she removed a silver flask from her bag and unscrewed the top. 'Perhaps you shouldn't then?' She held the flask over his tea, ready to pour.

'I think perhaps I should. A big one.'

'George's. He tells his underlings which drink he favours, then collects bottle upon bottle at Christmas.' She poured a good measure of brandy into his tea, gave herself the same amount, then took a nip from the neck.

'You have fifteen or so years, Simon. Make sure you don't follow in his footsteps, or those of the odious Nige. He's doing rather well, by the way.'

'I can imagine.'

'I sometimes read historical fiction. I keep promising myself that when I am older, or happier, I'll read the real stuff...' She paused and replenished their cups from the flask. 'Nevertheless, mixing with Georgie's associates and courtiers, living with Georgie, I forever return to the conclusion that little has changed. Nige,' she pronounced his name with an accompanying grimace of extreme disdain, 'is one of those who is moderately good at a trivial, unproductive and quite unnecessary occupation. It simply provides an arena within which he can thrive by satisfying the desires of his seniors. He is a pimp, your friend. Did you know that? A shitty little pimp.' She emptied her cup. Simon was about to pour tea but she stayed his hand and emptied the flask. 'Having reached the level of increasing professional incompetence, and gained further ground through his activities as a sycophant and pimp, will he now advance to assassination? Men of his type use blackmail and character assassination. I have seen that. Georgie himself is good at it. But do such people still murder as in earlier days?'

Lifting her cup she found to her disappointment that it was empty. 'Oh dear. So soon. Why not take me to the cinema or something. My treat,' she said. A five pound note had appeared, caught between the fingers of her hand like a cigarette. She waved it gaily in the air, then placed it on her unused plate. 'I shall soon enter my shitty shite stage, darling. Then we can both have a jolly good laugh.'

Simon's denim jacket was folded in the bottom of the small rowing boat, his floral tie curled snake-like on top. Even with his sleeves rolled and his shirt open the effort of rowing had him sweating heavily. Hilary watched him from her seat in the prow, her face easy with laughter. They had bought a quarter bottle of brandy and shared it almost equally. Hilary flung the empty bottle in the air and it entered the Serpentine with a pleasing *plop!*

'You look much happier. You look lovely.' Simon rested on the oars. Against the city rumble he enjoyed the liquid hiss of the boat as it cut through the murky water.

'Thank you kindly, sir.' She twisted her hair which flowed down the front of her left shoulder. 'I am glad you think I am lovely. And I look happy because I am happy, and I am happy for two reasons.'

'Go on.'

'Because your hair is dishevelled and you are sweaty and your trendy suit is all splashed.' She kicked his jacket. Cloud-blue pearlised leather shoe with a high heel. He made a mental note to check that nothing had fallen out of his pockets. Nothing of importance. Cheque book, wallet... The girder suddenly formed in his stomach, then dissolved. 'Go on,' he said.

'You won't approve.'

'Try me.'

'Are you going to take me to bed, Simon-quite-a-character-in-your-own-way?' There was nothing flippant in the way she asked the question.

'Yes. I'd like to. I'd like to soon. As soon as possible.'

'Still sweaty?'

'If you like.'

'Yes. I would like.' She leaned towards him, rocking the boat, and took his wrists in her hands. 'I would like very much.'

'Is that the second thing?'

'No, that makes me much happier than the second thing. And it frightens me.'

'What frightens you? Me?'

'No,' she said, releasing his wrists and leaning back with one hand over the side and trailing in the water. 'Simon-quite-a-character-in-his-own-right is nothing to be afraid of. I'm afraid of the novel.'

'Didn't know you knew about it.' He pulled on the oars to avoid a partially submerged branch which was entangled with rope and weed. 'That shouldn't be in here. It's out of place.'

'Possibly some shit brought it all the way from his duck-pond in the back of his shitty little Morris traveller, just to push it in the Serpentine and cause you a moment's puzzlement. Things are shitty and complicated I find.'

They were in Crouch End. He found himself thinking about the dust, the dirty sink the possibility of a cleaner. He almost forgot she was there.

'Is that what you wanted?' Her voice hard edged and distinct, as if speaking a foreign language.

Simon turned his head on the pillow. She was motionless, her face a death mask, gravity pulled at the flesh on her jaw. He began to say It wasn't what I didn't want then stopped himself.

'It wasn't what you wanted,' she said, a mixture of statement and question.

The skin behind her ear looked soft and unprotected, her long hair was in disarray, his head rested on some of it. He tried to kiss her ear. She pulled away and said, 'Don't do that. Don't!'

'I don't know what to say.' He found her groin then her hand, it was curled on her stomach. He took the cold stiff fingers in his, they didn't move.

'You wanted me. Wasn't that what it was all about?'

He raised his head. Her eyes were closed. Before coming to bed she had carefully removed her make-up, revealing the contours of an unfamiliar face. A flake of mascara was caught in the corner of her eye, like coal dust.

'I didn't want it to be like this. I wanted to be close.' He sat up and reached for his cigarettes. She pulled the quilt closer to her chin, hiding the bare shoulders and the swell of her breasts. Simon offered her the open pack of Bensons but she shook her head.

'How, then? How if not like this? Perhaps you were expecting me to be like a Romanian athlete? Perhaps you haven't noticed. I am over forty?'

'Not what I mean. That's not what I mean. You know that, Hilary. I know you know it.'

She said nothing in answer. He looked down at her. She opened her eyes and stared past him at the ceiling.

'What was the second thing?' Simon stubbed his cigarette out in the cheap pot ashtray he kept by the bed. She didn't register the question. 'Remember, you said two things were making you look happy, when we—'

'I know. I was wondering whether to tell you.'

'I see.' He slid down into the bed with the distinct feeling that he was taking up a temporary position.

'I'll tell you,' – her voice softer now. She turned to look at him for the first time. Her face sagged towards the pillow; she looked like someone else, an older sister perhaps.

'What is it?'

'Do you really want to know?'

'I really want to know.'

'Am I staying?'

'You answer every question with a question.'

'That's a shitty thing to say, Simon. I want to know what you want me to do.'

'What do you think I am, Hilary? I want you to stay, but I want you to do what you want to do. And I want you to be happy.'

'Men always know exactly what they want. Just tell me. Tell me. Am I staying?'

'Is that what you want?'

'What I want. What I want. Simon, I'm too old to know what I want. I've never done this before. I've never been with another man, not that he ever wants me as anything but...' Her eyes searched his face. For a moment they settled on his lips and he thought she was going to kiss him, then they returned to his eyes and she began to speak again.

'I thought that if we made love, if we lay together with no clothes, no watch, no rings or pearls, no make-up... I thought it would be different. Men have... propositioned me, made passes. I've never been interested. Half the time I felt that I was just a stopping place on their journey somewhere else. You were different. I watched you at the party, slumped in your chair. George and his fawning acolytes droned and barked. And I imagined life with you in a hut in a forest by a lake, with columns of midges catching the evening sun and nothing to disturb the silence but the whirr of birds and sometimes a fish would jump and ripple the water.' She closed her eyes and was silent for a moment. 'You made me very sad...'

Tears were squeezing between her eyelashes. Simon began to stroke the hair which looped down the side of her face. 'I don't know how to say what I want. I don't know how to want.' She paused again and opened her eyes.

'I only know how to be told what I want.'

Simon cleared his throat. He felt awkward and tired.

'Then stay. I want you to stay. I am telling you to stay. I know that you want to stay.'

She smiled and the tension sank beneath the surface of her face. He sensed her whole body relaxing; the bedclothes whispered.

'Now tell me what made you happy?'

She hesitated for a moment, then said, 'I have a half bottle of brandy in my overnight case.' She grinned, looked like a little girl caught doing something mischievous.

He was empty and cold, as if, somewhere inside, the moon had died behind rain clouds. The girder was back, pushing its jagged edge into his side.

*

Over the months she became voluble and energetic, he bobbed in her wake.

'The Chinks, Georgie and the Yanks assume, will cut little pieces of cheap leather to patterns provided by the firm. They will then send the leather to George who will have it machined and stick labels on the resulting sandals.' The first alcohol of the day followed a familiar route to her brain. 'George sends the wretched things back to China at a price which includes the cost of patterns and discounts the cost of raw materials. So the shitty world turns. Furthermore, darling, the shit regards this as a profit making venture, a tax fiddle, and a step on the road to a knighthood.'

Simon had been bullied into a weekend at her house, the husband safely away in what she called Red China, following in Tricky Dicky's footsteps, empire building.

She stood by the pool in a primrose dressing gown, a glass carrying traces of vodka and tomato juice in her hand, her eyes set on the beech trees lining the road some two hundred yards away. 'I do not care, Simon. I do not care. I would rather be puddled night and day. I do not care that your despicable Nige arranges for young girls to do things for Old Georgie and the Yanks. I do not care when Paddies are shot by our glorious boys in coloured berets. I do not care that the oh so exciting Olympic Games are receiving yet more attention, if that were possible, because Yids and Wogs are incapable of resolving their dispute without killing each other. Most of all, my darling, I do not care that all this,' she swung her arm around to take in the acres of park and a compact neo-Georgian mansion, 'that all this – conspicuous display – was bought with money resulting from the sweaty brows of the unfortunate and that highly prized mixture of hypocrisy, moral depravity and intellectual frailty which is known as good business practice.'

She had been holding her glass out to him. 'Thank you kindly, sir,' she said, and stepped to the poolside table. 'You are supposed to take the bottle and say "Should you?" then we struggle, then we make love, here at the pool side in the early summer light.' As she spoke she poured vodka, then added ice and tomato juice from a crystal jug. Simon accepted tomato juice but refused the vodka bottle.

'You used to be a good drinker, Simon. Remember that first time in London. Oh, brandy, brandy, all the way...' She took his hand, swung it.

'I'm watching it a bit.' The tomato juice fell cold and acid to the open sore in his stomach.

'I shall cook a special poorly tummy din-din because I love you, I love you, I love you.' She threw her empty glass into a flower-bed and pressed his hand against her groin. Her free hand, still cold from the iced glass, burrowed into his borrowed dressing gown.

'Would you like to go back to bed, Hilary?'

Her hand slid down to his cock which hung limp and shrunken. She twisted in front of him, her wide mouth laughing, her eyes shining and her face taut and tanned. She looked younger than her years, healthier than she deserved.

'Swim!' she said.

'I'll watch,' he said, and, pulling the towelling gown tighter round his chest sat down at the table and took cigarettes and matches from his pocket.

It was a big pool, lined with pale green tiles. Hilary swam well, her hair trailing like weed over her naked back. To begin with Simon counted the lengths. Hilary smiled and waved as she turned. Simon smoked. The sun began to blaze over distant trees. Hilary was lost in her steady breast-stroke and the smooth, regular turns. Water and swimmer were like a sophisticated mechanical toy.

It could only be obsessive swimming that saved her from raddled middle age, this and regular beauty care. Simon watched a green fly totter across the white wooden slats of the table. The relationship was dying. He didn't want it to end, it was useful, an interest, a way of pacing the passage of time, of his life. And for Hilary it was a reason for being – she repeatedly told him so.

Their time together was becoming ritualised. She no longer needed excuses to drink, no longer concealed half bottles. When they met she was on a plateau, having taken enough to keep the shakes at bay. Through afternoon and evening they drank heavily. Emotionally they were out of phase. Simon would feel loving, pleased to see her, glad to climb onto an island of warmth and caring after swimming in the cold and (due to his frequent absences and benders) increasingly rocky waters of O.A.R. But she would be brittle. They met for a while in the middle phase, she pirouetting on a peak of self-mockery, he mellowed by the first high tide of alcohol.

Love-making was rudimentary, then she sank into despair. As he helped her out, he became numb and hollow. It was always the same. He couldn't tell her. He acted. She was pathetically grateful, cried, told him of her childhood, of the pain inflicted by George. By then they were almost unconscious. When they woke she would refuel with white spirits and mixers and slip into the driving seat. He, dazed, a dull pain in his side and a fogged head, followed where she chose to take him.

Something cold and wet touched his leg. It was one of George's two King Charles Spaniels; the other was leaning over the pool, trying to drink, its small pink tongue curling inches from the green water. He lowered his hand to stroke the silky dome of its head, but the dog rolled on its back and mewled for him to tickle its belly.

'Is this Blither or Blather?' he called, as Hilary swam towards him, head clear of the water and hair like lines of paint down her cheeks, fanning over tanned shoulders and back.

'If its nose is scarred it's Blather.' She heaved herself out of the pool, her breasts swinging and, for a moment, trailing strands of twisted water. She pulled on her heavy yellow robe and began to dry herself. 'Call the little shits Blother.' Both dogs trotted to Hilary and fawned about her feet. One licked her toes and she kicked it away. 'You should swim. Makes you feel so good.'

He walked to her and rubbed her back through the robe. 'I've always been happier sitting at the side and watching. How do you do that?' He stepped back as she twisted a yellow towel into a turban that held her long hair out of sight. She had her back to him and for a moment the sight of her neck and the fair hair that grew there softened him. She was the best there was, kind, funny, clever, complicated, and independent. She asked nothing more than he should be there.

On the preceding Friday he played squash with an R.E. whose father was a junior Minister. Simon had beaten the young man, of course. When he was showering, the boy, for that was all he was, stepped into the cubicle, drying his stylishly long blond hair. 'Anything you want, Sime?'

Simon leaned out of the steaming needles of water. 'Like what?' Angry that promotion meant public school propositions in the showers and bad squash.

'You know,' the boy said. 'Anything to make you happy.'

'What the fuck is happy?' – pulling back into the shower. 'Nobody ever promised me fucking happy'

He wrapped his arms around her and she leaned back into him. 'Breakfast, then laze in the sun,' he said, pressing his face into her cheek.

XI

Thirty people sat on the floor in the Civic Hall. Heavy oak tables were pushed against the walls and littered with bags, clothing and leaflets. Rex and Helen had joined the local branch of C.N.D. and were amongst its most active members. Simon caught Rex's eye and smiled. The young punk had smartened himself up and was wearing ironed jeans and a sweater of cream and pink bands that made him look substantial. Helen sat beside him knitting. A question floated above them, pinned to the pale oak wainscoting, scrawled in purple and green on recycled paper: *Are you psychologically prepared for arrest?*

A square-faced woman in her early twenties hoisted herself onto a solid oak table, crossed her legs, and introduced herself as Trudy. She wore chunky trainers and heavy corduroy trousers. A bottle-green sweater smothered her trunk, brown hair hung in waist-length plaits interwoven with scraps of rainbow cotton. Her message, repeated in several ways, to stay 'cool calm and collected' during Non-Violent Direct Action.

Simon leaned into Lindy's side and whispered, 'She's very cool calm and collected, don't you think?' Lindy pushed him away and said, 'Sh!' Mary cupped Simon's ear and said, 'I'll go bloody scatty if she says it again.'

Trudy unwound her legs and slid from the table so that she half stood, half squatted. She tied a loose knot in her plaits and rested her wrists on it, her hands hung limply through the loop of hair.

'I want you all to feel free to ask me anything... anything. You'll have another chance to put questions after Rupe has taken you through the role-play and experiential exercises. But, for now, just ask away, okay?'

Rupe sat cross-legged by the wall. When Trudy mentioned his name he smiled around the room and waved as if his hand trailed rose petals. He was in his late sixties, thin, leathery face, craggy eyebrows and a mane of iron-grey hair. He could have passed for a prophet in a Hollywood movie, but for the lovat tweed suit and Fair Isle pullover.

No one offered questions. A prolonged silence, then Trudy nodding her head rhythmically said: 'Okay. Okay. I do think we

84

should just float a few questions before Rupe takes over. Anything, okay. Anything.'

There was a general rustling and murmuring. People turned to those next to them and outlined questions they would like to float, asked when the first break would be, discussed vegan sandwich fillings.

The first person to speak was a pullover-and-brogues man in his late thirties. Bright eyed and shiny headed, he raised himself to a crouch. One hand rested on the floor, giving support, the other smoothed his scalp as he spoke: 'I would respectfully suggest,' and no-one, thought Simon, could better communicate a respectful suggestion, he had to be a vicar, 'that in the interests of those of us who do not wish to be secondary smokers, primary smokers desist from here on?' His voice raised to form a question.

There was an outbreak of mixed responses to the vicar's respectful suggestion. The Blythe brothers, well over a century of politics between them, were quick off the mark: Derek's voice rang above the general hubbub: 'Move to a vote! Move to a vote, Chair!' From another quarter came Jed's authoritative demand for a 'ruling from Chair, Chair.'

Rupe rose to a crouch and, weaving his way between the campaigners, approached Trudy. Obviously the vicar had set the style for the day. Rupe stooped, his brow was wrinkled, he trailed one hand on the floor, even his muttered 'Sorry brother!' and 'Excuse me, sister!' added to the simian impression. Reaching Trudy, they spoke in whispers, or perhaps, Simon thought, head movements.

Conference over, Rupe returned the way he came, holding one hand palm outwards, as if to stop oncoming traffic, and offering a face made clownish by raised eyebrows and open-mouthed smile. Trudy cleared her throat several times, and the gathering settled into silence.

'Okay,' she said, replacing her hands in her looped plaits and nodding, 'I hear you request a vote. I hear you request a ruling from the chair.' She stopped nodding for a second and surveyed the room with a smile. 'Not the way we take decisions in the N.V.D.A. movement, okay. We have no chair. We, well, I, yes,' she began to nod fast, as if to catch up for lost time, 'I, I might, I suppose, be called a facilitator. But even that is over authoritarian for someone like me. No vote; no ruling from the chair. What we are going to do is this...'

Simon sank his head onto Lindy's shoulder and said, 'Oh, God!' Lindy said 'Sh!' and pushed him away.

Trudy flicked her fingers straight so that her hands were spread like the wings of a soaring bird. 'The essence of Non Violent Direct Action is a group reacting as an organic whole to any turn of events. We are going to take this particular issue of primary and secondary smoking as an opportunity to explore our capacity to reach decisions in a flowing, organic fashion, okay? I want you to turn to the person next to you and exchange opinions on the issue. Say, for example, *Although a primary smoker myself, I do not favour the imposition of my exhaled smoke on others, what is your position on this question?* Or whatever, that's only an example of what you might like to say. Just give it a try. Okay, in your own time.'

There followed a chaotic outbreak of urgent whispering and scattered laughter. Mary tapped Simon on the shoulder. 'Raise your bum, man. I'll look and see if you're sitting on her marbles.' Lindy asked, 'Shall we suggest the room splits into primary and secondary smokers?' And Simon said, 'Sh! Give us the matches.' Several primary smokers lit up.

'Okay, everybody!' Trudy increased her nod rate and clapped her hands without unhooking them from her plaits. 'Turn to the person on the other side of you, or behind you, or in front of you if you want, and tell them how the person on the side of you feels about primary and secondary smoking. And how you yourself feel about it. Okay, off you go again.' She flicked her fingers to emphasize 'again'.

A hand settled on Simon's shoulder and turned him. He found protruding brown eyes set in a grey face. 'My name is Peter. Glenise, who I exchanged views with, is a non-smoker herself. Glenise feels that smokers should be allowed to smoke in their own rooms. I feel that smoking is an affront to the liberty of non-smokers, there should be a ban on all smoking. What is your view as an obviously addicted smoker who is unable to control his unnatural craving for nicotine and the sensation of cigarette smoke flowing down your throat and billowing in your lungs? One can beat the addiction, you know. I did!'

Simon inhaled deeply, then blew a plume of smoke through

the corner of his mouth. He noticed that a lot of people were coughing heavily. Some coughed, he assumed, because, like him, they were making the most of their last few puffs; others, being secondary smokers, indicated how beastly the primary smokers were being, and some, he didn't doubt, were genuinely suffering.

'My name is Simon, Peter. Sorry, I mean my name is Simon... Peter, not Simon Peter. Anyway, Peter, my name is Simon and I can't tell if you are being serious or sending somebody up.'

'I thought you might say something like that, Simon.' And Peter eased back into his lotus position before whispering to someone who might or might not have been Glenise. Simon stubbed his roll up on the sole of his boot and putting it in his pocket found that Lindy's hand was already there. I am an ashtray, he thought.

'Okay.' Trudy raised her voice and clapped her hands. 'Now you see what is happening. Gradually we reach a sort of organic consensus. But we have a problem. Each of us now contains the views of three group members, but we are stuck in space, okay? Yes, we are located at one point. What we need to do is share our findings with others. To do this we must move about! I'm going to hand over to Rupe now, because the exercise is moving into movement and starting to overlap with Rupe's area of expertise. Movement! Rupe.'

Rupe moved at the crouch into the centre of the room. Still crouching, he began to turn slowly, his arms partially extended in front of him, his hands flat, as if displaying a model of St Paul's Cathedral made from spent matches.

'Moving,' he said, then repeated it, making the first syllable sound like a child's imitation of a cow, the second like the cry from the martial arts. 'Moo...ving! I move. You move. We moove. And... and... important to bear in mind *they* move.' It was very clever; one toe acted as the point of balance, the other turned him. 'Mooving! It's a word we don't think about very often. Mooving! Mooving! In a moment... I shall ask each one of you to move. And each one of us shall move. But before we do move, think, *Moove! Moove!* And as you think *moove* try to hear the soft throb of blood as it surges in your body, through your arteries and veins, push push through the aorta, shush shush into the lungs where biochemical miracles take place. And that, brothers and sisters, is how we are going to move. We will move like blood flowing through the body. Together we will be one body! Trudy!'

In the silence so skilfully created by Rupe, Trudy whispered, 'And when you have mooved, share the three views you hold with those of others. Just moove and flow.'

'Let's start mooving now.' Rupe began to move slowly, dreamily, his lips silently forming and reforming the word... mooving.

Derek, an evil grin on his pink face, mooved on hands and knees, like a child playing dogs. Simon followed suit. Some were mooving like crouched Isadora Duncans; Lindy, body upright, knees fully bent, gave the impression of urination on the moove; Mary favoured a bottom dragging approach which employed arms and legs. Peter squirmed like a worm, or a snake. Helen and Rex, hand in hand, mooved together, trailing their free hands and sticking very close to Rupe's own gait. Russophile to the last, Jed grinned like a split melon and mooved Cossack fashion, arms folded and heels kicking.

'They're cracked!' Simon said, when he and Derek met in the middle of the room and, still on all fours, raised their heads to speak.

'Eh, I know,' Derek said. 'But, listen, Simon, shall we cock our leg at door post?' Derek's clear peals of laughter caused one or two people to hush him, and others to join in. Jed, red in face and values, reached them having kicked his way through the body of campaigners.

'So, Comrades, how do we feel about this dirty imperialistic habit.'

'What's that, Jed?'

'Mooving, lad. Mooving!'

Derek entered a state bordering on terminal hysteria and Simon put an arm round his shoulder hoping to calm him. This gesture had the reverse of its intended effect. 'Jed, get him off! Get him off me! He's trying to mate with me!'

'Well, I've always liked you, you old bugger.' Simon withdrew his arm and pressed his head against Derek's. Jed took a kick step forward. His heavy leather shoe caught Simon's elbow. They fell in a tearful tangle.

Not everyone had taken the exercise so seriously. Some had

broken the unstated rule and were standing in order to talk. Others had gone out for a quiet smoke. One small group had broken into their packed lunches and stood with their backs to the body of the room.

Gradually order was restored. Trudy and Rupe had, they informed the meeting, spoken to almost everyone in the room and, just as they knew it would be, a consensus had been reached. There would be no smoking, No-one objected... everyone knew what the result would be before the exercise started.

'Okay! Okay!' Trudy knelt on the table, hands together as if in prayer. 'That was a lot of fun, and N.V.D.A. can be fun. But can you imagine taking that decision, in that fluid, organic, essentially what we call the reticular democratic fashion, while a squad of angry, overworked, frustrated police drag us from a blockade?'

For a few seconds the room was still and quiet, then the vicar rose to his perfected crouch and asserted the voice of the reasonable, sensible tendency.

'With the greatest of respect to those present, Trudy? I do feel that some friends were rather too light-hearted in their approach? And, with considerable respect, I would propose that we face up to June 9th with... well, perhaps a little awe?'

'Don't!' Lindy said, as Simon and one or two others rose to the occasion and said 'Awe!'

The vicar gave a light, dry laugh and sank back to the floor, then rose again and added, 'By the way, I feel that all ex-secondary smokers will second me in expressing my appreciation to the primary smokers for showing such selfless concern for our health by reaching the non-smoking consensus? Thanks everybody... it's for your own good as well, you know?'

Rupe announced that he was going to tell them a few things about breathing.

Simon, Lindy, and Mary sat arm in arm, heads together.

'Oh, dear sweet Jesus,' Simon breathed, his chest stiff with the memory of laughter, 'I love it. I love us all. We are absolutely crackers. Do you know that? We are all absobleedinglutely crackers.'

*

He traced a line round an onion with the point of a knife and then, using his thumb nail, removed the outer skin. The miners frightened him. They were a race apart, strong and physical. The May Day march had given him a strengthened sense of history, of the dignity of standing by what was right regardless of the moving standards of common sense. He harboured no doubts about the correctness of the miners' case. The State was attempting a huge step backwards, crushing communities and families as it did so; politicians were lying to the public. Many in the press and media in general were building up credit to spend in some future Thatcherite heaven. The running battles of Orgreave were a loud and clear declaration that Thatcher had enough policemen ready and willing to break bones for double time. Thatcher, unemployment and double time, he concluded, were inextricably linked.

It would be a long and bloody fight. No matter what the public were being led to believe, it would be the blood of miners that ran most freely. But, in the manner of these things, within his limited understanding, right would overcome might, the miners would win and Thatcher would go the way of Edward Heath. The question was, what part could he play? And why feel ill at ease about Lindy and Mary visiting a pit village with clothes for a jumble sale?

Sarah had called the night before to say she was back at Kirkfield Chance and would stay for a few days, helping in whatever way she could with the Women's Support Group.

'It's the women I'm going to see, and Sarah, dickhead. I'm not thinking of making a pass at Arthur, you know. I don't know why you're not coming.'

Simon squirmed and said, 'Will you be back for lunch or are you staying longer?'

She had a way of cutting through the crap. It was why he loved her. It was why he lived with her. It was why she could make life so bloody miserable. To leave her would be to turn his back on truths about himself, unresolved truths, areas of stunted growth. To leave her would be to become somebody else, and he wasn't fully himself yet.

The knife sliced into the side of his left forefinger. He felt a jolt as it hit bone. Nausea spread from the pit of his stomach. Blood the colour of blackcurrant wine tumbled out of the cut and paled to rose as it soaked into the perfectly sliced onion. He watched in amazement.

He ran the cold tap onto his finger and felt disgust and despair as the water revealed blue-white flesh pinpointed by tiny springs of blood. The cut ached with a throbbing intensity far outreaching its size. When the finger was numb he squeezed it dry with a tea cloth then clenched his fist and secured the rough bandage with his thumb. The onion, almost half of which was sliced, had fine red lines across it where the knife had been. A thin pink juice was spreading from its base and staining the wooden cutting-board.

'Fuck it!' he said gripping his cut hand in the other and pulling it tight into his chest. 'Fuck, fuck, fuck, fuck it.'

From a biscuit tin in a drawer he took a proprietary antiseptic cream and a piece of lint. Opening the fridge door he withdrew a plastic carrier which carried the bulk loader for black and white film, some cassettes of assorted film, and a roll of broad adhesive tape. He cut a three inch strip of the orange tape and then replaced the carrier in the fridge. The red lines on the onion were fading. Tea cloth trailing from his clenched fist, he dashed to the attic darkroom and fitted a zoom on the Contax.

Downstairs he found the back lighting from the window strong enough to shut down the lens and take three shots from different angles. He took a couple more, changing the exposure. His hands were trembling too much to rely on the first shots. He sat down for a moment, putting the camera on the table beside him, rhythmically tapping his damaged hand on his chest. He looked at the discoloured onion for a few minutes before adding the knife, a bulb of garlic and half a beefsteak tomato. He laughed as he took three more shots.

Each time he focused the heavy zoom more blood soaked into the white and green tea towel. Now there was blood on the focussing ring. He sat down. He was shaking and light-headed; was it the throbbing cut, or taking pictures?

Lindy and Mary came back at half past six; they had Sarah and Dave with them.

'Don't worry,' Lindy said, as she let them in, 'When Simon makes a curry there's always enough for the road, then some.'

A sheet of pale green paper was pinned to the scrubbed

kitchen table with the heavy knife. She read the message, first silently then aloud.

'This bastard done nearly cut me frigging finger off. Fiddled about a bit, but upsetting colour balance of decor. Gone to LGI to let experts tie it up. Don't worry, it's nothing but another bloody mess I've got myself into.'

Lindy held the sheet of paper for them to see. It was smeared with blood and the message, in pencil, was signed in blood; a bubble of it still looked sticky.

'I hope he's alright, Lindy,' Mary said, taking the knife and sticking it back on the magnetic holder by the sink.

'He's a dramatic bleeder,' Lindy said, folding the note carefully. 'Still that's no excuse for him not having the tea ready.'

When Simon returned he looked sickly. 'There was a day when I could have afforded a sodding taxi. Look, they've stitched me. Two sodding stitches. Still, didn't hurt much and I like this finger thing, makes me look interesting, eh?'

The kitchen was warm with the smell of curry. Lindy stood at the stove, stirring the pan with a wooden spoon. Mary sat at the table, a pint of homebrew in her hand.

'We've got guests, Sarah and Dave are in the front room. There's a meeting at the Trades Club. They say Scargill's coming.'

Simon took the pint that Mary offered him and drank.

'That's good. Curry smells good. At last, a chance to meet the highly regarded Sarah and Dave. And Scargill's coming. Knockout! Do you want to see my stitches?'

He began to untie the finger stall, holding his left wrist on his knee and working with his right hand on the tape. Lindy blew on the wooden spoon, then touched the tip of his nose with it. 'Shouldn't bother if I were you,' she said, returning the spoon to the pot and ruffling his hair with her free hand. 'Go and take a look at Dave's.'

'Dave's?'

'Ay,' Mary said, 'he's got his head sewed up by a demon cobbler.'

'You've been upstaged, love.'

The two women looked at him in silence.

'Orgreave?'

'Some bastard tried to knight him with four foot of timber, then arrested him for resisting arrest and assault!'

'Jesus.'

'We've watched it on telly, Simon, and we've said how they were being selective in what they showed. Wait until you hear what really happened.'

Dave and Sarah came into the kitchen, Dave leading, an empty pint glass in his hand. From a raw black eye a graze ran like a stain down his swollen left cheek. His Come Home To A Real Fire T-shirt was just as Lindy had described it, but Simon would never have recognized this battered face from her description. Warm, open, serious, but the first indications of laughter lines, she said. (Needles of jealousy had moved in Simon when she'd talked about Paul and David the night she brought Mary home from Greenham.)

David's face was pinched and grey, a deep cleft sunk between his eyes which were surrounded be tightly knotted flesh. His lips were thin and mottled and he had them pressed tightly together. But even as Simon watched, the mouth opened in a grin and the eyes seemed to brighten.

"Ey up, our kid,' Dave said, turning and seeing Simon's bandaged hand, 'you show us thine and I'll show thee mine.'

Sarah eased the young man further into the kitchen, cupping his elbows. Simon saw a stretch of shaved skull and a crusty black wound with its comic book criss-cross stitching.

'Jesus Christ!' Simon said, taking the hand that David offered and shaking it.

'No,' said Dave, 'but we're expecting his dad at meeting.'

XII

Lindy propped the paper bill against the big mirror on the mantelpiece and gave a credible impersonation of Chris Rowntree: 'I hope we'll be seeing your face at the meeting dear, you and your husband. Honest John'll be looking out for you. Party before everything, that man. Party before everything. Suggested I twist your arms. His very words, "Call by and twist their arms for them, Chris," he said. Comic, you see. No edge.' She paused to fiddle with imaginary pens. 'Deserves all the support folk can give. Not called Honest John for nothing, you know, oh dear me no. Here's your bill, dear. Four weeks overdue.'

'We ought to stop getting that Tory rag every Sunday.' Simon was drying, Mary washing.

Lindy said, 'You'd miss lying in bed, drinking coffee and saying "Oh Christ! Oh God! Oh Jesus!" It's the nearest you get to a religious experience.'

'It's transcontinental man, or whatever they call it.' Mary dropped the sports section onto the floor beside her chair. 'Should let 'em keep that and get a rebate. And happen the business news'

'No, I like interviews with bright young things who haven't let their father owning the company stop them working their way to the top.'

Lindy took hold of his arms and moved them. 'Have you noticed how this model can't talk and dry pots at the same time?'

'Best not upset him, Lindy. He'll show you his cut.'

'I feel like a gooseberry, me.' Mary said, twenty four hours later. She was fixing Coal Not Dole stickers on Simon's lapel. 'Don't forget to make the buggers take a collection.' She was going to Wakefield to hear Scargill with David and Sarah, Lindy and Simon were off to their first Labour Party meeting.

Sarah helped David into a black donkey jacket. The pair of them were at ease in each other's company. They spoke rarely, apart from rudimentary, functional exchanges. Simon watched Sarah setting a green and brown bush hat on the young miner's scarred head. She stood on tip toe. David stared ahead with a dreamy look on his face, hands hanging by his sides. He said,

'Can I ring Chance and get Gozzer to feed hens?'

It was a clear evening, the sky holding rumpled sheets of soft grey cloud, smudged pink in the West where the urban valley's final curve faded in a haze of pollution. Simon folded his arms and leaned back against the stone wall which separated their yard from the narrow back road. Lindy gave a last salute as the Mini pulled out onto the road. She turned and held her arms straight then fell forward so that he was trapped against the wall. Although their bodies didn't touch their faces were only inches apart.

'Nice people,' she said.

He kissed her nose, then said, 'I think Mary's the first real friend we've ever had.'

'She's been through a lot, has Mary. She offers everything whenever she meets anybody, it's her way of coping. And she takes what's on offer without making demands and imposing things. What about Sarah and David? You didn't mind me bringing them back?'

Simon raised his arms and took hold of her waist under the heavy grey sweater. 'I'm glad you brought them back. We live in a class ridden society and they come from nearer the extremes than us. It's a privilege to have them around. Proves the barriers aren't impregnable. Why isn't the world full of them – nice people?'

She bent her arms and slid them behind his neck and they hugged each other. From down the road came a cry of mock indignation.

'Eh! You can just stop that for a start. You mucky little devils.' It was Derek Blythe, shopping bag swinging. 'Get your mind off fun and games. I've come to take you to the meeting.'

*

'Abandon hope all ye who enter here,' Derek intoned, one hand tucked in his jacket front, the other holding out his glass of soda water to a cluster of Party members who were leaving the bar through a side door. He lowered his head so that the he, Lindy and Simon looked like conspirators. 'That was the SBT: Silly Bugger Tendency. If you like Tommy Cooper, you'll love Tippy Milgarth. Oh heck! And another thing, don't offer to buy King John a drink whatever you do. He'll do anything to avoid buying you one back, and his drinks are like his standards. Know what I mean?'

Lindy and Simon indicated ignorance.

'Doubles!' Derek's cheeks were flushed with excitement, this was his element. The waspy old Socialist had made the tittle-tattle and back-stabbing of local politics into an art form. 'Oh, you don't get full benefit until you join the dance.'

'Doubles!' Simon repeated with a groan. He waved over Derek's shoulder in acknowledgment of C.N.D. friends Danny and Katrina.

'Oh, 'ey up, Alice is here. Evening Ms Pile.' Derek raised his glass to a voluminous woman in a maroon cloak. She ignored him as she swept through the room.

'Come on, that's Alice Pile, the rump that got the chair after a split vote. You'll soon pick it all up. Look at this soda water, I'll make it last all night me, you watch.' He picked up his bag and shepherded them to the door.

Twenty or so people sat round the narrow room. They were shuffling papers, whispering, laughing, shouting greetings. Most had drinks before them on small round tables. The air was hazy with smoke from cigarettes and a couple of pipes.

'We'll sit with Tippy. He's as daft as they come, but you won't get categorised straight off.' Derek led them to a table flanked by stools and a section of banquette seating.

'Tippy,' Derek dropped his bag and sat beside a morose man in his mid-forties, 'I'd like you to meet two new comrades, Lindy and Simon.'

Tippy was a tall spare man, built to a pattern unknown to tailors. His brown tweed jacket faced in one direction, Tippy another. Immediately Simon wanted to make a portrait. Smooth colourless flesh like molten wax smeared downward to the contrasting black beard which sprouted from the surfaces under jaw. Small tufts of black hair also protruded from nostrils and ears. His hair, of the same bristly black, was bent rather than styled in a nineteen- fifties short back and sides.

'I AM VERY PLEASED TO MEET YOU,' Tippy said, slowly and with great force. Each word pumped the musculature of his face. As he shook hands, Simon understood the linguistic development of the expression to shake hands.

'ANY COMRADE OF DEREK'S IS A WELCOME ADDITION TO THIS BRANCH LABOUR PARTY, I LOOK FORWARD TO WORKING ALONGSIDE YOU IN THE STRUGGLE TO RETURN A LABOUR PARTY MEMBER TO PARLIAMENT FROM THIS CONSTITUENCY, AND IN OVERTHROWING THIS FOUL, HYPOCRITICAL AND TOTALLY DISASTROUS GOVERNMENT.' The speech of welcome, aided by the vigorous hand shaking, transformed his face into a healthy, pink sphere. In this inflated state, Tippy's was a face that could be inverted to reveal another.

Lindy sat between Derek and Tippy and said, 'Thanks, Tippy, it's nice to meet you. This is quite an event for us, our first meeting.'

'YES IT IS,' Tippy said, placing before her, one at a time, four sheets of paper of various sizes and colours. 'MINUTES... AGENDA... MOTIONS... AND A DUPLICATED DOCUMENT TOO FADED AND DISTORTED TO READ, BUT I AM SURE ITS CONTENT WILL BE CLARIFIED DURING THE COURSE OF THE MEETING.'

Alice Pile clapped her hands, stamped her heel, then banged a heavy glass ashtray on her table. She had taken off her cloak to reveal a chunky crimson sweater which carried a Labour Party badge. A fringe of salt and pepper hair sprouted beneath a purple velour hat held in place by a hat pin which ended in a plastic gooseberry. Similar green balls hung from her earlobes and a string of them undulated across her broad chest like mossy stepping stones in a river of blood.

'Come on! Come on! We've got a lot to get through and we're five minutes late.'

A burst of laughter came from the table to Simon's left where Katrina and Danny sat with Terry Skinnow and a man in his early thirties. Simon recognized Charlie Yates from peace marches and demos. It was clear that Danny had dropped one of his dry comments and Charlie was making the most of it.

John Harmer got to his feet and bellowed, 'Through the chair, shut up or get out! This is a Ward meeting, not a fairground. '

For a couple of minutes the room erupted into cries of 'Sit down!' 'Shut it!' and expansions and contractions of 'Point of order!'

'UNFORTUNATELY, LINDY, THIS IS TYPICAL OF THE MAYHEM WHICH OCCURS NOW THE BRANCH HAS BECAME A BATTLE GROUND FOR EXTREMISTS.' Tippy jacked himself up to his gangling six-foot-two and waved his papers like a football rattle. 'IN THE NAME OF SWEET REASON, WILL YOU SHUT UP, THE LOT OF YOU? LET THE CHAIR SPEAK!' Tippy's cry from the heart silenced the meeting and ended in opposition to one voice alone, that of the equally forceful Alice Pile.

'Sit down, Comrade Milgarth. Sit down and shut up.'

'EXCUSE ME, COMRADE CHAIR, I WAS SIMPLY ASKING THAT—'

'Sit!'

Tippy's jacket turned to Lindy as Tippy turned to Derek and said, 'THANK GOODNESS ALICE IS FINDING SHE CAN WIELD A LITTLE MORE AUTHORITY. POLITICS APART, DEREK, WE MUST SUPPORT THE CHAIR IF WE ARE NOT TO SEE THE PARTY DESCEND INTO ANARCHY.'

'Shut up or I'll send you out of this meeting,' Alice said, banging her ashtray again.

By nine o' clock Simon and Lindy were gaining rudimentary insights into the local Labour Party machine which was, according to a whispered comment from Lindy, a cross between a steam driven threshing machine and a mangle. They already had a basic understanding of the democratic structure and proceedings of the Party; the practice came as a surprise. Simon, who had known the cut and thrust of business and research meetings, was astounded by such a brusque, indeed, rude, chairing. Alice Pile regularly asked of a member, 'Alright, what the heck is it now?' and cut into people's speeches with a curt, 'Alright. Sit. We've heard enough,' or, 'I know you have a right, but shut up anyway.' And at least half the members appeared to pay attention to the proceedings simply in order to ensure that they never missed an opportunity to jeer, sneer, or fire acerbic asides into the hot fumes that were circulated by a noisy fan.

For the moment it was this fan that stirred the meeting.

'Right. Right. Alright then. I will.' Danny, a snappy-dressing social worker, was on his feet, struggling against abusive shouts from Harmer and the Right, and, it had to be admitted, the vociferous support of the Left. 'I now move... I move...'

'Good, out of the district, I hope.'

'Get on with it!'

'Sit down!'

'Order! Order!'

'I move that this Branch Labour Party does, as of that point in time when such a decision be taken by a fair and democratic vote, undertake to hold the remainder of the present meeting, and all future meetings without—' The background noise now had Danny shouting. 'Without, I said, Comrades, without the dubious and divisive so-called benefit of the noisy and inefficient ventilation fan.'

There followed a few moments of reaction: cries of 'Hear, hear!' and 'Rubbish!' The mild and flaky Chris Rowntree asked, 'What's in it for you, you smart-arsed little bastard?' Finally Alice brought the meeting to order. Tippy was, as usual, the last to fall silent: 'CHAIR! CHAIR! WE MUST HAVE ORDER, CHAIR.'

'Shut it, Comrade Milgarth, I've had enough of you for a bloody lifetime.' Alice was on her third pint of mixed and had rolled up the sleeves of her jumper and pushed the velour hat to the back of her head.

'Now, we have a motion on the table, I'm not taking amendments. I'm not taking more than one speaker and Comrade Page has, if he's going to insist on it, the right of reply. Comrade Sneath.'

Peter Sneath, Derek whispered, was a fair enough comrade in his own way, but he worked for the Council: 'King John's got him on a lead and King John decides how long it is.'

'Comrades,' Sneath said, eliciting a few jeers and sneers from the Left. 'Comrades, I am appalled and ashamed that we should be discussing such a trivial issue as whether or not to have a ventilation fan on. I tell you, if Margaret Thatcher came into this room now—'

'You'd ask her for a job!' Charley Yates pulled his cap forward and pretended to eat it.

'I will ignore that comment. I'll take it in good part. I want to see this Party unified, working together towards the overthrow of the Tories. We are at the moment living in a country torn apart by a violent and vicious industrial dispute.' The room fell silent. 'Near enough two hundred thousand miners are bearing the brunt of an attack which has been orchestrated by Margaret Thatcher and which is directed at the whole of the working class. If the miners fall... we all fall... and the Labour party falls...

'Later tonight we hear from a comrade in the N.U.M. and I would like to think that this Branch Labour Party will be able to say to that comrade, with hand on heart: We are unified. We can win this dispute. We must win this dispute. We will win this dispute...' Several members were now tapping their tables in support and offering quiet *Hear, hears.*

'I'll tell you something, though, Comrades. We won't win it, and we won't deserve to win it, if we spend our time playing politics and passing motions about ventilation fans. Comrades, I appeal to you, for the sake of the striking miners, for the sake of the working classes of Great Britain, and for the sake of our Party... let the fan be left on. I oppose the motion, Chair.'

Simon put his mouth close to Lindy's ear, so that he could be heard over the din that followed Sneath's impassioned opposition to the motion. 'I don't believe it. I mean you expect it from the prats in Westminster, but... Do you want another?'

Lindy touched her empty pint glass, but Derek refused the mimed offer, pointing with a happy smile to his half full glass and mouthing, 'I told you so.' And Tippy had already told them that HE DIDN'T DRINK AT MEETINGS.

As the door swung behind him, Simon heard the predictable cry: 'CHAIR! CHAIR! ORDER, CHAIR, ORDER, IF YOU PLEASE! LET'S HAVE SOME ORDER!'

A middle-aged man in flannels and a pale grey quilted anorak was climbing the stairs. 'Good meeting?' he asked. Simon was surprised to hear himself answer, 'Not so bad.'

When he returned, carrying two pints, his arm was taken by Charley Yates who said, 'We only just won that one, no thanks to you, you neo-fascist pillock. If the Left don't stick together they'll kill us, man.' Yates then gave a peal of laughter that ensured that no-one in the room heard Alice Pile announce the speaker. Danny and Katrina smiled, but their attention was directed towards Alice's table, where the man Simon had passed on the stairs was preparing to speak.

When he began his voice wavered, but he soon gained confidence. He stood upright and still, one hand clasped a few sheets of notepaper to his chest, the other rested on the table, his knuckles flat on the darkened brass, his thumb moving to and fro like the antennae of an insect.

'We're solid in Yorkshire,' he said. 'If it takes till next year we'll win. And it might do. Make no mistake, we're not talking about gentlemanly conflict. Coal Board and Government are set on winning... regardless of cost. Coal Board have played it mucky since day one. Before day one, to tell truth. That's why we're out.

'We didn't go against Plan for Coal. Board did! We didn't lie about closures. Board did! We didn't move men to Cortonwood and tell them they'd got five year there before closure... then announce closure two week later. And we didn't appoint a butcher to run our industry. But the Coal Board did.' He paused and drank from a half pint glass. When he spoke again his voice was low, and his eyes moved slowly from face to face.

'One lad's dead. I'm not saying he were killed deliberate, but I am saying this: if Coal Board had behaved decent, that lad'd be alive today. There's others in hospital, in intensive care. There's lads up on serious charges with bail that means they can't stop in their own homes and they can't step out of them. There's families with debts mounting that'll take years to pay off. There's young lads, young single lads, as get nothing, nothing from state. And there's kiddies learning there'll be no holidays and no birthday presents and no comics and no spice 'til this is all over.

'People say that miners are getting what they asked for. They say we're greedy. We're dinosaurs and Luddites. But we didn't ask for this. We didn't choose it. We had no choice and that's God's truth. We had no choice.

'They say Arthur Scargill's a tyrant who twists us arms and makes us do as he tells us. He's not, you know, he's a democratic leader doing what we pay him to do. Doing what my union elected him to do. I tell you, there's no union got a better leader... there's no party got a better leader. And I'll tell you something else, and it's important is this, if the impossible happened, if we went back without our demands being met, we'd have lost nothing. If MacGregor has 'is way, we've got nothing. Don't think I like being out 'cos I don't. Me personally, I'm not all that far off retirement. Bad as it is underground, and if you haven't been underground you don't know what it's like, but for all that, I'd have liked to have worked out my years in peace.

'I go back to pit ponies, I've been fined more than once for riding them underground!' He grinned and the tension eased, but only for a moment. 'Well, they got shot of ponies. Now they've decided it's our turn. I'm telling you straight, they've another think coming. They can't put us out to grass, they can't send us off to t' knackers yard. Margaret Thatcher's got something to learn: you can't treat people like animals.'

Several members began to clap and cheer. Hands were slapped on tables. The miner drank from his glass again, wiped his mouth with the back of his hand, then sorted his notes. The room fell silent.

'Well, we're not greedy. We' not asking for extra pay. We' not asking that pits stay open for ever like some folk are saying. We're asking that the normal procedures, the procedures agreed by Union, Board and Government, are stuck to. We're asking that Coal Board stands by its own rules.' His voice had risen to breaking point. He paused for a moment and drew deep breaths. When he continued he had quietened again. 'We're asking that our lives, our wives and kiddies, our communities, are given some value when it comes to assessing the economic viability of a pit. And that's not Luddite, you know. Some of the pits, shut them down and you shut a small town down... how much'll that cost in Social Security benefits and all the other problems that go with unemployment? I don't need to tell you people about that do I?

'But such things cut no ice with Tories. It's nothing to do with economics, you know. Nothing! She's out to put the clock back. She's open enough about it, isn't she? Do you remember? Do you? A return to Victorian values, that's what she said.

'I'm not an educated man. What I know I've picked up since I left school and there's all too little of it. But I know what Victorian values means. It means dire poverty. It means kiddies dying in rags. It means no Welfare State. We all of us here know what it means. It means the strong depriving the weak. It means rich living on backs of poor. And it means an end to strong unions and a massive pool of unemployed to keep wages down. That's what too many of our people voted for when they voted for Margaret Thatcher. They did it out of ignorance. They did it because of the lies told on television. They did it because of newspapers dedicated to them good old Victorian values: Bingo! Young lasses with no clothes on! Scandal and titillation! Lies,

lies, and more damned lies!

'I wasn't at Peterloo when working men and women were cut down by soldiers on horses. None of us was born then. I'll tell you something though, by God I'll tell you something, I've seen working men fleeing from coppers on horses. I've seen men battered to the ground and ridden over. If you'd told me a year ago that I'd see that in my own country, I'd have laughed at you.

'Well, we' not laughing now. We' fighting. We' fighting for us lives.' He emptied his glass, and nodded thanks to Charlie who slid a pint beside his clenched fist as it banged in emphasis.

Once again the speaker started low, almost whispering in the tense silence. 'I want to say a couple of words about Arthur Scargill. I've known Arthur on and off for a good many year now. People say he's careerist. Maybe he is. If wanting to get to top of Union and do best he can for it is careerist... well he's guilty.

'When I say what I'm off to say now... I don't speak for Wales or Kent or Lancashire; I don't speak for miners in Scotland and Derbyshire, in Durham. And I don't speak for bloody Nottingham... I speak for Yorkshire, I speak for Yorkshire miners... Arthur Scargill got where he is because he spoke out for what we believe in. He doesn't tell us what to do. We tell him what we want, and he does it with us.

'If Arthur had just said, "Aye, go on lad, close it down, break your word, Cortonwood means nowt to me" – he wouldn't have been President for long. I'll tell you another thing, he wouldn't have showed his face on Yorkshire coalfield again either. It's not Arthur's strike, fine leader that he is, it's our strike. It's the miners' strike.

'And in the end, you know, it's your strike. It's the old story: miners in the front line. If we lose, you lose. And if you lose, this country loses and this country'll take a long time to get back to where it were.

'So that's why I say we'll win no matter how long it takes. That's why I say we've got no choice. And I do believe we'll win. And I'll tell you why – because we're not standing alone. I've been in mining all my life and I've never seen ought like this before. We've got wives and kiddies on our side, well, that's to be expected, though we're grateful for it. But we've got shopkeepers and doctors. Even the vicar's wife comes and helps with the Women's Support Group.

'What about leadership of TUC and this Party, your Party, my Party? Well, they can't all be Scargills... the rank and file are great. And it's not just in this country. We get letters and donations from all over the world. I tell you, you never know who'll turn up at pit gates next.

'We had some women from Greenham come to see us a couple of week back. It's the same struggle, you know. It is. I didn't know that a few month ago, but I do now. You can't kill the spirit, that's what they say. Well that's it, that's what tells me we'll win no matter what they throw at us. We'll win because you can't kill the spirit.

'We're four month in dispute and we're more solid than the day we downed tools. So them lasses are right... You can't kill the spirit.

'I'll give you an example, a for instance.' He drank from his glass and slid the notes into his trouser pocket. 'There's a lad in my pit that were renowned for misery. Talk about doom and gloom!' There was laughter for the first time since the miner began to speak. He waited, his small tanned face immobile and serious. 'We picked that lad up off ground last week. He couldn't stand on his feet though he were trying. We carried him to an ambulance. His cheek were flapping open and his mouth were the worse mess I've ever seen. You felt sick to look at it. He were pulling at my arm and trying to say something but his jaw were broke. His mouth were broken teeth with blood bubbling out. I kept trying to hush him up, telling him he'd be alright, trying to comfort him like. Then I realized what he were saying.' He paused for dramatic effect. '"Never mind my bloody gob," he said, "you should see coppers boot." And he laughed. That lad laughed.

'There's a spirit moving on the coalfields, and it's waking in the Labour movement. It's a spirit that's slept too long, but it's awake now. It's awake and alive... and it's growing. Please God it never sleeps again. Thank you.'

He moved to the side of the room, taking his drink with him, and stood, a small, slight figure, crumpled, leaning against the wall. There was a moment's silence, then the room erupted into applause and cheers. Simon clapped until his hands were stinging, then he turned to Lindy. Her hands were curled in her lap and her head was rested back against the wall so that she appeared to be looking at the ceiling. He knew she was crying and that he, like many other people in the room, clapped long and hard to keep tears back.

XIII.

Echo of a departing tube. Empty platform. Stale air. Curl of froth from the pear shaped opening in the Guinness can.

Simon flicked the ring-pull with his thumb. Would it flash on the live rail? Which is the live rail? And can you stand on the live rail and, so long as you don't touch anything, survive? And do you need to be wearing rubber soled shoes for this experiment to succeed? And is survival success? And what chance of jumping onto the live rail without wobbling and falling off? And which is the live rail? Or is it rails? Must you stand with a foot on each to be jolted into the next world? And why think like this? Suicide is not my scene, not in this grubby hole in the ground. Quiet, maybe, by a river, on a surfeit of liquorice.

He drank from the can, pressing his tongue against the sharp edge of its opening. The Guinness was cold and tasted of metal, not what he needed. He stepped back from the edge, sat down, put the can on the bench seat, returned to Hilary's letter.

'... a surgeon friend says there is almost certainly nothing at all to worry about. But, really, what is gained by delay? So, please, my darling, for my sake, to set my mind at rest... promise...'

Curving beyond the line was a poster carrying the image of a young woman. She held her left foot in her hands, locking the right foot. Her legs crossed at right angles and formed a stable base to advertise her dusky brown tights. A kite-shaped area of darkness bounded by her legs and the rippled hem of a tweed skirt. He couldn't tell whether it was a uniform darkness or had gradations of shade. He wasn't supposed to know. He was supposed to be fascinated by the ambiguity, to stare and wonder, to feel a twitching in his groin, to imagine his hand or his head or his cock moving into that darkness. He was supposed to be mesmerised by this blank space until sexual expectation and this particular brand of tights were associated. Simon knew all this because:

'I personally agree with Pete. There is still an element of threat here.' Account Director. 'PH37 and threat do not mingle. It's located in the feet, I think, and I feel we should try covering the feet with pastel shoes –'

'Ballet pumps, nothing hard, shiny or pointed.' Client Marketing Officer. 'Nothing to suggest an immediate hard-on. It's strong at the moment, jolly strong, but we mustn't go over the top and push half the punters into feelings of sexual inadequacy.'

'Exactly, Pete. Exactly. What we have here is the most erotic image to date.' Account Executive. 'Distant, alluring, warm, moistly sexy. Threatening, yes, but only to others, and, and this is the big number... inviting! Pastel ballet slippers might be the key. Not new, slightly bruised at the toe'

'So far so good. So far so good.' Research Director. 'Doesn't stray from the implications of our first dip in the field. We'll need to think carefully about the shoes.'

'Shade: yellow. Don't ask why. Intuition dictates. Save time if we go on yellow now. Pete'll say flesh pink, then change his mind in seven days. Yellow's the man, chaps. Yellow's the job.' Artistic Director, receives appreciative laughter, creative people are allowed to be blunt to client... not too blunt.

'If we have something so powerful, and I'm not convinced we have' – Market Research Director, statistics – 'what's our line if there's an outbreak of sexual assaults? Specifically, women strangled with Pete's PH37s.'

Silence.

'Simmy, old son, see your quack.' Client Marketing Representative.

'So long as the buggers use a new pair every time it'll be a welcome blip on the sales figures?' Account Executive. Laughter.

'Dark night, deep colours, glistening Thames, trilby, very Strand, very Frank Sinatra, very Raymond Chandler.' Artistic Director. 'Coat collar up, trench coat. Hands out, PH37s stretched between them. Young woman, blouse torn, swell of titties, leaning back against stone parapet, thrusting pubes, slit skirt, bare legs. Caption: "He'll kill to get you in PH37s".'

'What a swinger. Smasherooney!' Account Executive.

'Very Strand, very let's flush that one down the hole, eh? Slogan's okay, but we don't want a re-run of the best failure ever designed. Got Simmy going though, off for a quick one with Madame Fist and her five daughters.' Client Marketing Representative; settling a score. Very appreciative laughter.

'Back to warm cunt then?' Account Director.

Simon screwed Hilary's letter into a ball and threw it at the poster. He stared at his feet, the buffalo hide boots were scuffed beyond casual elegance. He needed new ones. And his rust suit was looking in need of cleaning and pressing. He should go home. He should see the doctor. Anxiety immobilised him. It had gone on so long, the bleeding, three months since the meeting. Three months.

No shoes in the end, instead, ('I'm creaming!'), a small hole in the tights on her right foot. It was located over the space between the middle toe and the one to its left. The research and photography was billed at seventy-three thousand pounds, excluding salaries and expenses. Slogan: "This little hole could cost a pretty penny! PH37s. Perfection for you!" Appreciative laughter, serious acknowledgement of excellence – chance of an award!

There was nothing to look forward to. No structure for tomorrow. Nothing.

The rattle and push of a train.

He remembered Lindy.

He remembered Lindy. Stood. Flung the can. Guinness spurting and tumbling.

He remembered Lindy and walked, forcing himself to take bigger, more forceful strides.

The doctor asked him about his diet; any causes of anxiety; state of general wellbeing?

'Hop on the table and we'll take a look, shall we?' Simon wondered who the we was, would it be done with mirrors, or perhaps the mother with the sniffling little girl who was the last in the queue would be brought in. And why did the doctor de-personalise things? 'Trouble with the rectum. Blood from the rectum? Aha! Numerous causes – blood from rectum. Common complaint...' So his was a small share in some communal problem. Dear Sir, as a rate payer of many years' standing I can no longer forego the necessity of asking: why does the Municipal Rectum bleed? These days we can put a man on the moon, but we cannot control the all too numerous causes of rectal haemorrhage –

A finger went up, encrusted with glass. Simon writhed. The doctor muttered.

And then on his back having his stomach pummelled.

'I see. Yes I see. Not pain – tenderness. And here, yes, here.' On and on. Then she was at her desk, scribbling.

'Seems to be a little tenderness down there on the left.' Fastening his belt, Simon was about to ask how much she got paid for knowing something like that, when the flat of the monkey wrench hit his head. 'Any history of cancer in the family?'

She gave him a sealed envelope with questions on the back for him to answer, the whole to be posted to the local hospital.

Back in the flat he opened the envelope. He tried to read the scrawl, could make few words out. Wanted to run to the shop, to buy glue. Couldn't run. Walked like an invalid. Sealed the envelope with glue. Numbness spread, his mind began to freeze.

Just to sit was no good. He drank half a bottle of brandy mixed with double cream. Someone had told him of this cure-all for abdominal troubles. It was a man in a pub.

The cure-all worked, it took away the dull pain, the tenderness, the anxiety. The only thing left was the gobbets of blood and slime that slid from him like cooked plums.

His name was called. A nurse ushered him through one of the doors facing the waiting area. A small room, a short corridor, door at each end.

'Take everything off from down below.'

'Shoes and socks?'

'Shoes anyway. Pop yourself in that gown and wait here. It'll only be a few minutes.' She slid an orange file under the far door then left by the one they had come in through. He undressed as quickly as he could, fighting the temptation to try the door and, if unlocked, run.

Everything took so long, buttons stuck, he felt fragile. I've taken my socks off, he thought. He wondered whether to put them on again.

The towelling gown over his olive and yellow striped shirt and knitted tie emphasized the nakedness of his buttocks and genitals. He took off his watch and put it in his boot.

Pray for a fall in the blood fall, pray for a fall in the blood. Prayer was out of the question, unless you went through a lengthy process of sussing out then accepting a god. Meditate then. He had started to move his lips in accompaniment to his thoughts. Oh Jesus doctor doctor.

Face facts. But facts, even facts of 'this is my foot, bare, on grey linoleum,' even facts of 'pants are in trousers, trousers rolled, boots on trousers which themselves are on bench seat opposite this bench seat on which I cannot sit with comfort,' even such facts have become hard to recognize, hard to grasp. Alien.

Something inside me is sucking away my recognition of colour. I know this dressing gown, this towel dressing gown which the nurse gave me, this dressing gown which does not fit... I know this gown is striped in white and blue and orange and yellow and red and green, I know that these walls are pale green, that the doors are duck egg blue, that the ceiling is grey and the floor is grey. I know my suit is brown. All these things I know but colours are no longer colours. And sounds are changed.

I am on a conveyer belt.

The door opened. He blinked, the lights in there were so bright. Jesus, would death be like this? Everything so slow, his leg so tense and stiff that his knee threatened to break rather than bend.

A nurse, the oldest nurse he had ever seen, or was she a Sister? A nurse, say, with a face like Auden and a voice so rough and throaty she must chain-smoke used bandages. A nurse then, this nurse, sculpting him on an inspection-table, pushing his ankles so that his knees came up to his chest. Saying, 'That's it, deary. That's it. Just relax. That's it.'

Simon repeated her words in his head. The nurse left him, bare bum pointing at God knows what; his eyes stop working properly, everything is fuzzy.

Voices. Her words still echoed, over the whispered conversation. That's it. Just relax. That's it.

A young New Zealander, square jawed, looking like Dan Dare, asks about problems with the Municipal Rectum. Simon raises his head. Nurse Auden says, 'Just relax dear, just lie still.'

Dan Dare inserts a replica of the Eiffel Tower, base first, into the rectum. No linguistic device known to medical science can persuade Simon that this rectum is communal property.

Dare began to stuff other things up the Eiffel Tower. 'Just going to pump, mate. You might feel this a touch.' Simon asked himself why he couldn't find the funny side. His stomach swelled, he would fart, the Tower would tear free, impale Dan

110

Dare, pin him to the wall.

It isn't funny because it hurts.

'Right, then, let's have a look around up here, shall we?' Dare waggled the Eiffel Tower like the joy stick on a stunt plane.

Simon tumbled into shock. It was all happening to the Municipal Rectum. There was nothing he could do about it but hurt.

Dan Dare drags out the rectoscope. Simon shouts 'Shit!' Nurse Auden grimaces, croaks: 'You were very good!'

XIV.

It was June 9th, the Heads of State of the Commonwealth were in London, and so was Ronald Reagan, President of the United States of America, ex-film actor, ex-right wing grass on Hollywood liberals and progressives; a man who claimed he qualified for office because he could put on his socks while standing; a man who believed in Armageddon and hoped to live to see it; a man who epitomized the new frothy fascism which controlled and repressed the greatest experiment in multinational democracy the world has seen.

Three demonstrations were to run in parallel. A legal march was heading for Trafalgar Square. An illegal blockade of Grosvenor Square, and thus the United States Embassy. (After much debate and lobbying, National C.N.D. had agreed to support this action). And thousands of campaigners on the wilder shores of protest had announced their intention to blockade, even invade, the meeting of Heads of State at Lancaster House.

Exactly what would happen nobody knew. It was this uncertainty as much as the early morning chill that had Simon shivering as he waited for the C.N.D. minibus.

Danny wore his blanket like a shawl, pulled tight under his chin. He was dancing Plains Indian fashion to keep warm. Katrina, who wore an expensive quilted coat, hugged a bright blue knapsack. She squatted on her haunches so that the coat gave maximum protection to her bare legs. Her white hair hung like silk and shifted with the nibbling morning breeze. Sarah, in her ski suit, where the rainbows and cobwebs and peace symbols now vied for numerical superiority with strike badges, leaned into Dave's side. And Dave himself, one arm wrapped round Sarah's shoulder, leaned back against a lamp post and endlessly whistled 'Here We Go'. Mary had covered her knobbly joints with a massive knitted coat, bought at a jumble sale and personalised with badges and coloured wool interwoven with the grey cable stitch. Lindy wore a green military jacket which carried a few badges and good luck charms on the breast pocket. She topped off the mossy look with a green knitted scarf and a grey-green beret, flat, like a plate, on her spikey hair.

Simon opened his blanket to Lindy, whose face was white

with chill and anxiety. 'I'll share my body heat.' She stood close to him and he pulled the blanket round both of them.

'Bet its Jed and Derek holding us up.' Lindy said, turning to see out of the blanket. 'They'll be arguing over who gets on first.'

'Hold tongue, Squaw!' Danny pointed a finger at her from the folds of his own blanket. Turning, with the finger still extended, he addressed Katrina: 'Little Nose Running remember fire water?'

Katrina raised her chin from its resting place on top of the blue knapsack, smiled her slow milky smile and said, 'Danny, there are people trying to sleep.'

A white minibus took the corner wide and bumped to a halt. The first person Simon saw was Tippy, his excited face pressed against the window.

There was a charabanc trip atmosphere in the confined space of the bus. Derek and Jed were sitting at the back on separate double seats. 'Ooh, hurry up,' Derek shouted, 'get the door closed, you look like starved rats.' Jed, not to be outdone by his elder brother, held his clenched fist in the air and sang, 'Arise ye starv'lings from your slumbers, arise ye criminals of want.'

'WELCOME, COMRADE PEACE WARRIORS.' Tippy said, and then, pointing to a woman with smoke-yellowed hair and lined face, he added, 'THIS IS MY MOTHER AND SHE WOULD LIKE TO BE CALLED CORA.'

'I AM EIGHTY-SIX AND I HOPE TO BE THE OLDEST PERSON ARRESTED AT GROSVENER SQUARE.'

'Eh, Simon! Simon!' Derek leaned between Tippy and Cora. 'You'll be alright with your finger, mind, driver's a doctor.'

'The driver, Simon,' Jed said, using his formal, serious-business voice in which each vowel was delivered by forceps, 'is an old comrade of mine and, I should add, a very fine physician to boot.'

Simon realized she must be the Dr Jo to whom Jed often alluded: an active member of Scientists Against Nuclear Arms, the Medical Campaign Against Nuclear Weapons, and the Communist Party. She turned in her seat, and, kneeling, with her head bent to allow for the roof, said, 'Ignore Jed. Is everybody here?'

'Well, I'm not sure about Tippy!' Derek said, pushing Tippy

113

in the shoulder and laughing.

'I thought I'd symbolize purity.' Simon opened his blanket to reveal that he was dressed entirely in white, apart from a flat cap with several badges.

'Oh, I see,' Jed said, 'you're not selling ice cream then, lad?'

'Purity! Purity! Ooh, I like that, Simon, but listen, don't you think Purity might have found time for a shave. I'd call you Ethnic Minority in that get-up.'

Twenty minutes later Helen and Rex had joined them and Jo swung the bus onto the M1. It was Katrina who suggested that noise might be kept to a minimum for a while.

Simon, hunched inside his blanket and hoping to sleep, looked around the bus as Jo settled into a tyre-thrumming seventy. Katrina, Dave, Sarah, Helen and Derek were sleeping, the latter sitting bolt upright, head nodding like a snowdrop. Cora was knitting with thick wooden needles. Tippy sat brooding, his face deflated, grey and molten. Jed caught Simon's eye and raised his own skywards and grinned. In a voice just loud enough to be heard, he said, 'This is what D Day should have been like, but wasn't.' Simon smiled and tipped the peak of his cap with stiff fingers. Rex wore a personal stereo which leaked a sound unrecognisable as music, his eyes were closed, but his lips moved slowly as if he was reading something difficult; Simon wondered when Rex had taken the decision to go punk again. Mary sat beside Jo and talked quietly. Lindy and Danny did the *Guardian* crossword.

Simon cushioned his forehead against the cold window with his cap and watched the industrial wasteland moving like a river of monstrous flotsam. Strings of yellow lights snaked through field and factory then tunnelled into the humped backs of slag heaps and tips. The landscape was littered with immobile pit winding gear.

A junction approached and he saw policemen in glowing orange tabards, several blue transits were visible on the hard shoulder. A bridge was lined with squad cars. His stomach felt heavy.

The previous evening they had talked through three bottles of red wine. Would they be turned round before they left Yorkshire? Would they be stopped in London before they reached Grosvenor Square? How many would be arrested? Would the peaceful blockade turn ugly and violent? It wasn't beyond the police to plant agents provocateurs, then move in.

On and on, round and round.

He heard Jed draw Derek and Tippy's attention to the police, and then the first possible brush with the law was behind them. Simon breathed slowly and deeply, instructing himself to relax. What would be would be.

Gradually, holding his attention as he hovered on the edge of sleep, a huge orange sun began to dodge in and out of the broken horizon. Soon it was floating in a violet sky strewn with wisps of bruised cloud that caught and held a tinge of ochre. He had never seen such a sunrise. He nudged Lindy and she and Danny leaned towards the window.

'Incredible,' Danny said.

'I hope it's a good omen.' Simon inclined his head towards Lindy, smiling weakly. She found his hand and squeezed it. Only she knew how frightened he was. It wasn't just the fear of physical violence from the police, though that was as intense and bright as fresh blood. It was the thought of having to hold himself steady through a day of unambiguous opposition to an increasingly repressive state. It was the knowledge that no matter how he viewed and understood what he was doing, to the Government and the shadowy establishment that now ruled the country, he and Lindy, and the rest of them, were, at best, subversive trash.

Noon: the sun blazed on a scene that Simon would remember forever. Rising above the rumble of traffic he heard the sound of women singing:

We are women, we are strong
We are strong, we are strong
We say no, we say no
To the bomb, to the bomb.

He felt dizzy and sick as a wave of anxiety flowed through him, but he also felt that there was nowhere else he would rather be.

'Right, comrades,' Jed said, taking the lead, 'let's do what we came here to do.'

Crowd control barriers blocked the entrance to the Square, and behind them, shoulder to shoulder, stood a line of police; a further twenty or so clustered to one side. The intense mid-day heat had them in shirt sleeves. They were cheerful and relaxed. In the Square itself, police moved like ants, some were paraded at ease, others formed knots in the shade of trees, many more moved about, hunched over radios. High-ranking officers were apparent, and men in civilian dress.

About a hundred and fifty campaigners were sitting on the road in front of the police barricade. Most were in groups of five to a dozen and many of these groups were squatting round sheets or piles of bags. Some were eating, or handing drinks around. There was a Rupe clone sitting with his legs stretched out and his back resting against the crowd control barrier, he was reading a paperback book, face concealed by the white hair that hung like water flowing over a rock. A woman in loose green cotton trousers and floppy pink T-shirt decorated with a green web was offering each policeman in turn a spoon holding strawberries and cream.

Simon spread his blanket on the ground some feet away from a group of women in their teens. Gradually they settled around the blanket. Derek opened his striped fishing stool and offered it to Cora who vigorously rejected it: 'I DO TWENTY MINUTES' YOGA EVERY DAY!' One of the young women watching them smiled a greeting, the others broke into song, all had joined in before the third word had taken flight:

Stand up, women, take your choice
Create a world without nuclear war.
Now together we are strong
Break the nuclear chain.

One of the young women strummed a guitar, another, dressed in baggy overalls of purple and green satin diamonds, juggled with an orange, a banana, and a bright red apple. At each side of the street, where the barricade met the walls, people clustered, watching the protesters; most held C.N.D. logos on canes. A ripple of applause and laughter ran through the gathering as a young man in green silk shorts raised himself into a handstand on two wine bottles.

Drinkers from a pub, pint glasses in hands, jeered. A group including a nursing mother, in the shade of a banner carrying an applique picture of flower-strewn hills, began to sing to the accompaniment of guitar and flute:

After the bombs have fallen
See the victorious view
We are the angry cinders
They are the crisps in blue
After the war is won lads
Lift up your fried scampi hands
Cheer for the roasted royals
Who reign over featureless lands.

Next the first group of women sang bright and loud, some kneeling up, others juggling or hand jiving:

Sitting in a saddle down in Washington
They call him Ron with the neutron bomb
Brave and courageous with his Stetson on
He'll solve it all with the neutron bomb

Many joined the rhythm section, 'Ba doom, ba doom' and flutes, guitars, whistles and a fiddle rose with the chorus:

Oh, my heart stood still
Ba dum, ba dum,
Everybody else's will
Ba dum ba dum
If we let him drop that bomb
The neutron bomb Ron, the neutron bomb.
Laughter, then silence for the second verse:
He'll send his fleet to Nicaragua
He'll call it manoeuvres, but we'll know it's war.
He landed soldiers on Grenada's shore
He thinks he's above international law
Well think again.
Ooh, my heart stood still
(Ba dum ba dum)

Everybody else's will…

'Simon!' Lindy offered him a bottle of Hock.

'I was lost,' he said.

The wine was warm and mellow; the last of his fears and anxiety slid from him. 'It's beautiful!' he said, holding the bottle towards the blazing sun, 'Jesus, it's just beautiful!'

Danny and Katrina, out of fire water, sloped off to the pub for a top-up and to phone home and check on the well-being of Hal, their two year old son. Simon lay on his back, floppy white trousers rolled to the knee, shirt open, chest to the sun. The blockade thickened around them.

C.N.D. Stewards moved from blockade to blockade carrying information and encouragement. Telegrams of support had arrived from all over the world. Four thousand peace campaigners were breaking the law around the Square; no arrests had been made. No news from Lancaster House, but the stated intentions of activists in Leeds suggested that as many campaigners would be blockading the meeting of the Heads of State as were now blocking off Grosvenor Square.

Duke Street was a joyful carnival, impervious to a couple of drunken onlookers: 'Bruce Kent fucks Joan Ruddock!' they shouted, medallions swinging over their sunburnt beer bellies. A burst of laughter greeted the suggestion, a group of women gave the considered response:

It ain't just the care, it's the love and affection
It ain't just the way, it's the sense of direction
It ain't that we're good, we're just bloody perfection
That's what gets us by!

One of the men squashed his beer can and threw it at the laughing women; before it reached them a hand caught it and balanced it on a stubbled head painted with the C.N.D. logo. Snarling obscenities, the two men walked back towards Oxford Street.

'POOR DEARS,' Cora said to Simon, smiling down at him from her semi-lotus position, 'THEY'RE LIKE HURT CHILDREN. WANTING TO LASH OUT AND DESTROY. I'M GLAD THE RETALIATION WAS GOOD-HUMOURED. I'M

SURE BRUCE AND JOAN WOULD HAVE APPROVED.' She offered Simon a grape from the bag on her lap, holding it over his mouth and letting go when he grinned and opened up. 'I THINK WE ARE IN COMMAND OF THE SITUATION, DON'T YOU?'

Simon agreed. At one stage smiling coppers had broken into laughter and clapped when the arrival of a new group to replace them coincided with a friendly rendition of *Twenty hot coppers defending Grosvenor Square*.

Mary walked over and asked Cora if she would like to meet some Greenham women. Simon watched the pair of them stepping over strewn bodies. Dr Jo and Tippy had already left in an attempt to assay the situation at the other entries to the Square.

'Awake?' he asked Lindy, who lay beside him with her eyes closed, her face pink with sun.

'Hmn. What time is it?'

He sat up and took hold of Derek's wrist to read his watch. Derek gave him a swift tap across the knuckles without breaking off from his energetic discussion of the strike with Dave and Sarah.

'Just after two. You alright?'

'I'm fine. Want to move about a bit?'

Before Simon had time to answer he was approached by a Rupe clone. Not all campaigners looked alike, but he had to admit that half of the campaigners he'd ever seen fitted one of half a dozen styles. He wondered if he fitted a stereotype. The man brushed greying hair from his eyes and put his mouth close to Simon's ear:

'Things are about to start happening now. There are rumours, but nothing confirmed as yet, that the police are going to take out a sort of symbolic cavalcade of cars. A steward has suggested that Binney Street is not well covered. He suggested, but put it no stronger than that, that some of us from this blockade might like to move on. It is also the case that several groups are now contemplating a first strike on Oxford Street. I personally do not favour this move, but, once again, there is no pressure. Just talk about these suggestions with your group and then act on your consensus. Good campaigning.'

'Cheers.' Simon turned to Lindy and began to relay Rupe II's message, mimicking his genteel accent and articulate finger language. A skin headed woman with an orange C.N.D. logo stencilled on hair and scalp was already passing on the message to Derek, Sarah and Dave. But before a consensus could be reached a sweating steward squeezed between the crowd of onlookers and announced that an attempt to take out a convoy on the far side of the Square had failed. Campaigners had been dragged about but it was thought no-one had been arrested. However, the police had marquees in Green Park, ready for processing after mass arrests.

A handful of protesters laden with bags and cameras moved onto the pavement. Most were legal observers whose task was to avoid confrontation and collect information on who was arrested by whom and at what time. Adults led away young children, but some family groups, including the nursing mother, stayed in the blockade.

There was a palpable tension in the air. The police were still smiling, unable to overhear the steward's announcement, in obvious ignorance of what had happened across the Square. Puzzled by the activity in front of them they shuffled their feet; a few exchanged words with those next to them in the cordon and, hunching their shoulders, linked arms as if expecting a sudden charge from the colourful, sun-dazed campaigners.

Lindy, Simon, Sarah, and Dave, with several others moved off, quietly telling those around them that they were heading for Binney Street.

'Good luck, Comrades.' Derek squeezed first Lindy's then Derek's arm. Simon grinned and said, 'Over the top.' His anxiety showed. Lindy took his hand.

Beyond the crush of onlookers and legal observers were empty roads, then the narrow chasm of Binney Street. A few people stood in the middle of the street; thirty yards beyond was Brook Street where a confusion of police and demonstrators could be seen. The new contingent joined up with those already standing and organized themselves into a double cordon, sitting with arms linked and legs crossed.

A thin strip of blue sky was drawn taut above them, but no sun shone onto the road and Simon found himself shivering. Lindy hugged his arm against her side.

It was obvious that the police could clear them up in a matter of seconds. The double cordon reformed into a knot, broad enough to ensure no vehicle could pass, tightly interconnected to make removal of individual bodies difficult. Dave's back was pressed against Simon's knees. The miner's bush hat covered all but the final inch of the scar which traversed the back of his head. Simon felt a great softening as the urge to somehow protect the healing flesh from further damage swelled inside him. Some pigeons fluttered down from the blue and began pecking the pavement.

A Scottish accent suggested that reinforcements should be summoned from Duke Street. Mary disentangled herself as a great cry reached them from Brook Street. Two figures hurtled round the corner and sprinted towards the small blockade as if carried by the wave of sound.

They were women, one in a patched track suit, the other trailing swathes of orange, yellow and russet cotton. For a moment they seemed to run on the spot, the road racing beneath their pounding feet. Then the pigeons rattled into flight.

The women were shouting, calling for help. Police were trying to take cars through Brook Street. Thirty or forty campaigners from Duke Street, summoned by radio, came round the corner and Simon watched as shadow sucked the colour from them. He wanted to be calm, to offer the reasoned position, wiser to stay where they were, wiser to hold the small blockade on Binney Street. But it was no good, the confusion in him was too great. No time for analysis: no time to ask if the reasoned position was a rationalisation of fear. Tight hold of Lindy's hand he ran along the narrow road and out into sunlit Brook Street.

Police and demonstrators swirling together, shouts, screams, songs, whistles, loudhailers, laughter, keening, moaning, the whine of revving engines, car horns; a texture of noise unlike anything Simon had ever experienced. Lindy pulled him down the street, into the thick of it.

Several cars were nose to tail along the right hand side of the street, protected by a double line of uniformed police, arms linked and faces grim. The pressure of the milling crowd was intensified by cordons of police, arms linked, who divided the demonstrators into small pockets.

Simon's perceptions became brief and episodic. A push forced him onto a knot of squatting demonstrators. Lindy's hand slipped from his grasp. He heard voices singing *We Shall Not Be*

Moved, a chant of *229 – We've got your number, 229*. He tried to say sorry to the bodies he was crushed into, then felt himself hauled backwards by his shoulders. 'Come on, lad!' It was Dave. Grinning. Sarah stood at his side, creating space, radiating calm. Lindy was there, she took Simon's arm and shouted, 'The front! We sit at the front!'

They squeezed forward, avoiding strings of police, catching words hurled into the air, snatches of song, groans, screams, a steady call of 'Calm! Keep calm!' Ceaseless brief interactions with people in the crush.

Bursting through a gap between two groups of police they were ahead of the cars. Simon squeezed into a mass of bodies.

Something haunted the edge of his vision, an image sticky as mucus on the cornea. Two lanky men dressed in the fading black rags of politicized punk, arms out as if crucified, floating through the press, moving without hindrance like an oil stain topples smoothly over a choppy weir. And the look of ecstasy on their thin grey faces. Who are they? What are they? What do they know?

Still agitated, he came to his senses, took stock. He was in a clot of bodies. Behind him police attempted to cut the demonstration into manageable sizes, stop people joining the blockade. It was quieter down here. He tried to breathe slowly.

The leading car was ten feet away, police round it like ants on a fallen plumb, four or five attempting to clear a track through the rows of cross-legged demonstrators. The police worked from the side, taking hold of a campaigner and dragging or lifting. Occasionally a pair would drag a protester backwards, through the crush and away. Some protesters were dropped or bodily thrown out of the car's track. The car moved forward a few inches at a time.

Someone shouted, 'Watch that red-faced bastard. Watch that red-faced bastard.'

The noise level swelled again, but not before Simon registered motor drives whirring film across pressure plates and the dry hiss of camera shutters like cicadas in a Mediterranean dusk. He tried to speak but was tongue-tied, trying to say two opposing things at once: We were right not to bring the cameras, and, I wish we'd brought the cameras. Looking over Lindy's shoulder he saw a wedge of police cutting through the crowd. He shouted to Lindy, 'We're trapped!' She gave a tight smile and pressed against him.

The car was three feet away. He was not directly in front of it, but unless he moved it would run over his ankle. The police, angry and dripping sweat, wouldn't see his foot, or if they did they'd leave it there, let the black shiny rubber roll over it. The wheel would hit the joint, or, if he flexed, it would hit the foot side on, lengthways, twisting it through ninety degrees before crushing it into the tarmac. He began to tremble. Someone fell on him from behind, then the weight doubled and he strained not to collapse. The police were piling bodies on bodies. He began to panic, to lose his senses.

Then he saw Katrina, pink-faced but calm, cross-legged in front of the leading car. He seemed to zoom in and his viewpoint was filled by Katrina's profile, a black uniformed leg, and the star flower of a Mercedes Benz. He jerked his head to refocus but he was still under the weight of a struggling body and his head refused to move. A body fell from nowhere and landed across Lindy's shoulders and his lap. He pushed back and up with all his strength. Gulping breaths and a searing pain in the base of his spine as the weight lifted from him. Lindy was talking to the relaxed body which draped over them, limp and soft. It was Trudy from the workshop in Leeds. The two women were laughing.

He tried to focus his attention. He wanted to say, 'We can't keep on meeting like this,' to be cool, calm, and collected, but he was screaming: 'Don't hurt people!' Lindy put her finger to his lips.

A policeman lifted Katrina by her shoulders, then dumped her like refuse on the far side of the car's path. The red-faced bastard grabbed the free arm of a man in his early twenties who had been linked with Katrina. The copper yanked the arm then took hold of the man's hair with his other hand and lifted him. The man had been staring straight ahead with a concentrated smile, his face contorted as his arm twisted at the shoulder. Splashes of sweat from the policeman's glistening forehead fell onto the man's shirt, grey teardrops on white cotton.

A man in a fawn raincoat (why a raincoat in this hot sun?) with an armband saying NCCL Observer. He tried to calm the red-faced bastard and an elbow in his chest toppled him backwards. Simon shouted, tried to stand. Hands settled on his shoulder and pressed down, it was Sarah, her head over his shoulder: 'Okay, Simon. Okay.'

A jab of bright pain as his leg was booted from under the car wheel. The car moved forward and Simon saw a distorted tangle of bodies reflected in the shining black door. The car stopped. Inside was a small man, glistening skin stretched over high cheek bones, crimped chestnut hair, staring straight ahead, his eyes steady, his lips a cupid bow. Even through the thick glass he stank of money and power and the ultimate depravity and corruption of being this way in a world where children starved. Simon began to bang and claw on the glass and shout 'Bastard!' Dave pulled him away.

They tried to move ahead of the cars again, but now the crowd was almost stationary, divided into triangular groups by hundreds of police. Scuffles were breaking out. Police numbers shouted, then taken up and rippled through the melee.

The cars had moved forty or fifty yards since Simon entered Brook Street. A solid wall of police now blocked the road, others were lifting, dragging bodies. A matter of minutes before the blockade was cleared and the cars reached a major crossroads.

Suddenly a fresh wave of demonstrators appeared behind the police line. The police wavered. Simon was carried forward in the crush. The police lost control. Demonstrators mingled with Saturday shoppers, another carpet of bodies formed behind the double cordon of police.

Suddenly a cheer rose from the crowd. Turning, he saw the cars reversing rapidly back the way they had come. All around people were clambering to their feet, waving their arms. Lindy hugged Simon, trapping his hands above his head. 'We did it!' she sobbed. 'We did it!' Hand in hand they ran after the retreating cars.

It was a real victory, but hollow: the cars turned up Binney Street and broke out... or so it was said. It didn't matter. The State had thrown everything at them in that one all-out confrontation, and the State had retreated. Yes, they could have charged horses, yes they could have driven over bodies – but that would have been at least a loss of face on their part... and in front of so many whirring cameras and foreign television crews. Thatcher didn't have her hands on the collars of Dutch, Swedish, New Zealand television. Not yet...

Simon and Lindy were high. They had lost contact with the others, but identities were merged. It was as if everyone had known each other for years.

In ten or fifteen minutes the blockade would end, it seemed unlikely that the police would attempt another symbolic break-out. Lindy and Simon sat at the Brook Street entrance, sharing food and drink with a group from Plymouth. The pied juggler was standing close by, her hands moving smoothly, fruit turning and tumbling. A woman in her twenties was crying in a doorway, her face twisted with pain. Several demonstrators argued with a policewoman. The injured protester was led away to an ambulance which stopped a few yards down the road.

The first phase was over, the sense of unity dissipated like mist, Simon felt something leaving. He began to whistle.

XV

For three days he never left the flat. At first he took the telephone off the hook, but the G.P.O. employed a screaming device. He was in bed, in a daze. He wondered if he was dying. The noise became louder and louder. He put the receiver back on its cradle, soon it was jangling. How could he speak to anyone from O.A.R.? Or Anne, perhaps, saying she'd just had a Jaguar or a Lotus Elan (she now had presents from her estate agent like other women had babies or lovers). Worst of all it could be Hilary...

He stayed in bed and stared at the red telephone. There was a cigarette burn on the side nearest him. He couldn't remember doing that. He couldn't remember much at all. He couldn't think. Every time he tried to take hold of an idea it slid from him.

The phone stopped and settled like a dog preparing for sleep. Then the ears pricked and it was jangling jangling jangling.

Some part of him registered surprise that the instrument could be ripped from its wire exactly as he had seen it done so many times on television. It could.

He got up, got dressed. He had eaten little since the hospital – a few slices of bread, several pots of yoghurt, some cornflakes. After drinking half a pint of apple juice, he had reverted to water. No alcohol since the day before the hospital. At first he had pushed yellow, bullet shaped wax suppositories up his arse, felt them move of their own accord, slide into him. Now he had a kiddies' plastic hypodermic to fill from an aerosol, then squirt the expanding foam into his bowels to grow and leak back, a sticky, stinging mess.

Something was working. Today he was hungry.

He inspected a tin of tuna and experienced a fleeting impression; his tongue sliced lengthways on the crinkled edge of its lid.

The blood was easing off. He felt lighter, he assumed that he was lighter, but feeling lighter was more important. It was a sense of lightness about his stomach which radiated to other parts. He used an unfamiliar phrase: I am getting my health back.

The phone was dead. He remembered ripping out the wires. Swirls of confusion moved around him.

He questioned his sanity.

A block of three-dimensional graph paper; a monster rider on a monster horse. An alien thing. He often doodled while on the phone and was content to draw an ever-expanding network of old fashioned television aerials in the shape of an H. The new sci fi doodle disturbed him, he could not remember drawing some parts of it. His watch told him he had worked on it for two hours.

The window overlooked a street of Edwardian semis, broad grass verge and cherry trees in heavy, dirty leaf.

Soon it would be time for Nigel's party. Soon it would be a year since he met her. The tightness of her body, the smell of her hair, the warm softness of her tongue, the sound of her laughter. He shivered. As if walking on the lip of a high cliff, he felt a pull at the centre of his being.

He had spent a year thinking, feeling knowing that she felt the same. And yet –

He was standing with his hand on the door knob when someone knocked on the door and the knob twisted in his hand.

'Who is it?' he asked, surprised now by the sound of his voice.

'It's me, Hilary. Let me in.'

Keeping his right hand on the knob he released the Yale catch. The door wouldn't open. It was bolted. He couldn't remember doing that.

'Oh, Simon, Simon. I didn't know what to think. Your phone is out of action.' She hugged him to her, pressing her cheek onto his shoulder, then drew back and looked at his face.

'What is it? What's happened?' She raised her hand to stroke his cheek.

He turned back into the bedsitting-room. There was a leather settee loosely covered with old papers and books. He sat in the centre of it, wooden, limbs stiff but joints well lubricated. He stared at her as she stood in the doorway, facing him.

'You haven't shaved. You look so white and drawn. What is it, Simon?'

'A New Zealander banged stuff up my bum,' he said flatly. 'I haven't been out. I feel... raped, I suppose.'

'What did they say?'

'Avoid anxiety. Avoid anxiety and come back next week. I'm anxious about going back next week...' He laughed. Hilary didn't respond.

'I can stay for a few days,' she said. 'I'll look after you.'

'No!'

'No? Why not?'

'Just no. I don't know why not.'

'Simon, you're in a state. I won't take "no". You've let yourself go, let anxiety get the better of you. I'm staying.'

He stared at her in silence. She was carrying her overnight bag and a bottle wrapped in brown paper. She must have put them down before she hugged him, then picked them up as she followed him into the room. He felt dazed and tired.

She called from the kitchen, but what she said was lost in the sound of a running tap.

He got into bed without taking anything off, then pulled the bedclothes over his head and cried with increasing ferocity, writhing and biting the sheet. No because he was going to die and his only hope of survival came from the rightness he experienced that night with Lindy... and his only way to Lindy was through Nigel, and the thought squirted blood into his colon. No because he had used Hilary, like he had used so many others. No because Hilary smiled and beckoned death every time she raised a glass.

He woke sticky with sweat. The room was dark and airless. He pushed bedclothes off his face. It was night. Hilary slouched in the armchair. He remembered the bleeding. Then the dull ache was back. He eased the bedclothes further down. From the quiet hiss of night it was three or four in the morning; before the metallic sounds of dawn. Hilary had a bottle in her hand.

'You cried yourself to sleep.' Her arm dangled. She held the bottle by its neck, it leaned at an angle of forty-five degrees, its base resting on the floor.

'Not much left, afraid.' She raised her arm and took a long drink from the neck.

'Scotch?' Simon stretched, then hunched his shoulders, as if cradling some newborn thing in the pit of his stomach. Stretching threatened to anger the thing inside.

'Mm. Scotch!' She stood, wobbled, 'Oops!' She took two steps towards him, bottle held out like a timid child offers grass to a cow. When she stumbled, the bottle hit Simon's breast bone. He grunted. Hilary began to giggle, rubbing the spilt whisky into his shirt. Simon said nothing, tried to sit. Something would tear inside if he exerted himself.

'What the shit?' Hilary's face took the rusty light like metal; deep, black shadows and shining highlights. She was an old woman, toothless, characterless, decade piled on decade piled on flesh. Her voice was harsh. 'Matter with you, darling? Matter, hmn?' She pressed her splayed fingers into his chest and pushed herself up, tottering a little as she gained a balance. She was sitting on the bed now. Simon propped himself against the head board.

'Drink!' she said, an order not an invitation.

'I can't. I haven't since…'

'Drink. Simon, drink.' She pushed the bottle into his face so that its top pressed his upper lip towards his nose and he could feel glass on his gums. The smell of whisky slapped and caressed, screamed and cajoled.

'Drink, you... you fucker.'

Simon took the bottle from her and drank from the neck. It hit him like a train, crashing into his mouth then surging into his stomach. He drank again. Whisky splashed from the corners of his mouth and when he lowered the bottle Hilary licked his chin. She took the bottle and drank like a child drinks lemonade, her thumb half blocking the neck, sucking spurts of whisky. When she lowered the bottle she was breathless, she wiped her mouth with her free hand, then pressed it against his cheek.

'Better?' Her voice had softened.

He was wide awake and acutely aware of his senses, as if he had woken into a static mosaic of smell and vision, touch and sound. The scotch had anaesthetized everything in its path leaving a visual image like the silver track of a snail.

'Better,' he said, hearing the graininess of his own voice, noting the cold flatness of it. 'Much better.'

Hilary slapped him hard across the face, rocking him sideways on the pillows. He raised his hand to the cheek. His teeth hurt and his head felt as if a delicate machine had been knocked off balance.

'Jesus,' he said, 'I can see stars.' She hit him again. He fell sideways onto the pillow. As he started to sit up he saw her swinging the bottle at his head and tried to protect himself with his arm. She lacked co-ordination, the bottle thudded against the bed head, Hilary let go and it fell onto his upturned face, hitting the bridge of his nose and splashing whisky into his eyes.

Hilary slid off the bed and crumpled on the floor like a discarded coat. Simon sat up, rubbing his eyes with his sleeve. Patting his stinging nose. On impulse he drained the bottle into his mouth.

'Jesus.' He stood at the side of her and she flipped her head backwards so that it rested on the bed. For a moment her eyes hovered, out of control, then she stared at him.

'Kick me,' she said, her voice slurred, saliva catching the light and burning down the side of her face. 'Kick me, fucker. Shite bag, KICK ME!' She took hold of his foot and tried to swing it into her side. Simon began to lose his balance. He saw his intestines misting with sprayed blood. He pulled his foot away and went into the bathroom.

The neon light flickered and hummed. He held a flannel under the cold tap and inspected his face. A neat blue cut on the bridge of his nose oozed blood into his right eye. He squeezed the flannel before pressing it against the cut. Suddenly he wanted to crap like his stomach would burst. He locked the door and lowered his trousers, putting the flannel on the edge of the bath. There was a small scimitar of blood on the flannel. He pressed it back onto his nose.

Holding a double sheet of toilet paper on the flat of his hand he caught the shit as it fell, then he eased himself back onto the seat and inspected the paper. They were like small plums, slick shining purple coating around tiny faeces.

She was in the kitchen, swearing quietly, opening and closing cupboards. He went in after her.

'I can do without this, Hilary.' She swung round from the big stripped-pine cupboard and focused on him. She was swaying, a blue and white jug in her hand.

'I can do without this, Hilary,' she sneered, giving a whining edge to her mimicking.

He held up his hands, symmetrical, as if about to clap them like a child, finger to finger, thumb to thumb, then he let them fall to his side.

'I don't know what it's all about. I don't understand what you want of me.' He took a step towards her and she lifted the jug as if to defend herself. He stopped and looked at her. She was crumpled over to the right, her body twisted, damp patches on her yellow blouse, hair bedraggled. He had never seen her as bad as this, her face full of hatred; eyes narrowed, steady on his face.

'Hilary,' he said, deliberately softening his voice, as if talking to a timid animal. 'Hilary, Hilary, what is it?'

'Hilary, Hilary, what is it?' She repeated his words, whining and snivelling.

'For Christ's sake –'

'For Christ's sake.'

'Listen –'

'Listen.'

He lifted his hand, moving towards her. She cowered against the cupboard, one hand raising the jug, the other scrabbling like a crab on the pale wood until it found a handle, then securing itself.

'Leave me alone!' She whispered, 'Leave me alone, shite. Fucking shite.'

He took another step towards her and she slid to the floor, trembling, her eyes wide now and her lips drawn back. Her face was grey, nerves twitching around the eyes. He turned and went back into the bedsitting-room.

The room was light, a grey flat light. A milk float passed beneath his window, its steady whine accompanied by the rattle of bottles. He stepped to the window and looked out. Across the road a man in a denim shirt and thick unruly hair was opening the sun roof in his Mini. Simon watched as the man poked his head through the hole in his car roof and waved to a young woman in the bay window. She was wrapped in a lemon sheet, her long auburn hair tumbling in curls onto her shoulders. The man allowed his car to roll forward without turning on the engine. When it was out of Simon's line of vision he heard the engine cough into life. He watched the woman lean forward and rest her forehead against the glass.

'I'm sorry, darling.' It came as a shock. He had forgotten Hilary.

The transformation was unbelievable. Her skin was tight, shoulders drawn back, head erect. Even her hair seemed to have sorted itself out and hung straight and ordered, neatly splitting at her shoulders, quarter this side, quarter that side, half hanging down her back. She came to him and rested her mouth against his neck. 'Forgive me, Simon. Please.'

He put his arm across her shoulders but couldn't tighten his hold on her. The bridge of his nose was throbbing and stinging at the same time, and his left eye stung from its dousing with whisky and blood.

'Tell me you need me. Please, Simon. It is important to me. I must stay to look after you.' There was a hint of desperation in her voice, a hint of threat. He touched his distended stomach with his hand. She misinterpreted the movement and pressed herself against him.

Perhaps to escape he said, 'Stay. Yes, stay.'

Then, with a flood of emotion warming him he pulled her into his side and said, 'Of course you can stay. Of course.'

They became businesslike, undressing and getting into bed, she quickly tidying the crumpled bed clothes, he opening the window to let in morning air.

The warmth in him, the affection, was not for Hilary. It was a response to the absence of the other person, the grey twitching, cowering person. For a moment, as she slid to the floor in the kitchen, he had wanted to hit her, beat her, kick her. He had teetered on the edge of accepting her assumption. Now he was safe again.

She made love to him, gentle and considerate. He told himself how to respond: gentle and considerate.

He thought she was asleep in the crook of his arm. He watched flashes of light race across the ceiling as early cars drove along the road and caught the slanting sunlight.

'Why didn't you telephone?'

Simon pretended to be asleep. He didn't want to talk. He regulated his breathing and closed his eyes in case she looked. There was silence for a few moments, then she said again, 'Why didn't you call me, Simon. Why didn't you tell me what was happening?'

She turned in his arm and he knew she was looking at him. He heard her raising herself on her elbow and guessed she was inspecting his face. She moved again, resting her head on his arm. She began to talk quietly.

'I was desperate, darling. You must believe me. You must. I wouldn't have done it if you'd called me. I waited days and days, then I called and there was no answer. Your office said they had no idea where you were.'

Simon made a calculation and realized it was five days since he had been in contact with O.A.R. Tomorrow was the day of his meeting with the marketing people from a food, pharmaceuticals and entertainment conglomerate which accounted for a third of O.A.R.'s turnover. If he slept now he might safely expect to wake mid to late morning, he could then take himself to the squash club and have a sauna. He would call O.A.R. as soon as he woke, get into the office after lunch. Pick himself up... dust himself down.... start –

'He knew George was away, he told me so. After, after he'd... he'd shafted me. That's what he called it, shafting.' Her voice was trembling. She was crying and talking about Nigel. 'He... I got drunk, Simon. I loathed him, but I just kept on drinking and drinking, and he kept on pouring it down me.' She paused and pressed herself against him. Simon felt a great sympathy for her and tightened his arm around her shoulders. She sobbed for a while. He thought about Nigel and Hilary together and it meant nothing to him. He felt sorry for this confused woman who expected something that was not his to give. He kissed her hair.

'I said yes to him, I suppose I said yes to him. It's all so confused and horrid, Simon. I think he kept telling me how much he wanted to, how much I wanted to, whispering and stroking, then pulling back and saying how it must be mutual, how I must tell him, tell him... And he gave me vodka. Oh God. Oh God!' She sobbed for a while and he held her, his free hand stroking her hair. He was thinking about O.A.R. again, ordering the components of the presentation which, luckily, he would not have to give, but which might elicit questions for him to field. It was all there, in his head.

'You're okay,' he said. 'You are alright now, Hilary. You were drunk, that's all. Try to forget it now and sleep. Sleep. It's not important.' She stiffened in his arms and was silent, then he felt her body relax and she began to talk again.

'There had only been you and George, so it is important, Simon. To me.' He tightened his hold about her shoulder, said he was sorry, he hadn't meant it in that sense, said for her to sleep, sleep. Said sleep and time were what was needed. She listened in silence, then spoke as he paused, as if she had heard nothing.

'I wouldn't let him use the bed... No, no I wouldn't do that.

He… he shafted me on the floor. He was so… so full of himself, bouncy, he got up and poured himself brandy, not for me, just himself. He was so proud, Simon, telling me how he had thought it was time that he came round and gave me a bit of fun. And he was rough... ungentle. He talked and giggled about George, poor George, and he said how he had wanted to shaft me since first he saw me at the party. I didn't tell him about us, he asked... he asked what had happened between us at his shitty little party. I pretended I couldn't remember you.' She began to cry again. 'Oh, Simon, I am sorry, I am sorry. I pretended I didn't know who he was talking about. He said he thought you'd dipped your wick in me. Dipped your wick. I told him to shut up and get out and he started mauling me again and saying dirty talk would turn me on. Oh God, it was awful. It was hours before he would go. He kept telling me to call him when I wanted fun. He said he had a girlfriend but she knew what he was like and quite liked it that way. He said, Simmy gave her one at the party, then he said he thought you'd had it up us both in the same night. Did you, Simon, did you... did you fuck someone that night?'

Simon said nothing, his hand stroked her hair. He wondered if it was blood he tasted. There was a tightening of muscle under the corners of his mouth. He felt his lips pressing together. He felt the dull throbbing sharpen to a spike in his stomach.

XVI

Back in Duke Street Cora, Jed, Derek and Mary stood by the bags and blankets. Danny joined them as Lindy and Simon were hugged by Mary. Danny was tense, he hadn't seen Katrina for over an hour. They stood in a group, their excited stories marbled by anxiety about Katrina and Tippy and Dr Jo. Dave and Sarah were assumed to be safe since they had headed up Brook Street in front of Simon and Lindy. Then Dave and Sarah appeared with Katrina between them. She was flushed and grinning, white hair swinging like a shampoo ad.

'This one got herself picked up, then went back for another go.' Dave was laughing, his bush hat exchanged for a white canvas cap with a pink peak. Next came Tippy and Dr Jo.

'HISTORY HAS BEEN MADE! OXFORD STREET WAS BLOCKED! IT WAS WONDERFUL. BUS DRIVERS, MINDFUL OF THEIR UNION'S POSITION ON UNILATERALISM, VACATED THEIR BUSES. DEMONSTRATORS BLOCKADED THE ROAD BY DANCING! ROUND AND ROUND AND ROUND!'

'It was so wonderful,' Dr Jo said, breaking her normal silence, her serious face lifted by happiness. 'They didn't know how to cope. They didn't know who was who, so they stretched orange tape around everyone and said that anyone still inside after thirty seconds would be arrested.'

'BUT WOMEN WERE CARRYING SCISSORS, THEY CUT THE TAPE INTO SHORT LENGTHS AND DANCED WITH IT. IT WAS WONDERFUL!'

Simon moved to where the police barrier had been and looked back towards the group. A personal crisis passed and yet a feeling of nausea hung about him. The action as a whole had been a victory, but he was ambiguous about his own part in it. His intense fear and inability to think clearly in the pressure of Brook Street worried him. The women had seemed so calm and strong. Fearless.

It was typical of a C.N.D. demonstration that, as people drifted away, a squad of stewards with black plastic bin liners began collecting litter. And it was equally typical that the

135

demonstrators left little litter. Somewhere at the back of his mind he toyed with a pastiche peace song: we are gentle angry people and we never scatter litter... we are really kind and liberal and never ever bitter.

They walked towards Brook Street. This was where he ran, there he had stumbled over the sitting group. Here he had caught a glimpse of his own face reflected in a car door, distorted like a Bacon portrait.

He walked with Cora who told him that Tippy had never seen his father, an early volunteer in the last war who died as a POW in Malaya. 'HE WAS POLITICAL TO HIS TOENAILS,' she said, with pride. 'OF COURSE I SUPPORTED HIM, BUT HE ENCOURAGED ME TO FIND MY OWN WAY, I DIDN'T COME FROM A POLITICAL FAMILY, YOU SEE. HE WAS A GREAT BELIEVER IN THE EMANCIPATION OF WOMEN AND WORRIED THAT I WOULD SIMPLY TAKE ON HIS VIEWS BECAUSE HE WAS THE MAN.

'I DIDN'T HAVE THE SUFFERING OF THOSE WHO WERE TOLD THEIR HUSBANDS OR BROTHERS WERE MISSING BELIEVED DEAD. I KNEW LENNY WAS DEAD.

'WHEN THEY ANNOUNCED THE RESULTS OF THE FORTY-FIVE ELECTION I TOOK TIPPY TO THE TOWN HALL. THERE WAS A CAVALCADE OF VICTORIOUS LABOUR CANDIDATES. I HELD TIPPY UP, HE WAS THREE AT THE TIME. I DEDICATED HIM TO THE LABOUR PARTY. I TOLD HIM HIS DAD WAS DEAD, BUT THAT THE PRINCIPLES HE BELIEVED IN WERE MORE ALIVE THAN THEY HAD EVER BEEN IN OUR COUNTRY. AND I TOLD HIM THAT HE MUST NEVER FORSAKE THE LABOUR PARTY, BECAUSE THAT WAS WHERE HIS DAD'S SPIRIT WAS. AND I TOOK THE SAME VOW MYSELF.'

Cora had a look of satisfaction on her face, although whether it was satisfaction at telling him, or at what she had told him, Simon couldn't decide. He said, 'Lindy and I have only just joined.'

'Then you have been saved a lot of pain and soul searching.'

'Derek said something like that.'

'I've known those two since the early days.' Simon realized that her speech had lost its studied formality. Shades of a cockney accent had entered her voice. She inclined her body to his as they walked. 'Never underestimate either of them, or their type. The Blythes of this world sometimes act like silly little boys, and they ARE CLOWNS, but Derek and Jed have remained steadfast.' She took his wrist in her cool, fine fingers and said, 'And that steadiness was never due to lack of intelligence or imagination. It is harder for men to adjust to the times while maintaining the principles and enthusiasms of youth. You will find this. Tippy lives in fear of becoming a laughing stock. I say to him, Of course you're a laughing stock, Tippy. But just look at those who laugh.'

They were following a general flow towards Trafalgar Square when they heard singing. At first it was a drone, then Simon recognized the hypnotic repetition of 'Break the nuclear chain'. Lindy, who was walking with Dr Jo, called over her shoulder that they were catching up with the tail end of the legal march. They hurried and joined the straggling marchers with their banners. Simon's spirits soared.

Stand up, people make your choice
Create a world without nuclear war.
Now together we are strong
Break the nuclear chain.

Simon realized that, for the first time, a march was going through densely peopled streets. Rich shoppers tripped in and out of luxurious shops. People with faces so hard they couldn't even express disdain.

'What a lot of death masks,' he said to Lindy and Dr Jo, who had waited for him and Cora.

'I can hardly believe this,' Dr Jo said. 'A march on *New Bond Street.*'

And then the march concertinaed together, thinned as those in front sat in the road, and there, a hundred yards ahead of them, a solid wall of police.

It was not the official march, but hundreds of like-minded people moving from Grosvenor to Trafalgar Square.

And so Simon found himself in the thick of a second act of non-violent civil disobedience. Things seemed calmer this time.

The presence of more children, laughing and waving peace flags was reassuring to him. He and Lindy walked up the pavement to find out what was happening. They arrived within a few feet of the police who were locked together three deep.

A tanned, athletic man in open-necked white shirt and jeans was shouting at the protesters: 'Charge the fucking pigs, for fuck's sake. Come on! Come on! We can push the bastards away like the fucking shit they are.' He hardly seemed to pause for breath. People around him were telling him to calm down, but he shook them off and carried on shouting. Any of four or five policemen could have reached out an arm and collared him. It didn't make sense.

A Rupe clone rose above those around him who were cross-legged or sprawled on the road.

'Time you went off duty, Officer,' he shouted in a clear voice. 'There will be no charging... from either side I hope.' Rupe III sat down to cheers and hand clapping. The shouter almost proved the point by leaving the square through the police lines. Arms unlinked to let him pass.

'I don't understand,' Lindy said. 'Are they stupid or do they think we are?'

A few moments later, as they were about to return to the rest of the group, Lindy and Simon caught sight of the mounted police. Shouts of protest arose from others standing near the entry to Oxford Street. Crash-helmeted horsemen were drawn up behind the police cordons. Simon felt his stomach sag.

'Oh, Jesus, not them.'

'Come on,' Lindy said, 'Let's get back to the others.'

The crowd started to count down, chanting taken up and spreading:' 99... 98... 97... 96... 95...'

'They've said they'll let us through in two minutes,' a punk told Lindy.

'Two... One... ZERO!' Nothing happened.

Tippy was quietly confident: horses would not, could not trample seated people, it was a well-known fact. The group took little comfort from the gangling socialist.

'Are you sure they don't just refuse to trample people who wear socks with sandals?'

'SIMON, YOUR HUMOUR CARRIES OVERTONES OR

AT LEAST UNDERCURRENTS OF ANTI-PROGRESSIVE
SENTIMENT.'

Tension was easing when police transits squealed to a halt
behind them. It was an impressive entry, a display: thirteen
vehicles from left and right, parked in a herring bone pattern. A
couple of constables stood either side of each van, others waited
inside.

The protesters were caught between two plugs of
constabulary. If horses were used people, including children,
would be injured, perhaps some killed. The vans blocked off any
retreat.

*'Let's buy rubies,' Hilary said. 'Let's buy rubies and pearls
for blood and tears.' New Bond Street: they stood hand in hand,
peering into a jeweller's window, she so elegant and costly. He
wore an expensive rust suit with broad lapels and flairs. His
image in the window frightened him.*

A heavy-chested man with a chunky gold chain round his
wrist squatted beside them. 'This is it,' he said, his voice earnest
but enthusiastic. 'The pigs have blocked us in because of a group
of anarchists up front. They've being trying to get them for
months. In a few minutes the pigs are coming out of the van and
charging up through you lot and making arrests –'

'Hang on, man. Hang on.' Mary put her large hand on his
shoulder to slow him down. 'How you know all this?'

He looked about him, then said, 'A copper told me.'

'Oh, a bobbie, I see.' Derek raised his eyebrows.

'We're going to charge the line.' The man was sweating.

'Who's this we?' Lindy asked.

'All of us. If we don't break the pigs they'll get the anarchists,
right. There's enough of us. We'll smash 'em, right.'

'Which peace group are you with?' Dr Jo asked.

'Never fucking mind that. Just smash the fucking pigs.'

'I think, Comrade,' Jed said, giving him an understanding
smile, 'that we are concerned about your credentials. It is
singularly stupid to suggest that this mixed crowd, which
includes the old and infirm, toddlers and infants in prams, to
suggest that such a group attack two hundred police and a
contingent of potentially brutal mounties to my mind,' he went
on, using the Party technique of leaving no space for interruption,
'and I believe I am expressing the general feeling of this group,

139

your lack of intelligence and failure of imagination is more consistent with police thinking than that of the peace movement.'

The man stared at Jed and grappled with the implications of what he had heard. Then he silently moved off to another group several yards away.

'An agent provocateur, that's for sure,' Jed said clearly pleased with his observation and his French accent.

'Or a silly bugger!' Derek added.

In the event there was a gradual leakage through the covered arcades. They had waited twenty minutes.

By the time the group from Church Hill left New Bond Street police outnumbered demonstrators and all was still.

'Some of our friends from the media are down here. I believe the BBC has already announced that this demonstration has only attracted seventy thousand people.' Bruce Kent's voice rang over the packed Square. 'Let's tell them, shall we? The C.N.D. estimate is not seventy thousand, it is two hundred thousand.' He led them into shouting the number one, two, three times. Simon wondered how the hacks at the front were taking it. Later on they would be turning in their copy – would they write two hundred thousand and expect it to be cut by subs, or would they just write their own lies?

He was standing barefoot on the smooth crown of an iron bollard in front of the National Gallery. The rest of the group were pressed against a stone balustrade several yards away. Thousands of people were crushed into the square, waving banners, cheering, clapping.

People milled about at his feet: grinning, loving, vital people; silly, mooning, loony people; people of all ages, races and religions. People who knew that all life is connected. People who believed that in the end the answers were simple: you put life before death, you put love before hate, you put courage before fear, you put bread before bombs, you put peace before war, you put people before governments.

This was the best time, the right time, the time closest to fulfilment in a disordered and cruel world.

A cheer erupted and spread through the Square, a cheer so solid it was almost visible above the packed bodies, like heat shimmers on a summer day. Simon joined in, feeling the strength of his own voice boosted beyond belief. He couldn't hear what had been said to provoke the cheer, but he knew why he cheered. Simon, and all the crowd, were cheering themselves for being there, for being who they were, for offering themselves hope while governments strutted and postured and offered mass death.

It was dark and chilly in the covered car park. The minibus stood alone. Simon said, 'God, I'm tired.'

Dr Jo fiddled with the keys, trying to open the van door. Jed said, 'This has been the day, Comrades.' Then he put his arm round Derek's shoulders and they sang together, clear, strong tenor voices echoing through the deserted car park:

We peasants, artisans and others
Enrolled among the sons of toil,
Let's claim the earth henceforth for brothers,
Drive the indolent from the soil.
On our flesh long has fed the raven,
We've too long been the vultures' prey;
But now, farewell the spirit craven,
The dawn brings in a brighter day.

Dr Jo, Cora and Tippy had joined in softly, now half the group surged into the chorus:

Then, comrades, come rally,
And the last fight let us face,
The International
Unites the human race.
Then, comrades, come rally,
And the last fight let us face,
The International
Unites the human race.

A slow hand clap came from behind them. Standing by the entrance, straddling the razor-sharp division of sunshine and shadow, were two police officers.

XVII

One day, he would think of this as the first reconstruction. There had been rehearsals.

We always live at the forefront of time, he told himself.

Hilary slept noisily. He dressed and drank coffee, stomach distended, but no pain. He could face the day, only the cut on his nose nagged, Hilary's bag lay open at the side of the bed. He left a scribbled note on top of it: *Gone to town to get ready for work. See you. Love, Simon.*

Mid-morning Tube, airy, empty, rattling. Sunray and sauna, then Jermyn Street for haircut and shave. Hot towels twirled and twisted on upturned face. Soft fingers. Powder.

From Liberty's, a violet cotton shirt and navy cotton socks (to be blessed by, he told himself). From Austin Reed, a ready to wear grey chalk-stripe wool suit with wide lapels; for good measure, a grey, white and pink silk tie.

By the pub door, beneath O.A.R., he found a dull grey pebble traced with pale green lines. He touched it to his tongue (pretending to cough), then put it in his pocket.

I bleed, therefore I am, he thought, I bleed, but will not be beaten. I'll magic my way through.

Shoulders back, head up, new wardrobe swinging in the Reed carrier.

Entering the office block.

'Simmy! Simmy! Where the hell have you been? Top floor straight off.'

A mouse? A mole? A moth? Something moving in his colon. He slid his free hand inside his shirt, felt tight skin.

'Chronic enteritis, squits, chunder, the lot. Bloody phone kaput! Better now. Guts still dickie.'

Lift stops. Door's hiss.

'Looking good, old son. Sure you haven't been truanting?'

'Reconstructed myself, all sham, natch. Inside this shiny shell I bleed for the world and all who sail on her.'

Bypass Doreen the Dragon, into Furnace's office by the directors' door. Furnace standing at window. Haze over London. Cut flowers on glistening, empty desk.

'Furnace, what's new?'

'Good God, Simon! Thought you'd defected.'

'Not yet!'

He explained. Furnace wasn't listening. He went to his office, opened mail. He left early, pleading a medical appointment. He worried he was tempting fate. He knew he was 'walking to tube' and 'it is raining', other than that he didn't know what he was doing. He stopped and thought.

'I am going back to the flat.'

XVIII

Summer days. They worked in the darkroom, illustrating a book on local history. It was an underpaid activity, pleasing enough to spend July taking pictures, but now, in blazing August, seven long days in red light irked. And so they decided that Sunday would be just that, a day of sun.

Simon walked to Rowntree's paper shop for tobacco. Lindy set a pink-and-white-clothed card-table in the yard. By the time Simon returned the table was spread with fresh bread, boiled eggs, toast, marmalade, coffee, and a small vase holding three marigolds.

When they had eaten Simon said, 'Guess what I have,' and pushed his hand into the pocket of his baggy khaki shorts. Lindy wiped crumbs from her mouth with her hand, then wiped her hand on her denim cut-offs.

'Is it perfect?'

'It's perfect.'

She began to make a roll-up, then grinned and unmade it, returning the tobacco to its packet and screwing the sliver of white paper into a tiny ball.

'Gaulloise!'

'Oui!' he gurgled, 'Le fag bleu pour la belle dame de mon vie.' He opened the packet and held it out. 'Avey vous une de cette while les autre est ready.'

Cigarettes lit, they made displays of appreciation, then Lindy said, 'That's the book profit going up in smoke.'

'Aye, Lass,' he said, assuming an accent. 'By God, don't we know how to spend it?'

He picked up the *Observer* from the floor beside his chair and opened it out to show her the headlines. 'I have an idea,' he said, refolding the paper and rhythmically striking his bare knee with it. 'I suggest that we make fire lighters of this crap and leave them in the hearth for colder days. I can't face the black and white bits, and the coloured bits are always worse.'

She took the folded newspaper from him. 'We'll save it for the crossword, and maybe a quick peep later on. I mean, in the right mood it makes funny reading – and there isn't another

Sunday this side of Attila the Hun. Shall we drive out to the Chance and see if Sara and Dave are there, see what's happening? Or shall we stay around here, walk up and see Kat and Danny? Go down to the river?'

'Nothing can be more political than lobotomized *Sun* readers hitting their kids and giving them shite to eat.' Simon swung his arm in the direction of the river, the park side of which would be crowded. 'Let's see Danny and Katrina.'

'It's too early for a bottle, don't you think?'

'What time is it anyway?'

'Half-tenish.'

'So, say eleven when we get there, and this being Sunday, and what with doing twelve to fifteen hours a day for seven bleeding days, taking everything into consideration, I'd say you were right. Far too early for a bottle.'

'Home made or store bought?'

They decided to take homemade, and then have the option of clubbing with Danny and Katrina for store bought.

A steep, overgrown path led to the cottage. Danny claimed the path gave him security, Katrina said it would someday enclose them with rambling roses. 'And who will fight through to kiss us awake?'

It was a small, double-fronted house of stone which pre-dated the Victorian expansion of Church Hill by two centuries. Owned by an obscure charity, the cottage brought with it the annual duty of reporting on the condition of the windows in three local churches. Katrina had taken lease and responsibility several years earlier. In those days, before Danny, she had hoped to keep herself as a painter. Danny changed all that. Now she was one of the growing population of social workers, the unemployed of the ideal society, doing well by doing good.

Danny greeted them with a carafe in one hand and a trowel in the other. 'Some say cut lettuce and leave its root in the soil to rot, put back nitrogen or grow new mini-lettuces. I believe the lettuce should be gently raised by the root with the assistance of a trowel or small fork. Rex and Helen are here and Kat has insisted that the lettuce should be dug exactly one hour before it is consumed. I take it you're intent on getting pissed in the sunshine?'

Lindy held high the litre bottle so that sun sparkled in the pink wine.

'Pass, friends. Rex has some home-grown dope.'

Time passed paradoxically, at the speed of light and a snail's pace.

'This is very nice, Rex.'

'It is very... pleasing. My sister grows it under glass in Devon. She parcels the harvest into equal shares, then gives them to friends and relatives. She keeps two shares for herself so that she can always be hospitable. As good a way as any to organize society. But how to sell the concept, Simon. You tell me, marketing man.'

'The only propaganda is the propaganda of action,' Simon explained. 'No good telling people what to do or what to think. For everyone you convince, you will create one who opposes you. The result will be a world divided.'

They were standing face to face in Hal's paddling pool.

'You can't talk. You're in the Labour Party.'

'Take more than the Party to stop me talking, sunshine. Point is, just do, just be. In the final analysis there is only example. Only example is influential. Never ever push anything except yourself.'

'And that joint you're holding onto.'

'And this joint I'm holding onto. Helen's in the Party, why aren't you?'

'It offers nothing. Compromise and sell-out. I'm not knocking you or Lindy, or Danny and Katrina, not even Helen, it's where you choose to do your thing. Can't tell me you fit snug though. There's a lot we all want you'll never get through your branch, let alone Conference.'

'Go on. What?'

'Veganism.'

'Right, what else?'

'Homoeopathy, animal rights, pacifism, food additives, de-schooling, bare-foot medicine... Need I go on?'

'No, Rex, thou need'st not. Problem is, you should be inside the Party, not outside. You should come and fight your corner. I agree with you, a lot of comrades would, but, I suppose, at the moment, there's the immediate press of the strike and the disarmament debate.'

Rex handed him the joint. 'Two more sell-outs. Kinnock won't be seen dead with the miners. Mealy-mouthed git. He's on his own side, like all the rest of them.'

Simon drew long and thoughtfully, then let the smoke ease back out into the scented air of the garden. For a short while he could smell the intermingling of the scents of nicotiana and roses.

Katrina said, from somewhere: 'You two!'

'Don't you agree with people being on their own side, parties of one? Isn't that what you're all about?' He handed Rex the joint.

'Dicky argument.'

'Yeah. You're right. Shite leadership, but only to be expected. Tell you this though, you can work to improve the Party, but only from inside. And another thing: there's money going to the strike from the Party.'

'And other parties. And individuals.'

'You two!' Katrina called.

Exactly how Simon came to be standing in the pool, Simon couldn't remember. He remembered eating and drinking and smoking.

'You two! Look, you two, go and sit over by the hut, out of the way.' That had been Katrina. Lindy was content to stretch out on a sun bed and close her eyes, not even opening them for her lips to greet the glass.

And so it happened that Simon found himself during the early afternoon of a scorching August day, seated on a vast plateau of intoxication. This plateau featured stumps, ruins and freshly dug foundations of ideas; some new structures were taking shape; some conceptions of incredible architectural beauty and integrity, mounted on frictionless trolleys, shied from his close inspection. A slim-fingered hand eased through his vision and he recognized the tightly packed paper tube as another joint, a J, a Jimmy James.

'Thank you, dear boy.'

He accepted the joint and dragged smoke and air deep into his lungs, he felt it putting solid flesh on his body, a round belly, pads of rosy stuff on his cheeks and chin, a thickening of fingers and wrists, a pouching beneath the eyes. And clothes: a black waistcoat with bone buttons, a slim gold chain; nothing ostentatious. Hair slipped back into the top of his skull and grey side-whiskers sprouted. He felt the sweet touch of a nicotiana-scented zephyr.

'And then the dog collar to... God bless you, Rex, my boy, did you know I am a man of the cloth?'

'A wrecked rector... I'm Rex the wrecked rector, I drive a red tractor, I plough every furrow I can...' The tune was vaguely Burlington Bertie. Rex drew on the joint. Simon crossed his chubby legs and admired the shiny black shoes and gaiters, then waving his ringed fingers in the air he added, 'My make-up's Max Factor, and my benefactor's a jolly and generous man...' Then the giggles came.

The tubular metal and striped canvas garden chair whimpered and squeaked as he slumped back against the garden shed, exhausted, aching from the crescendo of laughter. He opened his eyes. Rex sat opposite him. Their bare feet touched. Rex was beautiful, dressed only in lemon trunks, his slim, hairless body burnt gold, his black unkempt hair and beard, glistening from days spent swimming, his face, usually so tight and neurotic, relaxed and happy. Happy... intelligent... sensitive! And all around him a glorious outbreak of rambling roses reverting to wild, pale pink, mixing to white and could it be pinpoints of blue and green before the amazing citrous heart of each blossom?

'Happy, intelligent, sensitive.' Simon caught up with his voice. 'It's not a very common combination on a face these days, Rex. Hold it as long as you can.'

'You two!' Katrina appeared in his field of vision. She wore a bikini and carried a fat-bellied jug of home-made rose petal wine, mint, gin, and soda water.

'Lethal!' Rex said as he slowly offered his empty pint glass.

'Lethal lethargy. Lovely!' Simon emptied his glass and held it out.

'I planned on doing something today. Danny's too far gone now. Oh, well.' As the wine twisted down into Simon's glass he had a deja vu: liquid twisted like a swaying rope.

'Lovely drink, Katrina.' Rex offered her the joint and she straightened and took a couple of quick drags.

'Take it to the others,' Rex said, letting a long arm dangle to the lawn. His fingers scampered like spring lambs, found the cigar box, flipped up the lid and withdrew another King James amongst jimmies. 'No, take 'em this. We'll finish that one.'

Simon accepted the joint from Katrina, swigged the freshly mixed drink, took a quick pull and coughed. 'This day is heaven, this organic dope is bliss, this cup of wine is anthraxian – No, I don't mean that... what do I mean?'

Katrina stood, a long thin streak of white, a pink flush, like a figure drawn in rose petals. Her white hair tied in bunches, her mouth a gentle curve of contentment. 'I don't know what you mean, Simon. I never know what you mean. Do you?'

'Occasionally dear lady, occasionally.'

'Enjoy!' She walked out of his field of vision.

Very slowly he stood up and turned through ninety degrees. Like some prehistoric creature making the transition from water to air, he flapped his arms. Pink jewels of drink floated from the rim of his glass. 'Katrina!' he called, his voice trailing like the wisps of cirrus high above them. 'Katrina!'

She turned, still smiling. 'What?'

'Ambrosial... no, nectar. It's nectar. Tell Lindy I love her.'

Katrina laughed and walked on to where Lindy, Danny, and Helen sat around the pool. Hal sat in the water, a T-shirt protecting his white skin from the sun, a floral sun hat covering his white hair.

'Rex,' Simon said, handing back the joint, 'I'm going to turn my chair and observe the little gathering by the pool for a while, but, before doing so, I must tell you that you look lovely against the roses. Lovely.' He turned his chair. A page turned in his head, a big page like the sail of a yacht, a flood of ozone and the cry of sea birds, then the question as the garden re-established itself:

'How did we get here?'

'Fats Waller!'

'Fats Waller?'

'Hmn. Big bird. Fat swallow.'

'Large insect plays jazz cornet?'

'Big Spider Beck!'

Hal walked towards them on his short rubbery legs. He carried a slopping seaside pail in each hand. When he reached them he flopped his bare bum onto the warm grass as a prelude to letting go of the handles. Leaving the two buckets, one red, one orange, he trotted back to the pool, then staggered back to them with a wooden box.

'It's his wee wee box,' Danny called. There was a lot of laughter by the pool. Simon and Rex watched with drug-induced curiosity. Simon sang snatches of Waller. Hal climbed onto his wee wee box and carefully emptied the orange bucket over Simon's head. Simon sang on as he cupped Hal's bottom in his hand, saving him from the roses. Hal dragged his wee wee box a couple of feet, then emptied the red bucket over Rex. Rex had prudently moved the dope box with his foot. Somewhere a long way off, people were laughing. Hal trundled off, dragging his wee wee box behind him.

'I don't know.' Simon said, inclining his dripping head towards Rex.

'You don't know what?' Rex asked.

'I don't know.' Simon said.

At Menwith Hill Peace Camp, outside the American spy base, two men take a decorator's plank and push it through the window of a caravan, shattering the word 'Peace', which was written in pink paint.

In his one up and one down terraced house, close by the Chance, Gozzer sits in the corner of his bedroom. The room is bare, like the downstairs room is bare. He has a pile of clothes, a carton containing two tins of beans, and a carton of kitchen utensils. A few personal belongings are safe at his mam and dad's. He stands and walks to the window, spits into the garden (he is thirty-four, there is coal dust in his lungs).

'This is fucking daft, this.' His voice is soft in the night and he is surprised to hear a cough from the deep blackness of the garden hedge. 'Who's yon?' he asks. 'Got any fags on thee?' No answer. Anxious, for this must be an intruder, Gozzer slams the window and stretches out on the floor, his head on the jumper and underclothes. A blanket curls at his feet like a faithful dog. Gozzer cries.

XIX

On the Tube, carrier between his feet, he looked up and she was smiling at him. They didn't speak until they had walked a couple of hundred yards. Simon was three or four houses behind her, but he could tell that she knew he was there and who he was. He trotted to her side.

'I live opposite,' he said.

'I know. You always appear to be hurrying somewhere. And you whistle a lot.'

On the Tube he thought it. Walking behind her he thought it. As soon as she spoke he knew it. Why not screw the night away? Preparation for the presentation. Her name was Jenny. Jenny was available. Jenny was convenient.

The road was warm and dusty. 'I must have a shower first,' she said, when he suggested eating at the Acropolis.

Good idea. Not too fast, don't suggest sharing. Softly softly catchee… what? Clap hands here comes rosy.

As they parted, agreeing to meet in half an hour, Simon took the bare muscle of her upper arm in his hand. 'Don't be late.'

She leaned towards him, as if expecting to be kissed. He pulled back. 'I won't' she said.

She was wearing a yellow dress with no sleeves. As she crossed the road he got a kick of excitement. Heat and the revealed outline of her body hit his groin. It had been a long time – except Hilary. It would do him good. It would help him through the night. She turned and waved. He waved back. As Nigel would say, pushovers are for pushing. Forget Lindy. Fly!

Hilary had gone. No note, no nothing, It was what he expected. It was what he wanted. Had she been there he would still have gone out with Jenny... why not? Why fucking not? He stared from his window and fought away the memory of Lindy and Nigel. Smother it with cunt. Why fucking not?

It was better than he expected. Jenny was funny, athletic, good at physical sex. They played at reducing her philosophy to the shortest and simplest statement possible. She rejected *Copulate!* in favour of *Live!*

151

It was not in his nature to lie about himself (apart from deliberately allowing his body, face and movements to create wrong impressions – tenderness, sadness, passion, etc., etc., and so on, and on, and on... the everyday stuff of swingers!) but he had intended lying to Jenny. In the event he didn't, he played down the bleeding, he made light of Hilary. And this openness brought them closer together, created a capsule of warmth and security.

'Why don't you write poetry?' she asked. 'Everyone should write poetry.'

And:

'I thought you were a push-over.'

'I was. So were you.'

'I approached you.'

'I came and sat in front of you and willed you to look up.'

'I didn't know that.'

'Success! You've just admitted ignorance for the first time.'

She was an ergonomist working with a small company that designed interiors for civil aircraft. 'It's possible that I know more about variations in shape and bulk of the human bum than any other person, living or dead.' Seats were her speciality of the month, the year really, she told him.

Sitting on his back, facing his feet, moulding his buttocks with her hands: 'About sixty-fifth percentile for your volume-to-height ratio. Bet you wriggle about a lot when you sit.' She wriggled herself deeper into the pit of his back. 'Like this?'

And:

'John's a drummer, session man, a vicar's son. Wants to marry me. We're involved in a long engagement, eighteen months so far. We have weekends in the vicarage in Wiltshire. Mother's related to Enid Blyton by marriage though you'd think it was by blood. Call him Noddy and he hates it. Nicest, kindest, gentlest man I ever met, or woman come to it. I want out, but don't know how. If I tell him about us, he'll forgive me and say he can't blame you.' She was straddling him, gently rising and falling as she spoke.

'Sounds like a nice feller or a smooth blackmailer.'

Jenny fell forward and bit him hard and fast on the neck and shoulder. 'Sounds like both, but don't throw stones.'

152

They were good together. The second time he came he called her Lindy and cried. Later he called her Jenny and laughed.

He kept his eyes closed and enjoyed the lightness of the bed covering. This was the first time under a quilt, a *doony*, she called it. He guessed it was sometime before seven and decided on six fifty-three. She was moving about in the kitchen, that was what had woken him. He trailed his hand out of the bed and found he was on a mattress on the floor. He'd forgotten that. He found his watch, after a full ashtray and a wine glass. With the watch in front of his face, he opened his eyes. Six fifty-three!

'I'm squeezing oranges.' Jenny put her head round the kitchen door and smiled at him. 'Hang on.' Her head withdrew, then she tripped into the room. She clutched a yellow sheet to her shoulder. She was as he'd seen her the morning before, when Hilary collapsed in his kitchen. She knelt on the floor and kissed him, spurting fresh orange into his mouth. It came as a surprise.

He was reliving the previous night as Jenny, naked now, returned from the kitchen with boiled eggs, wholemeal toast, marmalade and coffee.

'I know no other woman like you. You play a beam of gentle self-mockery over the intricacies of your life. I admire it.'

And:

'I've got to go.'

'I know.'

And Jenny, naked curve of her spine in the corner of the bow window, knees up to her chin, brown hair tumbling over her shoulder, watched him dress. 'Like a knight into armour,' she said, then, softly:

'"Rouse now, my dullard, and thy wits awake;
'Tis first of the morning. And I bid thee make –
No, not a vow; we have munched our fill of these
From crock of bone-dry crusts and mouse-gnawn cheese –
Nay, just one whisper in that long, long ear –
Awake; rejoice. Another Day is here!"'

As he left Jenny's front door, Simon said, 'Wish me luck!' and Jenny said, 'You don't need luck, you need education.'

'What do you mean?' he asked, stepping back into the tiled

hall and taking hold of her soft, warm hand. He was in his new uniform: chalk stripe and everything. In the breast pocket of his jacket he carried the magic stone; it had been charged with energy and good fortune: in his mouth, in her mouth, elsewhere.

'I give our relationship two more nights, then it will be empty of all significance.'

'Where has this come from?' he asked, a look of pain on his face. 'I feel like I could stay with you for ever.'

'Thanks. I feel we are into rapid sexual discharge, a massive exchange of things, tremendous mutual gains. I'm not knocking it. I just don't think it will go on for more than three days. And when it peters out, I shall be terminating the relationship, okay? Knock it on the head before we reach diminishing returns.' She was dressed in a fawn linen suit with lemon shirt and a double string of cheap beads round her neck. She looked radiant.

'Why have you suddenly started talking like this when I'm just leaving for an important meeting? For Christ's sake, Jenny.' A note of irritation sounded in his voice.

'That is why, Simon. Exactly that. We were good together last night. A few hours later you're doing your *I'm away to the office now, darling, important meeting* routine. That's why you need your eyes opening, to see yourself standing at my door, after one night together, expecting me to peck you on the cheek and wish you luck at your important meeting.'

'There's nothing wrong with asking you to wish me luck, is there?'

'No. I do wish you luck. I was wishing you luck. I also wish you realized that three penile insertions doth not a little woman make.'

'Ah! I see. It's the ladies' liberation bit. Got you.'

Jenny withdrew her hand and said, 'Piss off. As I see it, you are a statistician with a mild internal haemorrhage, probably because your life's a mess. I'm an ergonomist in a pretty well balanced state, as far as such is possible in a crazy world. I'm not going to rise to your silly quip, which I assume you thought was an example of gentle leg pulling. Objectively it seems to me that you are the one who needs the gentle leg pulling. I just need to spend the next two hours polishing a report I'll be handing to my Director later today.'

Simon began to interrupt, but Jenny pressed her finger to his

154

lips, then followed the pressure with a swift soft-lipped kiss. 'We'll sort things out a bit tonight, eh? Swap a few ideas and have a nice time. But there'll only be one more after tonight, so don't go wasting time knocking what you don't understand. Now off you go to your important meeting.' She turned him about and pushed him firmly through the door.

'Maybe I'll fall in love with you, Jenny.' He stood on the step, looking up at her.

'You know nothing. We are in love. Enjoy! Grow! Learn! Grab it! We have forty-eight hours, then it's downhill all the way. Go on. Best of luck!' She shut the door.

He watched her blurred outline turn and vanish into darkness. Then, her words whirling in his head, the feel of her body and hair and tongue still moving on his skin, under the agency armour, he walked rapidly down the short path and into the road.

'I feel good,' he told himself. And the reason he felt good, he realized, or, at least, the fact from which his good feelings seemed to radiate, was that he had left his brown suit in Jenny's room. Turning the corner, he swung his briefcase, threw it into the air, allowed it to spin twice, then caught it neatly by the handle. Had he dropped the case, he would have accepted her assessment of two more nights. Since the double flip and catch had been so perfectly executed, he knew it would be more...

The Northern Line was empty enough for passengers to register each other as human beings. To Simon, like most other Tube travellers, a crowded compartment was as devoid of human contact as a deserted one. But a sparsely populated compartment forced home the recognition that the lumps of flesh and hair, clothed in summer colours, were people. Each had a life story, each shitted and pissed, ate solids, drank liquids, had hopes and fears. Each believed them self to be special in some way, understood life as a process in which they were the centre.

Thinking along these lines Simon saw his face distorted by double reflection in the sliding doors. The portrait, smeared and sneery, toppled him from the battlements of his Jenny-built castle of joy and speculation.

The descent was rapid and bumpy. He smashed Anne, Hilary, the board of O.A.R., Dan Dare with his probe, Jenny again (it was from her hands he slipped), Norma with the big mouth, and a grinning Nigel screaming: mouth, cunt, give it one, soft twat.

He came to rest in a trench of slime and offal, the white of sinew glistening in dark, bloody light. Naked bodies moved in the slime.

Pulling his shiny briefcase tight to his stomach, squeezing his buttocks together, he dispelled the image. Flashing a look around the carriage, coughing to secure his balance. No one had noticed. The fall had taken seconds, his eyes open to the tumbling images.

He found the report Furnace had given him the previous afternoon. Opening the folder at random he inspected a table showing usership of strong flour by geographical region and socio-economic grade.

His consciousness centred on the table, compressing the last of the visions until they were no more.

A proportion of the AB housewives would employ cooks. He'd ask an R.E. to look up the statistic. *Of course*, he would say, looking round the collection of eager faces, *point oh three of ABs never get their hands near flour: they employ a cook, live-in or daily. And, and perhaps this is a more significant observation in terms of market segmentation, an unknown proportion of the cases represented by these data are using strong flour in the service of others, that is, not for consumption within their own households. This unrecorded category includes cooks and, for instance, mothers who bake for married children. Now it may be that such users are of little significance to an understanding of the market. Unfortunately, predictably, and as ever, until we know more about them, we have no basis for assessing their contribution to the profile. Not my place to say it, but it strikes me that daily, cook and mother hen are potent images in the product area... Give us this day our daily's bread.* That would get a couple of snorts of laughter from the Client Marketing Director, whose idea of a brilliant joke was 'Cross your legs, mate, we've only got one nail left'.

Point out that... basic tagging questions on omnibus survey... indicate intensive investigation... cost effective, emphasise correlation not causation. Eyes on the columns of percentages. They faded. Lindy Nigel Lindy Nigel Lindy Nigel

Lindy.

He mumbled, 'Oh Jesus Christ Almighty give me ground to stand on'. A young man looked up and grinned, then whispered to the woman next to him.

XX

The summer progressed nicely. French, dwarf and broad beans were vibrant with health in the vegetable plot where Simon advised and Lindy worked. Early potatoes were dug as needed and eaten with freshly cut courgettes lightly fried in olive oil. Salads were eaten daily. Chilled runner beans (Scarlet Emperor, so beautiful it was a crime to cut them, except that cutting them brought more and more dangling seed pods) in garlic sauce with fresh home-baked bread. They ate in blazing sun, on the back step. Glasses of light home-made wine, taken in the heat of late morning could encourage a day to drift like cloud until the sun went down and the heavy red wines slapped into glasses. Dust settled on the television screen. Mozart and Bach off-set the dross of contemporary culture, but, late at night, when the alcohol had gentled them to a misty, soft-edged world, they delighted in all-time favourites. They cake-walked into town with Taj Mahal, they tiptoed through the tulips with Tiny Tim, they rode the yellow taxi with Joni Mitchell and, physically spent, they handed their souls to Louis Armstrong who blew them high above the polluted town and the corrupted present to a place where it rained rain, not missiles and dilute acid. And then, the room greying with reflected dawn, they lay and looked at each other, and their eyes were as blue as the first time they met, and their prolonged hedonism had driven everything from them but love and contentment.

Day followed day in a gentle maze of happiness.

'We are resting,' Simon said. 'Recharging. It just seems a long time since we did anything.'

'It's a week since we went in a shop. The State can tolerate rebellion, but what happens if they discover we haven't been in a shop for a week?' Lindy raised herself from the sun bed and hitched her bikini top into place.

'Guess we'd be in danger of being certified.' Simon sat in a garden chair, his feet up on the breakfast table. He handed her a cigarette and began to make another. 'I wonder how everybody is.'

Lindy moved onto her back and lit her cigarette, her hair had grown long, her skin tanned. She threw him the matches and said,

'I can't rest much more.'

'Now, or in general?'

'In general.'

'What do you want to do? Greenham?' The sun made the flame on the burning match invisible, he shook it several times before it died. Each time he had to look closely to see if the match was still charring.

'I sometimes get an empty feeling. Why aren't we working with the miners? Danny goes collecting every week. Terry Skinnow does as well, I think. And Jed is always making trips out to Kirkfield Chance and helping in the kitchen. I mean, while we were doing the pictures it was okay, we've got to live, but it's almost two weeks since we finished.' She sat up and stubbed her cigarette end on a flagstone then put the crumpled paper and tobacco into a pot of thyme.

'Right.' Simon flicked his screwed up fag into the same pot. 'It's the thought of wearing outdoor clothes! It's a week since I've worn shoes, I feel like Huckleberry Finn. But, you're right. Holiday over! What do you want to do?'

'What do you mean, "you"? You're making out I'm dragging you from something. I want to talk about it, that's all. I want us to talk it through and decide what we are going to do, like we always have done.' She took his big toe in her hand and tried to break it off his foot. 'You lazy sod.'

'I'll make coffee.'

'No coffee. Remember?'

'Oh, shit. That's that then, innit? We balance our re-entry to the capitalist, consumerist world by re-engaging the enemy. Buy coffee and plan our next assault on the state. Leave my bloody toe alone or I'll call you lovey.'

'Just try, that's all.' she gave his toe a final twist, then got up. 'Come on then, Huckleberry Hound.'

'Finn, I said. Huckleberry Finn.'

'I know,' Lindy said, pulling him to his feet.

'On, on into the breach dear friends, or block the thing up with our English dead. That Henry the Fifth was a hypocritical, murdering sod.' He looked at Lindy who stopped and turned before entering the house, she grinned and nodded.

'Like all the rest of 'em,' she said, then ran into the shadows of the back hall.

*

'A lad with a broken collar bone is arrested on assault and the copper who clouts him and jars his wrist is the one they report as injured. It's tragic, bloody tragic.' Paul Riding stood outside the Miners' Support Centre, a lock-up shop by the Markets. His open face had developed a deep cleft between the eyes since Lindy last saw him, a red and purple bruise crossed one cheek and carried an outbreak of small scabs where the skin had broken. Simon accepted the tin of roll-up tobacco and began making a cigarette.

'I could never have believed I'd see this day, you know,' Paul went on. 'They show nowt on telly. I've seen a lad dragged through a broken windscreen. They've set dogs about us. I've seen a lad in back of a transit, face down on t' floor and six coppers walk over him in their boots, then sit with their feet on him. I mean, it in't a sheltered life, mining, but I've seen things that'd shock if they happened in South Africa. Rule of law's gone out of window. Cops do what they want now, and they do it with impunity. They've learned a lot of it in Northern Ireland. I got this fair and square in a push.' He pointed to his swollen cheek with the wet end of a match-thin roll up. 'I don't begrudge it. But when you get a dozen coppers making a passage and they push somebody between 'em, seeing how much damage they can do with their boots and fists and staves – Christ. Bloody hell!' He dropped the tiny cigarette end and twisted his foot on it. Simon looked at Paul's trainers, they were too small for his broad feet, splitting at both sides, mended with string.

'I'll tell thee what though, Simon. We shall win. They've done their bloody worst and we' not beaten. We can't lose and I'll tell you for why. We've got support on the ground. If we lose, we lose everything, it's us livelihoods and us families and us kiddies' jobs after. Coal stocks is down. Wait 'til dark nights come and snow and fog and power cuts, eh? She'll not beat us into submission. Never!'

'Get waving them buckets and stop calling, you two. Men!' Penny Riding and Lindy walked back down the busy street and stopped in front of Simon and Paul.

'There's plenty with buckets, Lass. How's our Lindy then? We haven't seen you at Chance for a while.'

Before Lindy had time to answer two constables stepped into

the group. The smaller of the two put his hands on Lindy and Penny's shoulders and said, 'Move along please, you're causing an obstruction.' Paul turned on his heel and walked away.

'We're talking, is that an offence?'

'Move!' the larger copper prodded Simon in the chest with a knuckle.

'Come on,' Penny said, with a grim smile. 'We'll not obstruct these two officers any longer. I mean, I can think of better things to see in the streets.'

'Don't worry, darling. It's a little place in Majorca, thanks to you lot.'

Penny ushered Simon and Lindy across the road. 'I hope the bugger burns down with him in it.'

XXI

'There is no flood back to work.' Jed hit the table with his clenched fist. August: the C.N.D. meeting was down to half a dozen members: Jed and Derek, Lindy and Simon, Danny and Helen.

'There is no flood back to work because only a few drips have returned, and when I was at school a few drips made a trickle, not a flood.' Jed scrubbed his short hair with his knuckles and acknowledged a largely imagined response to his quip. 'The bloody Tories are running scared. It's months and they thought it would be done and dusted in weeks. But there's months more to come. The miners need every scrap of support –'

'Jed! Jed, I think—' Helen was trying to get her word in. Jed was having nothing of it.

'Support, yes, support. Solidarity! We must not let that woman who, by the way, I am assured enjoyed her parents wedding very much, she must not be allowed to starve the miners back to work. C.N.D.—'

'Chair! Derek, through the chair!' Danny was waving his flat hand, as if trying to chop Jed's words into smaller units. Jed carried on making his speech.

'It's no good, you know.' Derek shook his head and gave a sympathetic smile. 'Once he gets going only exhaustion or hunger stops him and he probably spent the afternoon in bed stuffing himself.' He grasped his brother's wrist. 'Jed, stop it off, there's others want to stir the pot.'

CND meetings were becoming like Party meetings.

'If I may be allowed to conclude, Chair?'

'Aye, go on then. Make it snappy.'

'I am sure we are all of one mind that the sine qua non of the C.N.D. is that we remain non-political in a party political sense, but equally the C.N.D. is an intensely political movement. I am arguing, doing my very best to explain in as cogent a fashion as I am able, without the advantage of a degree in political science or any of that damned nonsense' – his eyes sent a fusillade of arrows at Danny, who grinned and doffed an imaginary cap – 'to make the case that the industrial dispute in question, viz, the miners' strike, has now become equally non-political in a party political sense. Indeed both the miners and the C.N.D. are bringing about a broad left alignment which undercuts the ground that silly buggers like Kinnock and his vacillatory henchmen stand upon. We should therefore, and I say this with all the authority and force at my command, throw the weight of the C.N.D. fully behind the miners. Those comrades in the C.N.D. who argue that by so doing we align ourselves with the violence of the picket line are naive and misinformed. I wouldn't say that Kinnock enjoyed his parents' wedding, because by his present performance he is still so wet behind the ears that I doubt his parents have yet had the wedding...'

'Jed, for God's sake –' Danny raised his eyes to heaven.

'God doesn't come into this, Comrade. God's done about as much good for our cause as—'

'Jed, get on with it!' This was Lindy, coming out of a whispered conversation with Helen.

'I would like to do so, Linda, I would very much like so to do, given the opportunity to present my case without interruption. Let me simply state that Kinnock's inability to give a clear lead, his pusillanimous condemnation of violence on both sides, bodes ill for his leadership of the Labour Party.' Jed squared his flat cap on the pile of papers he had before him. He coughed, politely holding a curled hand in front of his mouth, he raced his eyes from face to face, then brought them to rest on his cap. There was a silence. His speech had ended.

'Well said, Jed.' Danny was grinning again. 'Speaking as a member of the party in question I agree with you entirely. Kinnock is behaving like a worm. To suggest that the violence is equal on both sides is to be misinformed, and he is certainly not misinformed. So we've seen an act of deliberate duplicity motivated by fear and a desire to win votes –'

'It's cowardice, that's what I say,' Derek said. 'Where's his sense of history? Where's his sense of proportion? Where is his dignity?'

'Speaking as a member of C.N.D.,' Helen said, sitting forward and putting both hands flat on the table, 'I think Mr Kinnock is right. We must condemn violence no matter where it comes from.'

Simon said, 'I appreciate your position, Helen, but don't you think a distinction should be drawn between offensive and defensive violence?'

'I didn't think you believed in the deterrence argument,' Helen said, a sarcastic edge to her voice.

'Let me finish, Helen.' Simon was controlling an increasingly eruptive temper. 'We're not talking about the miners saying "You clobber us, we'll clobber you". I'm not talking about deterrence in that sense. I'm saying that in the event of somebody knocking the shit out of you, you are likely to hit back, kick back, scratch back – retaliate. What's more, if somebody attacked you it's more than likely that any one of us round this table would attempt to defend you. Would you criticize us then for being violent?'

'That's not the point –'

'Helen, that is the point.' Danny sounded exasperated. 'You can't expect people to stand and let the police hit them with truncheons. And it's not law-breakers you're discussing. It's blokes trying to protect what's theirs.'

Lindy said, 'I think we should let Helen have her say without interruption. She's in a minority, let her make her case.'

'That's right,' Derek said, 'We'll take that as a ruling from the Chair, shall we? Helen, love, you carry on, although I must say, from the Chair, that you're talking a lot of damned nonsense and them—'

As Danny and Lindy said, 'Derek!' and 'Chair!', Jed took his brother by the forearm and squeezed. Derek, face flushed, snowy hair in disarray, said, 'Very well, Comrades, but it just gets up my cuff when I think of what them lads is going through and we sit here trying to paint black white and white black...'

'I'm not sure I want to say anything, if that's how things are.' Helen was shaking and obviously on the verge of tears. She started again.

'I'll try, but it seems your minds are made up. I'm not a great radical, I don't think that Mrs Thatcher is evil or that Mr Reagan is senile. I mean, I think that most people are well-intentioned –'

Derek made a huffing sound, Jed, increased the pressure on his arm.

'Well, yes, I even think Mrs Thatcher means well.' She was clasping her hands together to stop their visible trembling. 'She believes all that she says about trying to make the world a safer place; negotiating from strength and so on. I disagree with her. I disagree wholeheartedly. I believe in unilateral disarmament,

164

that's why I am here. I think that if we eradicate our bombs and weapons the world will be safer. And the money saved could feed millions. We all know that, we all know that the money spent on arms in a day would for a whole year feed, clothe, educate, and provide medical care where necessary for all of those in need of those services. I think this is the most important issue in the whole of history, and in the whole world. We've got to do whatever we can to bring the world to its senses before it's too late.' There were indications of agreement.

'I see the strike as rather insignificant compared to all that. Wherever violence comes from, it is wrong. Our credibility as a movement which argues for peace and against violence can only suffer if we take sides in a violent dispute.'

There was a moment's silence and then everybody began to talk at once. After having his own undisciplined say, Derek gave way to Lindy. She tamped her cigarette and addressed her answer to Helen, speaking quietly.

'Helen, I've seen the police in operation at Greenham. I've seen enough to know what's going on between the police and the miners. It's women at Greenham, it gives us an advantage. We don't have the same problems as men. We don't have the same need to appear big and strong; we find our strength in other ways. When the police get really wound up they try to humiliate us, they taunt us sexually, they maul us, they hurt us in sneaky ways, it's dislocated shoulders and bruised breasts. We're not hit with staves, or kicked. We don't even, touch wood, get punched in the face or kicked when we are down. In some sense we command the situation by being passive. We frighten their spirits by singing. The more they humiliate us, the more they humiliate themselves. The M.O.D. won't release the figures of how many of their police and squaddies are undergoing psychiatric treatment after a spell at Greenham.

'I wish the miners would use passive resistance. But they are tough working people who've been brought up to physical labour, physical games. They've been reared in a culture that glamorizes violence. We can't realistically expect them to sit down and sing "You Can't Kill the Spirit". Not yet anyway.

'When the police wade in, they try and humiliate the miners by physically beating them, and the miners try to maintain their dignity and their limbs, if not their lives, by retaliating physically.

You don't like it, I don't like it. None of us like it, but I can't put my hand on my heart and say I blame them for retaliating. And I can't and won't say that they are as much at fault as the coppers, because from what I know, and what I've seen, they are paid overtime to brutalize the miners. To spread the blame equally in that situation is to be either morally superior or morally lazy. I don't think we can afford to be either.'

Lindy flushed under her honey skin. Simon put his hand on her thigh and rubbed. She turned to him and smiled. Jed said, 'Hear! Hear! Chair, I feel that we must, as a group, fully endorse Linda's excellent contribution.'

'That's all well and good,' Helen said, fists clenched on her lap, 'but even if I accept all you say, I don't see what it's got to do with our campaign.'

'Chair,' Jed said, commanding attention from his brother by squeezing his forearm, 'I wonder if I might be permitted to elucidate?'

'Aye. Go on then.'

'Helen, what you say about our role on a global scale is indisputably correct, and very well stated, if I may make so bold. But only a damned fool would equate Moscow and Washington...'

Jed battled through the outcry, defending the good of the workers' bomb against the evil of the capitalist bomb. By the time order was restored the water was very muddy. Danny, who had been relatively silent, spoke to notes:

'I'd like to make five points, Comrades. One, I see nothing wrong in C.N.D. allying itself with right against might, wherever that conflict is fought.

'Two, the Government is deploying policing tactics against the miners which it has learnt in Ireland. If the Government win this struggle, the same tactics will be employed against the peace movement.

'Three, running down coal is a preliminary to massive investment in nuclear energy. Many of us oppose that in its own right, but within the context of our campaign I should point out that the production of nuclear energy is a by-product of maintaining the arms race. We are needed, that is, this island is needed, in order to reprocess nuclear material for the NATO alliance. There are other arguments there, breaking United

166

Nations rulings on the mining of uranium in Namibia; effects on civil liberties; danger of reactors leaking; long term health hazards of so-called acceptable levels of radiation, and so on.

'Four, solidarity breeds solidarity. Already there are pit banners that carry our logo, not to mention those of the feminists and gays and Anarchists. Whatever else this struggle is, it's a period of massive politicization for everyone involved. Our campaign has always had over-representation of the middle classes. The strike brings us into contact with the Left as a whole, but, more importantly, the working class. Do you know, Helen, what the strikers shout at scab drivers, amongst other things? I'll tell you: *Sun* reader! Biggest insult there is: *Sun* reader! Think about it. That's new. That's politicization. That's promising. Blokes who used to salivate over page three girls, now recognize poison when they see it.

'And five, which is related. The Campaign for Nuclear Disarmament is like all peace campaigns, like all moral campaigns, it is the people attempting to bring the State to its senses. You used a broad canvas, Helen. Well if you expand that canvas, I believe you find that the miners' strike and our campaign are part of the same gradual progression towards a real democracy rather than the jokes we have now all over the world.

'Our only hope as a species is to find some way of interacting which doesn't involve us electing fools to represent us. Well-intentioned, if you like, but fools for all that. Normal, healthy adults do not behave like so-called world leaders. And so-called world leaders have a clear tendency to behave, at best, like stupid, spoilt children. Maybe it's the power, maybe it's the type of person who strives for such power, I don't know. What I do know is that the miners are presently at the brunt of an irrational, unfair, immoral attack, just as is world peace.

'There is, I hope, a global pressure towards progressive values, it's a struggle, a battle, a world war, if you want... we each play our part in it on our own small stage. Just now there is a skirmish on our doorsteps. Our part in that, our part as members of C.N.D., is not to go and get beaten up, certainly not to go and fight coppers, but it's not to stand aside and pretend nothing is happening. Our role is to support those people who are struggling with the State.

'Jed wants to take our banner to Kirkfield Chance. To

display it there as a signal of support and solidarity. We don't have to defend every blow struck by a miner to agree to that. He wants us to donate twenty quid towards a scheme where kids get a holiday from police vans and horses and dogs. We don't have to agree with every word Arthur Scargill says to agree to that. I'm not saying every miner is an angel. I'm saying that our place is beside them, supporting them. If we ignore their struggle, our struggle becomes a little more meaningless. Why save the world if you don't intend to improve it?'

'Alright,' Helen said, 'alright, I agree. I am swayed, but not convinced. But yes, we should send the money, and Jed can take the banner.'

'Come with us, Helen,' Lindy said, 'Come and see.'

Mary washed the patina of dirt from her face to reveal heavily freckled cheeks. It was the sun did it, she told them.

And there was sun enough that summer.

Sun enough to sunbathe and burn. Sun enough to spend a day by the canal and for the two women to dive into a lock and churn backwards and forwards.

'Don't want to leave the cameras,' Simon shouted as they trod water and insisted he join them. 'Can't swim either.'

'You'll not need your bloody cameras then, will you?' Mary was exhilarated to be back. Lindy pushed her under, then squealed and swam to where soft green moss flowed down a post and turned black in the water.

They visited the Support Shop and agreed to take a pile of produce out to the Chance. Pleased to take a few more red, black and orange stickers and arrange them into a C.N.D. logo across the back doors of the battered mini-van. Happy to be together and doing something to help the cause which was gradually spreading its battle front into every facet of British life, and beyond.

The dockers were back and so those days of excitement were over. And Orgreave was sinking into folklore. Now news was of arrest upon arrest at picket lines, of collectors moved on and arrested.

The police were raiding village after village, entering Welfares and pubs, taunting, pushing with batons, swiping pints from tables. They alienated whole communities, not just the miners and their families but shopkeepers, farmers, even the scattering of middle class commuters.

And worse, young men were seriously injured, beaten whilst handcuffed, forced to run the gauntlet of police brutalized by greed and a desire to get on in Thatcher's Island.

But none of this, nor the meanderings of Silver Birch, a Notts scab, said by the gutter press to be turning Yorkshire miners by their thousands, began to dent the confidence of the mass of pickets and activists. Bronzed by an unfamiliar British sun, young men like Gary Riding were 'taking' to the summer of discontent, creating a carnival spirit.

But it wasn't only sun and a heart-filling esprit de corps and solidarity that miners flung like a flag around the shoulders of anyone who approached them with an open mind. It was new areas of expertise and confidence, it was miners who would claim that their formal education left them with nothing but 'a few strips across the arse' now visiting the capital cities of the world and making speeches. And it was men coming to realize the strength of wives as individuals, as fighters in the struggle.

Many battles were fought and won as the N.U.M. and their supporters faced the Coal Board and the State. For many the coalfields were an educational adventure, the summer a time of massive learning and expansion.

'In other words,' Lindy said, 'you can't kill the spirit.'

'Right, our lass,' Mary said.

The hedge gave way to fencing and they saw the Chance's pale blue lifting gear darkened by the summer sky. It looked liquid as heat rose from a field of ripe barley, splattered with a haemorrhage of poppies.

As Mary turned onto the pit road they saw someone wrapped in a heavy coat, sitting in the hedge bottom.

'God, he must be hot.'

'It's Goz!' Mary pulled across the road and stopped.

There was no footpath, just a grass verge, a ditch lush with foliage, and the remains of a once dense thorn hedge. Gozzer sat on the embankment, his back against a stump of dead hawthorn, his feet lost in long grass. He wore a black trilby and a heavy black overcoat, buttoned to the neck, its large collar pulled across his throat, one lapel concealing his chin.

"Ey up, Gozzer.' Mary stuck her head through the open window. 'It's me, mucky Mary from Greenham.'

Gozzer's narrow face was pale and his lips moved as if he were rolling a match stick. But there was no match stick, and there was no recognition of Mary. Instead he remained unmoved, staring through the car and its occupants as if they were not there.

'Hang on, Mary, let's get out.'

Simon leaned forward and watched the two women. Lindy sat in the grass beside the gaunt man, Mary stood, one foot each side of the ditch, her hand resting on her knee, concern on her round face.

'What is it, petal?' Mary asked. Simon saw the miner's lips move but couldn't hear what he said. Lindy put her arm on his hunched shoulders and said, 'Come on, Goz. It doesn't matter.'

Lindy helped him to his feet, Mary swung round and poked her head into the car: 'Poor bugger's in a state. He's messed his trousers.'

Gozzer, near tears, wouldn't join them. Lindy decided to stay with him while Simon and Mary went on with the provisions.

'What's up with Goz, then, Paul?' Mary asked. Paul and his two sons, Barry and Gary, were sunning themselves outside the picket hut. Gary, who wore nothing but bruises and a pair of white cotton shorts, stretched his legs and curled his toes, displaying hardened, dirty pads.

'He's down, is Goz. He'll not laugh like he used. I reckon it's being clouted but doctor says not.'

Paul stood up and the ancient settee moved, causing Gary to roll over onto the arm; he gave his father a punch on the buttocks. "Ey up, thee, nearly had us over, you clumsy sod.'

Paul laughed and stretched, pulling his vest out of belted trousers.

'Mind you don't get thee belly burnt.'

Paul scooped Gary's ankle into the air, pulling so that he was almost upside down.

Barry sat ill at ease on the bentwood kitchen chair. He wore a bleached denim blouse, matching trousers and expensive canvas shoes. Everything about him contrasted with his father and younger brother: Nikon S.L.R., neatly cut hair, enamel Labour Party badge. He sat with one knee held tight by the interlinked fingers of his hands. With a strained smile, eyes flickering with anxiety, he watched Gary repeatedly slam the flat

170

of his free foot against his father's side.

'Gerrim off us, our Barry,' Gary called, his voice strangled by contortion and laughter.

'You've made your bed, Gary, you must lie in it.' Barry stood up, turned the seat in his hand and sat down again, straddling the seat, resting his hands and chin on the curved back.

'We've brought some stuff across from the Support Shop in Leeds.' Simon sat down on an upturned box.

Barry hitched his lightly clad feet onto the cross-members of his chair and said, 'It's going to take a lot of that.'

'There is a lot of that, our kid,' Gary said. Breaking free, he draped an arm across his father's heaving shoulders. 'What we need is a bit more from the bloody leadership.'

'Kinnock! Kinnock!' Mary clenched her fist and made as if to rap on a door.

'Who's there?' Gary grinned.

'Well, it all depends who's asking you see, boyo.'

'There was this earwig –' Paul began, but was interrupted by Gary.

'Come on, Dad. You tell jokes like Thatcher tells lies: too often and to the detriment of the working classes.'

'Detriment, eh?' Barry said. 'Been eating dictionaries, Gary?'

'You've got to eat summat.' Barry winced.

'We get big catering tins from abroad.' Paul's straight face signalled a joke. 'Lasses at Welfare say we got goats' eyes last week. Enough to see us through to end of strike, eh!'

'Give over, Dad. What about leadership, Barry?' Gary asked, dropping back onto the settee and stretching his legs towards a long-dead fire.

'We get everybody here,' Paul said. 'We get S.W.P. and W.R.P. and C.P. and Militant; we get Greenham women, and one who won't stay away, will you, Mary?' Mary grinned; squatting on her heels she was eye to eye with the men who sat around her. 'We even had Bruce Kent come. Nobody'd blame him if he kept himself clear of it. Local Labour Party comes up trumps. Can't you do something about bloody Neil, lad? They're spelling his name with a K and two Es round here.'

'He's in a difficult position, Dad –'

'Oh, poor bugger,' Gary cut in. 'Have they stopped his food parcels? Cut his 'leccy off? 'Ey up, get collecting buckets out for

Kinnock!'

'That kind of sarcasm doesn't help.' Barry reseated himself for the third time, sideways on the chair with his foot resting on his thigh.

'Christ, why doesn't he just come and see for himself. Did you know he refused to share a platform with two lads from this coalfield? Did you, Barry? Turned up and said *Get them off or I'm not going on.* What kind of a bloody Labour Party leader do you call that?'

'One who puts the future of the Party before winning cheap glory with –' Barry hesitated; there was silence as the listeners waited. 'Neil has to take account of the complexity of this, he is up against the Tory media. He's going to have to face a general election. You're in dispute, buried in the most militant coalfield in the country. You've no idea how the electorate see it.'

'We know this much, Son,' Paul spoke quietly and slowly. Gary twisted on the settee to look at him. 'There's ordinary people, electorate as you call them, all over this country and they do more for us than our own Party leader. Your brother Gary here's done as much travelling round as you have, I should think, and so have I. I've been to places I didn't know existed, and I've been fed by people of every religion and every colour of skin as well –'

'And that's only in Bradford, Barry,' Gary threw in.

'Oh, forget it,' Paul said. 'We'll not argue. I'll just say this, there's a lot supporting us in this action as'd back Labour if Kinnock gave the lead Arthur does.'

'Arthur Scargill is alienating people every time he makes a public pronouncement. Can't you see that, Dad?'

'He's talking to us, Lad. To me and Gary, and to folk like Simon here and Mary, to supporters. Course he alienates Tories and merchant bankers and newspaper owners. He's leading a union in struggle. He's using every opportunity to exploit right wing media to talk to folk on his side. He's not pussyfooting about worrying about what Tories think. Barry, for crying out loud, what does Kinnock think Tory press are going to do at the next election? Say "Good old Neil"? Does he really think if he condemns picket violence they'll tell everybody to vote for him? Good God, Lad, you learned nowt at that bloody talking shop you went to. If he tries to please bloody Tory press he'll end up

172

licking their boots, then they'll kick him in teeth. He's newsworthy, he should take every opportunity to talk to the Labour movement.' Paul had spoken with increasing vehemence, now he was sitting forward, his face flushed. Barry's knuckles were white where he gripped his foot.

'He's right, Barry,' Gary said, stretching out a hand and putting it on his elder brother's shoulder. 'I don't say you're thick. You know plenty. But you've got to take account of what others know.'

'There is a huge bulk of voters who are not taking sides in this dispute.' Barry started chopping the air with his hand to emphasize each point. 'Labour needs those votes. If we don't get them they'll just pile up and up on the Alliance ticket. I'm telling you, this strike is damaging the Party. The mining industry's best chance is down to a Labour Government at the first possible opportunity. And don't go talking about '74 and bringing the Government down because that's so much hot air. We must be realistic. Neil cannot come out and say everything he'd like to say. Scargill has degrees of freedom with which he is irresponsible. You'll not win this dispute by combating violence with violence, nor by hurling your bodies at police lines. Let the working miners work. Obey the law. Influence the public.'

'*Working miners! Working bloody miners!*' Gary was on his feet, fists clenched, standing over his brother. Paul pulled at the only thing available, the elasticized waist of his son's shorts. Gary slapped the hand away. 'I'll not clout him, Dad. You've no need to worry, our Barry. I'll not spoil your London leisure wear, but don't talk about being fair to working miners to the lads or you might get more in your gob than a posh accent. They're scabs, bloody scabs. They're traitors, every last bloody one of them. Selling our jobs and our kids' jobs. Tell me one thing, our Barry, do you believe in trades unions or do you think we should shut up shop and let Thatcher walk all over us?'

'Don't get smart with me, Gary. I've forgotten more about the union movement than you've ever known.'

'That's sodding obvious, our kid. You've forgotten it all.'

Barry hesitated, shrugged his shoulders, then spoke again. 'It's all new to you: heroic days, exciting. Don't you remember before? You'd no time for politics then, you were too busy out boozing and birding. But now, suddenly you're the big union man. I'm talking about reality, Gary. I'm talking about the nineteen-eighties and a society based on credit and consumption.'

'Nobody's accusing you of insincerity, Lad.' Paul put his hands on his son's shoulders. 'Only thing is, it doesn't matter how complicated things get. The union stands for simple things an' all. You must never forget the simple things, Barry, they're as true as your complexities. And they're real. Without them we're nothing. We throw away everything we've gained since they were sending women and kiddies underground. That's what Gary means.'

'Aye.' Gary glared at his brother. 'You don't cross picket lines, Barry. You don't cross pickets. If you forget that you can take all your books and certificates and wipe your bum on them for what good you'll do working people.' Gary turned and ran, his bare feet soundless on the beaten earth path which led from the pit gates to the village centre. Barry smiled at his father and raised his shoulders.

'I'm sorry, Dad. It's not as simple as that.'

Paul fell back into the settee and smiled. 'I'm sorry, Barry. I'm right sorry. It's as simple as that. From where I'm sitting a scab's a scab.'

'Dad, let me—'

'Leave it, Barry. Leave it. You know plenty, I grant you. But you don't know how it feels.'

XXI

He fooled no-one at the presentation. Ashen, tongue of heavy dough, he gripped the table with both hands. After fifteen minutes sweat began to pour and he walked out. Blood trickled. His colon radiated pain and extreme discomfort from his skull and down to his feet.

He sat on the lavatory with his head in his hands until Furnace himself came and tapped on the door.

Furnace was good about it. The options were simple: one month's sick leave or three months' pay in place of notice.

Jenny nursed him for two nights, no sex, just comfort. She took him through the debate on feminism, on her stand against capitalism. But it was all low key. He slept a lot. He ached a lot. He brooded.

Jenny suggested hospital once, then left him to his own decision. Three weeks later he assured her he was much better and she left for the country and the vicar's son.

The bleeding was minimal, but he was weak and sickly. He lived on yoghurt and advocaat, mixing them into a drink which he sipped throughout the day. It seemed to do him good.

He told Furnace he needed more time and agreed to spend it at Furnace's villa near Toulon. Furnace directed him to see Carmel Sykes 'the company therapist' who Simon had never heard of.

'Get your psyche sorted out, Simon.'

The day before his flight he took a taxi to Harley Street.

It soon became clear that Carmel was Furnace's mistress, an ex-primary teacher turned lay therapist. She had a handful of clients most of whom were market researchers. On her consulting room wall hung signed photographs of a radio celebrity and a pop megastar.

'What was his problem?' Simon asked.

'I taught him to read, write and do his tables. That goes back to my teaching days. He was a dear boy.'

The air tasted sweet and fresh. He relaxed suddenly, muscles he hadn't realized were tense eased as if a switch had been thrown. He settled on a chaise longue and looked around.

'I prefer the photographs to the paintings.'

There were six naive paintings, each picturing a cute urchin undertaking some household task in the courtyard of a white farm house. He had given considerable attention to one of them, attempting to find something of value in the carefully controlled brush work and greengrocery colours. He found nothing, and the other five were simply variations on the theme: the same cock strutted in the same corner of each, the same dog curled by the same wall, the same mare's head and neck over the same stable door. Only the urchin changed: cleaning shoes, peeling potatoes, washing dishes, incongruously kneading bread, his dirty arms deep in billowing dough.

Carmel said nothing. She sat at his shoulder, spiral notebook in hand, broad Slav face impassive.

'Is this how the hours go by? You wait for me to say something? What shall I say?'

'You find yourself wondering what I want you to say! Why not say what you want to say?'

'The paintings are shite. Why do you have them? Who did them?'

'Miranda, Furnace's wife. She is a close friend.'

'Does she know about you and Furnace?'

'No. She sees me three times each week for therapy, and we have lunch twice a week as friends. If she knew about Furnace and me it would topple her into crisis. Miranda is a sweetie. I don't believe in causing unnecessary pain. Do you?'

'I don't suppose so. We might argue about necessity.'

'Furnace told me you'd had tummy trouble and it toppled you. He thinks it is sex. He thinks everyone has sex problems.' She turned and smiled, she had soft, full lips and grey eyes. 'Sex problems are easy to cure, Simon.'

'I have emotional problems.'

They moved to a low smoked-glass table and sat in armchairs. She took a bottle of hock from a concealed fridge and poured two glasses. The sight of a chilled bottle caused a brief wave of anxiety, then a sense of wellbeing.

'It's simple enough,' he said. 'I met someone a year ago and she haunts me. I got mixed up with an older woman who relied on me to give her existence meaning. I couldn't produce, now she's in a clinic for alcoholics. Her husband's business has gone dickie: oil crisis. So he ships her into a clinic. What proportion of people are treated for their partners' problems?'

Carmel remained silent.

'I see. Well, that's Lindy and Hilary. Next is Jenny who gave me one fantastic night and two nights of further education. We only had three nights because she has a theory that the first three nights can't be improved on, so why waste time running downhill. She nursed me for a while, as a friend. Anyway, that's okay. Lindy is the emotional problem.'

'But this is delightful, Simon. You are not impotent, you like to make it with members of the opposite sex... you can make it.' She looked at him, her face animated by a blossoming smile. 'You don't require your partners to dress up or need the presence of animals or toy cars... or anything?'

She laughed. He liked her.

'There is one thing,' he said, his voice deliberately heavy. He was rewarded when her eyes seemed to darken as the flesh around them tightened with concern.

'Tell me.'

'I like it best in bed. Does that count as a perverse sex aid?'

Carmel tipped her glass to him. 'With some of my clients that would count as an outrageous perversion. Tell me about Lindy.'

'I've read about love,' he said, holding out his glass as she twisted the bottle, 'I guess that's it. I think I love her.'

He talked and she listened. It was easy. He told her about Lindy, about the party and Hilary and how Nigel had, not long ago, shafted her. But, he thought, Nigel, shit that he was, could not be blamed for Hilary's complications.

He described the dreams when he felt Lindy by his side and how he woke to find himself in an empty bed. Worse still, in bed with someone else. About Jenny's rigid self-containment. About his disinterest in work and distaste for the company of his colleagues.

At last he stopped and sat back, feeling emptied and tired.

'Simon, I wish you had a nice sex problem. You realize I am nothing but a whore.'

'Literally?'

'Yes and no. Furnace sends people to me and usually he collects the tab, as in your case. It's his way of making an honest woman of me.'

'You're good at listening.'

'Therapy is more than that. But my analysis is a little... How should I put it? Pop!'

She glanced at the painting by Simon's shoulder. 'Miranda is the scruffy little boy getting on with domestic chores, Furnace the ever-present strutting cock, and I am the kindly horse, looking on from the side lines. Her interpretation, not mine.'

'Who's the dog?'

'Ah! The dog is her physical side, the side he cannot awaken. My analysis. Miranda is very, very happy in her ignorance. Would you disturb it?'

'I don't know. Why does she have therapy if she is so happy?'

'Beneath her happiness is guilt – no-one should be so happy. And she wants to be a painter. An artist. To express pain and torment instead of smug complaisance. Perhaps someday I'll reveal all... I don't think she would thank me, do you?'

Travelling light, he flew to Marseille and found his way to Furnace's house by bus and on foot. For three weeks he did little but eat, sleep, sunbathe. The local village offered good food. The ever-present scent of lavender eased his mind and muscles. It was a calm before the storm. He regained strength and stability, putting off thought of the future with an ever present refrain: there will be change.

178

XXII

They were in the back yard. A candle burned, steady in the still air. Lindy and Simon sat on the back seat of a 2CV, a psychotic car written off after their first, overloaded trip to Greenham. Mary and Goz had wicker chairs.

They had eaten outside: salad, spaghetti with a tomato and mushroom sauce, a two-litre bottle of cheap Italian red. The young miner's spirits were still low. A bath and clean clothes (borrowed from a smaller and broader Simon) had little effect; he stayed silent, face blank.

'Right, you buggers. I've got a good idea.' Mary's chair creaked as she sat forward.

Simon rubbed the tab of his roll-up into a ball and flicked it into a froth of nasturtiums. 'If it's the canal you're on your own.'

'Too right.' Lindy was wearing a black trilby. She flicked the brim, like a cowboy in a western. 'I'm opening a bottle of organic health drink.'

'I don't want to denigrate his Natsurin '83 –'

'Eighty-four, 'smatterfact. You denigrated the last bottles of '83 Monday night.'

'Will you let me finish, for Christ's sake. Goz, you don't know how lucky you are. Natsurin '83 – never again!'

'What is it?' Goz asked flatly, his glass of red untouched by a plate of picked-over spaghetti.

'It's wine he makes from rubbish, tea leaves and potato peelings, old socks. That sort of stuff. Brilliant for when there's nothing left.'

'Why's it called Natsurin?'

'Gnat's urine, Goz.' Lindy dropped the trilby onto his head.

'Aye, but not healthy gnats, sickly little buggers with warts and scabs and bad diarrhoea. No way do we want your '84 stuff, man. Not while we can stand, anyhow.'

Pooled resources produced enough petty cash and Simon went off in the Mini.

Ten minutes later he peered over the back wall, like Mr Wot, and said, 'I found myself facing a tricky decision. The pregnant sister in the offie was very pushy and suggested we put one pound seven pence on the slate and get a bottle of ersatz Pernod, rather than a half bottle of the real stuff.'

He opened the gate and walked to the table, clutching a plastic carrier to his chest. Tall glasses were on the cleared table, a Pyrex bowl filled to the brim with ice, a jug of water. Candle flames reflected in the ice chunks. Lindy held a pouring device, marked with the Pernod logo. Mary was wearing the trilby. Goz drained his glass in a manner that suggested he might enter the spirit of things.

'I suppose you made the right decision,' Mary said. 'Quantity over quality.'

Lindy reached towards the carrier, but Simon, a broad smile on his face, pulled back. 'Just look at him,' she said. 'Talk about cat with cream. Come on, what've you done?'

'I put two pound thirty seven on the slate and got a whole bottle of Pernod. Quantity and quality.'

'You do nicely for yourselves anyroad,' Goz said, watching as Simon unscrewed the metal cap.

'If you knew how much Natsurin and weasel piss we drink between bottles like this.'

Lindy made a display of carefully pouring a measure into each half pint glass.

'Should we have two measures first time round? Or shall we take just the one measure first time, two measures second time?' She looked up and waited, bottle poised, face serious. 'Goz, what do you think?'

'Me?' he took the trilby off Mary and slapped it onto the back of his head. 'I'm just wondering how you become one of you left wing intellectuals like – beats pit any day.'

As the Pernod bottle went down, Goz's spirits soared until suddenly he tumbled into deep depression. Mary almost carried him upstairs to the spare bed. Her own few belongings she took to the kitchen where she settled down on the hearth rug. 'Away, I've lost my taste for beds, man. Too many long sleeps in short ones. Happier on the dog shelf, me. You know what they say, a hard bed is good to find.'

Lindy knocked seven shades of shit out of her pillow, then said, 'He's lost his nerve. He's scared of going underground again.'

She rolled onto her side and drew her knees up into her

stomach.

Simon had felt a twinge of envy as Mary carted Goz off to bed; he knew his head might float off into dangerous waters. Too much booze. Too much tension in the back yard. He snuggled against her back, but found the knobs of her spine hard and unforgiving. He put his hand on her stomach.

'Sleepy?' he asked.

Lindy was silent for several breaths. Then she said, 'Yes.'

Simon rolled onto his back and stared at the ceiling. He squirmed a little inside, not wanting to play *Do you remember?* He heard Goz moving about in the next room and considered going and talking to him.

A train pulled through the valley, a long heavy train, its clatter accompanied by an unusual hissing. He'd heard it once before and wondered if this could be the nuclear train. The thought held him to the mattress. 'Maybe just a peep, just a little leukaemia.' The pun came of its own accord. Next, an image of Thatcher and a run of words: *Thou art more noxious than the smell of spew, and flowers die when you step in the room.*

Simon and Mary tidied the kitchen, carrying newspapers and leaflets hither and thither, debating the relative merits of duster and vacuum cleaner. The vacuum cleaner in question redistributed dust. They decided to dust – more organic. Lindy looked up from the typewriter.

'Don't do anything above six feet, it's covered in manky grease. It needs scrubbing.'

'I thought we'd leave that,' Simon said, flicking a check duster so that it cracked like a whip. 'Look at the pattern this makes, it's like bark.'

'Crocodile skin,' Mary said, inspecting the results of Simon's repeated flicking on the side of the gas cooker.

'How's it coming, Ms Smith?'

Lindy carefully removed the paper from the machine and said, 'What about this? *Greenham is going strong, even though there is a partial media ban on those fine women. But there is an almost total block on reports from the many other peace camps around Britain. Menwith Hill, just outside Harrogate, now has a permanent camp which needs all the support it can get – we should discuss a trip out as a group.*' She paused and made a note in biro on the paper.

181

Simon sat down and began to roll a cigarette.

Mary said, 'Don't tell me that's all you've done. You could have carved it on stone the time you've taken.'

Lindy raised one finger at Mary, then carried on reading: '*Do go as individuals, stay if possible: old world hospitality and friendship is alive and well and living in the peace camps which spring up like mushrooms all over the country. Another local camp is running at Fylingdales until August 27th – a bus trip to the moors would make a nice day out.* Then I've put a double space and a centred asterisk, right, then another double space, then... Is it okay so far?'

"S fine,' Simon said, handing her the cigarette he had just made. 'Let's our members know that there's more to peace camps than Greenham, but doesn't ram it down their throats.'

'Lovely when he's serious, innit?' Lindy bent forward to accept a light, then, after inhaling and blowing out smoke, continued. 'So this is the bottom half page, right? *We now have one hundred members and an ever improving reputation with both Leeds and Yorkshire and Humberside C.N.D.. Spread the news, come to the next meeting, bring a new member with you. Remember that the Government is actively opposed to our beliefs. One consequence of this is that you can't believe what you read about C.N.D. in the press: C.N.D. is made up of the people you know in and around Church Hill – ordinary, sensible, thoughtful, caring people. Remember that when an official news report says 100,000 demonstrators, that means roughly 400,000 people like us* – Sodding thing's gone out...' Simon relit her cigarette and she went on, '*Did you know, for example, that over 200,000 of us demonstrated in London on June 9th, that around 5,000 of us blockaded certain roads in London as an act of non-violent civil disobedience on the same day. According to the press it was 50,000; according to Scotland Yard only 216 of us broke the law. What does it mean when the likes of us become the target of such crude propaganda and censorship? It means we are winning. Let's keep it that way.*' She held the paper in the air and made a mocking trumpet fanfare. 'Tan-tara tara. What do you think, peaceniks? Beat the *Sun* in a circulation battle?'

'It's good,' Simon said. 'Don't forget the Peace Festival on September First, then there's the WONT trip to Greenham, and Labour C.N.D. at Blackpool.'

Mary watched the pair of them in the mirror as she despondently rubbed it with an old sock. Still eyeing their reflections she said, 'I ought to get back to Greenham, you know. I mean, it's good being here, but I do nothing really, do I? I'm neither here nor there. I'm just another number on the things you lot organize, haven't even paid my fifty pee membership if it comes to it.'

'You can stay as long as you like,' Lindy said.

'And don't go before you've finished the mirror.'

Mary threw the sock at him, Simon caught it and grinned, but she avoided his eye and turned to Lindy. 'I don't know where I am with things at the moment. You know you said you felt torn between here and Greenham? Well, it's not quite that with me. I suppose it's the strike. It's a bit... what? Ominous. Greenham: when you're there, you're there. Being there is it. You get on from day to day, get hassled, lose your bitty stuff. Just being there is what it's about. Bearing witness, like. But out here it's decisions all the time.' She sat down at the table and rested her chin on the backs of her hands. 'Lost my way.'

Lindy reached out a hand and tousled Mary's' unruly hair. 'Goz upset you.'

'Reminded me of that little sod I wed. He'd be full of himself one minute and so deep the next you'd think he'd never break surface again. Not a natural life. Not unless you're a worm or a mole. Wes'd sometimes be sitting quiet, watching telly and he'd suddenly say how many days it'd been since he saw daylight. He always knew.

'Some can cope and some cannot. Little Tommy Birn were one that couldn't... that's why he knocked me about. That an' it being all he'd ever known.'

'Trouble is, on the one hand you can excuse any kind of behaviour by social conditions and upbringing.' Simon paused to light a cigarette. 'On the other hand you can say that each individual is responsible for his or her own behaviour and values. I mean, this is the violence debate, isn't it? Their violence is a crime, ours is justified. I'd have laughed at an argument like that a few years ago. Violence is violence. Now I've taken sides, I feel for one side and not the other. Subjectively our violence is different –'

'It *is* different,' Lindy said. 'There's got to be a difference

183

between defensive violence and offensive violence. You must allow self-defence.'

'Yes, but Mary says Tommy clouted her because of the stresses of working underground and because he was brought up in a house where the man beat the woman, right? Well, you can build a similar argument for coppers.'

'Some people rise above it, you know, Simon. I mean, where I lived ninety percent of the people I knew were married to miners, but all them husbands were not same as Tommy. He'd got special problems, like.'

'Maybe the police attract people with special problems. I remember reading that the difference between police and criminals, in terms of psychological and sociological dimensions, was approximately zilch.' Lindy was drawing wine from a plastic brewing barrel. Mary brought glasses from the cupboard. She stopped, three wine glasses easily held in one big hand.

'Middle class, social-scientific bullshit.' She put the glasses down and sat at the table. 'I'm going to pronounce now, so pin your lugs back. You can talk about blacks and whites, blondes and brunettes, fat and thin, tall and small, and you're talking about something. I mean, all other things being equal, fat people weigh more than thin people.

'Well,' Mary went on, her knobbly face creased by a frown, 'you can't say the same about criminals. I mean a criminal is somebody who breaks the law, right? But laws change from country to country and time to time. Laws change. I mean secondary picketing is suddenly against the law, so something you could do one day and be a responsible trade unionist, do it now you're a criminal.'

'Well that's what I'm saying.' Simon hunched forward and stubbed out his cigarette. 'The difference is a matter of convention.'

Mary made a non-committal noise then laughed. 'Personally, I'd make a law against speculation on the stock exchange, all this dealing in futures and in money as such. I mean, we live in a finite system, you know, if one little group are clawing millions to themselves, a big group is losing millions, right? So what's criminal? In my system there'd be a big difference between coppers and criminals. Criminals would be them public school dumbos who milk working people and gamble with stocks and shares. Wouldn't need coppers... And people'd have more or less the same... no crime, right? Bar serving Natsurin.'

'Right!' said Lindy. 'Right, criminality is a class-based convention. I'll grab that.'

'Listen,' Simon said. 'There's no point in starting from somewhere else, is there? So what do we do about the cops now? I'll tell you.' He held out his glass and Mary filled it. 'You know the vice squad has pretty police that go round chatting gays up, then pounce. Well, I'd make all police pretty police. They'd all wear pastel shade uniforms, nice flowing cheese cloth numbers –'

'Spirit of the sixties, man!' Lindy drew on an imaginary joint and exchanged upward glances with Mary.

'No, listen, there's a real threat in the clothes they wear and they behave accordingly. Another thing, change the style and a different sort of person would be attracted. Leave them with as much power as they have, but change the constraints. Change all the myths – if you want a recipe for wholemeal bread – ask a policeman. Run police series on telly where they all fly kites and do origami.'

'That's right man, and put acid in their whistles – groovy! You'd get run out of the S.W.P. for talking like that, you know. Trendy libertarian revisionism. The bugger needs reprocessing, Lindy.'

'Let's put that on a skin and get it Roneod.' Simon flipped Lindy's leaflet. 'We can give them out tomorrow.'

*

Sarah and Mary were going back to Greenham, apart from that it was a perfect day. Sarah had phoned the previous night to say expect us early. She came with Dave, Gozzer and Gary and a dozen fresh eggs. The back yard was the setting for a late breakfast send-off. Sarah wore navy satin shorts and a floppy white blouse. She sat on the wall, banging her trainers against the warm stone. Dave, his hair almost concealing the scar, in 'Burn MacGregor' T-shirt and shorts to match Sarah's, leaned against her and every now and then held her foot still by gripping her tanned leg. Goz and Gary Riding had the wicker chairs. Gary wore faded, torn jeans and a 'Women Against Pit Closures' T-shirt. Goz wore baggy flannels and a granddad shirt with the sleeves rolled high on his blue-veined white arms.

Jed arrived on his usual Saturday morning visit: 'If you will give me something in the vicinity of one pound seventy five pee, I shall be content to take my leave, Comrades.' Jed danced from foot to foot, carrier of *Morning Stars* clutched to his breast, flat cap at a jaunty angle. 'Must complete my distributive duties.' He was visibly excited by the gathering in the back yard.

'Will you not have some coffee, Jed? No bother, you know.' Mary came from the house with more coffee.

Turkish mixed with Co-operative instant. But, in the blazing sun, it tasted, as Gary said, 'good enough to drink'.

'No, no. I must be on my way. I will see all of you later, I trust?' Jed addressed the question to Simon as he sorted out change.

'Not unless you catch me in the bath, Jed.'

'Simon, there will always be room for wit and repartee in the Socialist state, but I do sometimes wonder how you will gain admission.'

'We'll be there, man,' Mary said.

'Very good. Very well, I shall look forward to it. But not too soon I hope. Cheerio.' And he was off, pushing his cap forward to air the back of his head.

'How you feeling, Goz?' Lindy asked the gangly miner. They were in the kitchen, Goz watching the toast, Lindy making more coffee.

'Me? I'm alright now. Buggered if I know what were up. I felt as if they were all against me. I got so's I couldn't step out of house, tha' knows. When you found us I could no more have faced 'em at Chance than fly.'

'What about going underground?'

'Daft, in't it? You know Barry Riding, Gary's brother, he's big in the Labour Party. He came round to see us. He were right nice about it, sat on t' floor in me front room and talked about strike and Labour Party and how it were historic. Then he started on about casualties and such. Anyroad, I soon realized he were squatting there in his posh clothes with his posh talk and he were trying to help me.' He pulled out the grill pan and turned four slices, blowing his fingers after turning each piece. 'Soon as I saw what he were up to... I felt better. Him help me! It were amazing, as if I'd taken me jacket off an' pockets were full of lead. He were trying to do something useful, you see. I thought, bloody hell,

186

thank God I'm not him. I know where I stand, I'm solid with my mates, and they're solid with me. Not like that poor bugger, swanning round London, eh? Rather face two dozen pigs with big sticks than some of them sods at top of Labour Party. Know what they say about the Labour Party, never turn your back on a comrade... then you won't get stabbed.' He turned off the grill and began piling toast on a plate. 'Bloody politicians! Where'd we be without 'em?' Gozzer flicked his head in the movement that had given him his name.

The sun rolled round and the day rolled on. A day of argument, laughter and easy companionship. Dave took the trilby from Sarah and said: 'It don't matter what happens. We've already won this strike. This'll always be our victory, you know what I mean?' And they did. Simon felt the sense of rightness he'd felt when standing on the bollard at Trafalgar Square.

'There's nowhere I'd rather be,' he said. 'And no-one I'd rather be with.'

'That's it, cocker.' Dave said, slapping the trilby on Simon's head and accepting a glass of Natsurin '84 from a grinning Lindy.

As the sun and Natsurin went down an unspoken agreement settled on them. The return to Greenham could wait another a day. There were beds, sofas, armchairs and floor enough for all.

XXIII

Jenny pushed a last piece of baklava round her plate with the back of her fork; honey rippled. Simon smoked a Gitane. He was tanned, looked healthy.

'You appear deeply, profoundly, miserable,' Jenny said, giving up on the pudding and accepting a cigarette.

'I'm sorry.'

'Don't do that, please. You have your strong points, Simon. The insincere smile isn't one of them. What's the problem?'

'Everything!' He looked around the Acropolis. It had crudely painted walls featuring green mountains, sheep that looked more like dogs than the sheepdogs, stiff shepherds, ancient ochre ruins. A waiter in his late teens misinterpreted Simon's inspection of the walls and brought the wine list and a clean ashtray.

'We'll have more coffee,' Jenny said. The waiter replaced their ashtray with the clean one.

'Everybleedingthing!' He stubbed his cigarette in the wet, pressed-glass ashtray.

'You know, moaning is a useless seduction ploy. You'd be surprised how many otherwise intelligent, attractive men believe that, in the absence, I should imagine, of the slightest shred of evidence, they can moan their way into a woman's pants.'

'Thanks,' he said, lighting another cigarette. He caught the waiter's eye and ordered another bottle of retsina.

'I'm serious,' Jenny said. 'It takes two forms: "Come with me, I'll give you a really miserable time" and "Come with me, I'll let you cheer me up".'

The bottle came, Simon poured himself a large glass and then one for her. She nodded. 'This is a variation, of course: "You make me so unhappy I am driven to drink". In your case you have it in trumps: "You drive me to drink against the advice of my doctor".'

He drank the glass quickly and refilled it, staring at her with distaste, grimacing as the wine hit his stomach. She took an unused knife from the place setting and rubbed its blade with a napkin before offering it to him.

'Here.'

'What's that for?'

'Cut your fucking ear off.'

He grinned, amused by the explosiveness of her sarcasm, but his eyes prickled with tears.

'I wish I could stop bleeding bleeding.'

'Is it bad?'

'No, it's settled in, become a fact of life, like endless drizzle. In France I had a few days of feeling great, then it was back again. Anyway, sorry. Sorry about being so fucking miserable. Okay?'

'Stop being so sorry. The invitation was for an enjoyable evening out.'

'Yeah, I know. I'm sorry.'

She raised her eyes and then filled her glass and drank in silence. He pushed his glass to one side and drank the thick sweet coffee.

'Sorry about being so bleeding sorry.'

She said nothing, there was a period of silence, then he coughed and said, 'I slept with someone in France.'

'Right, tell me about that then.' Her tone was business-like, plainly saying, *Anything so long as you stop moping, anything to pass the time until I get back to my own cosy bed, on my own...*

'She was American, doing the tour with her mother. I picked her up in a hotel bar in Hierre. She wouldn't come back to Furnace's place, so we sneaked into her room. Strange, she was in her early twenties, worked in an insurance office somewhere with a foreign name, in California.' He emptied his glass, then half-filled it from the bottle, topping up Jenny's first.

'Go on.'

'Not much to say. I don't think I've ever met anybody so healthy. All white meat and cream and apple pie and strawberry and...' Jenny was smiling at him. He hesitated and recognized his own good humour flowing back. 'You know what I mean? God, Jenny, listen, she was a bit overweight, I suppose, but her flesh was made of something else. Did you ever read about that bloke in America who killed and ate his social worker? Well, if the social worker was like this, he was after health food! I mean everything about her was as perfect as a Coke bottle.

'I asked her about Vietnam and she said that her cousin had been killed there and *we don't talk about the war.*' He put on an American accent, then, seeing Jenny frown, realized how

189

heartless he must sound. 'She said it was just something that had to be done, the responsibility which came with being the bastion of democracy and freedom. That's what she said, democracy and freedom. Everything about her was healthy and polished and perfected.

'She had a sort of emergency renovation kit with her, slung over her shoulder, very casual. Then in her room she had a case with nothing but vitamins and cosmetics and stuff, the full repair kit, with manuals. At her age! Anyway, when it came to it – it was a two-person job to get her jeans off.'

Jenny cracked out laughing, took a cigarette from the pack which lay open on the table, and said, 'No.'

'Yeah. I'm serious. She said her mom would know she was with someone because with these jeans Mom always gave a hand. Twenty-five, Jenny. When we'd got her perfectly shaped legs out of her perfect jeans, I had to sit around like a spare while she got ready for bed: forty-five bleeding minutes at least. If that's democracy and freedom give me...' He stopped in mid-flow and smiled at her.

'What?'

'I was just thinking how lovely you look. I feel at home with you.'

'Crap. You were just moving into a chat-up. Anyway, now do you understand why capitalism will always restrain liberty? You say your work gives consumers choice. Your Barbie Doll in France is where that leads to.'

'Don't talk about work, for Christ's sake. Three nights, you said, then there's nothing left to say. Well I didn't expect the second night to be a seminar on feminism and the third one a Marxist critique of market research. I mean it's just how I make my living, for Christ's sake.'

'Do you understand now though?'

'Yeah, I understand, but not so well that I don't need another night when you can explain the great difference between what I do and what you do.'

'One more, then.' She reached across the table and stopped his hand as he began to empty the bottle, his face showing indignation, hope, despair, pain; signs of unforced laughter. 'But only one more. That's really it, okay. I'm going to John's on Monday, for a few weeks. Maybe for good, who knows? And you should give your life a shaking up.'

'Don't you think it's shaken enough at the moment?'

'Give it a couple of hours, Casanova.'

'Has it ever occurred to you that his name was Newhouse?'

'Andiamo!' She pulled screwed-up notes from her pocket and went to pay.

'What do you mean, they killed a friend of yours?' Simon propped himself on his elbow and looked at her for the first time in minutes. She was crying, big malformed tears caught in her long lashes.

'Jenny. Tell me. Please. Don't cry.' He kissed her wet eyes.

'He wasn't a close friend, he was a dosser. Alcoholic. I knew him from the park, sometimes gave him money. They arrested him one night and next morning he was dead. They said he'd assaulted two policemen and fallen down stone stairs trying to get away. That was '69.

'And then, in America, I was doing a postgrad course. We had an emeritus professor, a gentle, loving man. He drove to his office one morning and found the National Guard blocking his way. He stopped, one of them pushed a rifle butt through his windscreen, another tossed a cylinder of tear gas through the hole. He was in the college hospital for three weeks.' She sat up and grinned at him. 'East, West, North, South, any race, any colour, any political persuasion: pigs is pigs. Remember that and you won't go far wrong.'

'Seems a bit extreme.'

'I'm not here to convince you. I'm giving you the words so that you recognize it when others are still clinging to Dixon of Dock Green and jovial station sergeants. It's a fact of life. Authoritarian personalities are attracted to uniforms and power. Uniforms and power shape authoritarian personalities: you always get a higher percentage of psychopaths and sadists in the police and army than in the general public. Beware the future, Simon. Capitalism carries the seeds of its own destruction. There will come a time when a fully brutalized police force will change sides. People like you will be at risk before and after the revolution.'

He argued with her, carefully phrasing his opinion that what she said was over-dramatized, simplistic fantasy.

191

'Of course you think that,' she said, angry, sitting naked on the bed, her back straight, her hands gripping his shoulders. 'You are supposed to think that. You are not supposed to understand the Third World War. You are not supposed to see that we are eating the food and flesh of millions of dispossessed people around the world. You are not supposed to know that multinationals now have turnovers greater than the gross national product of the majority of nations. You are not supposed to link Africa, South America, Asia. You are not supposed to realize that in some countries people who hold certain views are honoured, in others they are bound with barbed wire, shot in the head and left by the roadside. You are not supposed to realize that every time you draw breath you are taking an active part in a global struggle. You are not supposed to dwell on the defoliation of Vietnam and to wonder what happens to peasants sprayed with defoliants. You are not supposed to know that the Americans are not only killing people there, they are killing millions of acres of nature... life itself. Mainly, my lovely, innocent friend... you are not supposed to think outside the system,'

She eased forward and kissed him gently on the nose, her anger spent.

'That's it then, is it? That's the end of the bleeding lecture?'

'That's the end of the bleeding relationship. We are ships which pass in the night, exchanging a little cargo.' She was smiling, stroking the back of his neck.

'You haven't had much from me, Jenny. I don't agree with everything you say, but you've given a lot.'

'You gave me laughter and word-play.'

'Superficialities.'

'Yes. Don't knock them. Remember babies and bath water, mate.' They dressed and parted for the last time.

XXIV

They had discussed the possibility for weeks when the first graffito appeared. It read, *TARMAC: BUILDING FOR DESTRUCTION AT GREENHAM*, a spray paint job in British racing green. The slogan survived for a month, then Tarmac painted it out, leaving a pristine white surface. Simon, Lindy and Katrina bought spray cans. The next day they viewed their handiwork: *WARNING: TARMAC CAN SERIOUSLY DAMAGE YOUR HEALTH*, with black C.N.D. logos at each end.

Leeds' Labour Council had declared the city a Nuclear Free Zone, but still gave the Church Hill Leisure Centre contract to Tarmac – a company involved in work incompatible with progressive values. But then, as Danny eloquently explained: 'The Party is a stultified hierarchical structure with a minority progressive membership attempting to radicalize and democratize its machinery. Active membership falls into two categories: those who are out to change the Party, and those who are out to improve their personal lot by serving the City power brokers – Sneath, for example. If Harmer said, "Rip your nose off and stuff it up my arse", Sneath would do it, and smile... and say, "Thanks a lot, John!"'

A silent battle ensued. Each time their slogans were painted out they replaced them with something else. When Tarmac left *CRUISE IS BAD NEWS* for three months, the trio painted out their own slogan, replacing it with a giant logo in blue, silver and gold and half a dozen posters for the October demonstration in London.

The fence as a whole was a pleasing enough sight. C.N.D. and the ever changing pop posters kept down the swastikas and National Front slogans which decorated so many public surfaces.

When pop posters appeared on the C.N.D. patch, it took half an hour to locate those responsible. An apology was made and a promise that the posters would be removed. And they were; within fifteen hours the C.N.D. site was clean as a whistle. Twenty-four hours later it featured holly, candles, a Christmas tree and *NUCLEAR DISARMAMENT –THE ONLY SANITY CLAUSE*, and, beneath, in red and green script, *Happy Christmas and a PEACEFUL New Year*.

One night in mid-November, Lindy and Simon ate at Danny and Katrina's. It was a reasonably boozy occasion. They stretched in armchairs in front of an open fire which reddened white walls and added depth to Danny's favoured photo reproductions of air-brushed American classic cars.

'Alright! Alright, so you like them. Why have such fucking awful plastic frames?' Simon sipped a cocktail of vodka and Grand Marnier: the Lenin Stinger. On the slate coffee table stood a best buy from the local car boot sale – a dozen small bottles of assorted liqueurs.

The game was Name This Cocktail. Nobody knew who was winning.

'They're not plastic, they're wood.'

'Yeah, I know, pressed white wood with shiny varnish – what's more plastic than that, for Christ's sake?'

Lindy urged them to drink up as she had an idea for Bandierra Rossa.

'I suppose you feel we should have your photographs on the wall.' Katrina glared at Simon.

'Certainly not. I would feel, dear lady, mortally affronted to have my pictures hung alongside such trash and, secondly, I would fear that my work had lost its cutting edge if it were to be displayed in the home of soft-booted social workers.'

Katrina said, 'Shit!'

Danny wagged his finger: 'Community worker! I am a community worker.'

'A pissed community worker,' Katrina said, watching Lindy draw the cork of a bottle of red which had somehow survived the meal.

'Yeah, okay, a pissed community worker.'

Simon put his finger over the top of a bottle of Kummel, shook, licked his finger. Then he stood, swung one arm and placed his hand tight over his ear and in a drawling folk singing voice offered, 'Yours is the future caring boot upon the human face.'

'Ignore him.' Lindy had mixed the Bandierra Rossa in a jug: Spanish red, anise, the final drops of vodka and a fair slug of slivovitz. 'I thought we should have a longer, more soothing drink after the Lenin Stinger!'

As she filled glasses they exchanged views on who was

194

responsible for their shared tendency to become pie-eyed whenever they ate together. Danny terminated this mini-debate: 'We are a sort of hedonistic co-operative, it doesn't make sense to allocate responsibility – we share the glory, Comrades. '

They drank to it. The Rossa was excellent.

'Seen the leisure centre fence? They've painted everything out, posters, graffiti, the lot.' Simon lit a fuse that would splutter for months.

It took over an hour to decide on the slogan. In the end it came down to the deliberately ambiguous TORIES ARE SMASHING PEOPLE! or a lengthy, considered reference to a pit disaster which still echoed in the hollow statements of Government and Coal Board. They decided on the latter and drafted and redrafted, counted words, allocated tasks. Katrina drew the short straw and agreed to stay home with Hal.

Lindy was look-out and prompt, Danny took the top line, Simon the bottom. They worked with large brushes, Danny had gloss white paint, Simon gloss pink. It was a magnificent, twenty-yard graffito, filling a whole section of prime site where, each morning, a traffic jam formed.

'Fantastic!' Lindy pocketed her prompt sheet. 'Let's get going.' They walked up the road, swinging carrier bags in which were tins of paint and brushes. Then Danny remembered that Katrina wanted the C.N.D. patch decorated. They turned about and walked back. Two men were reading the slogan. One was uniformed.

'Just keep walking,' Simon said.

'Oh, yeah. Act normal.' Danny was laughing quietly.

'Shall we do a runner?'

'Come on, just walk. They'll get one of us if we run, then the thing's blown anyway.'

They strolled on, swinging their bags. Simon wore decorator's overalls and his badge-bedecked demonstration cap. Danny still wore a rubber glove on his painting hand. The policeman walked towards them then stopped so that he blocked their path.

"Ello! 'Ello! 'Ello!' Danny whispered, scarcely controlling hysteria.

'What are you doing?' the copper asked, when they were stationary, three abreast in front of him.

'Walking.'

'Walking?'

"Sright, officer, taking the evening air, strolling.'

'What's in the bags?'

'Paint and brushes, officer.'

'What you been doing with them, then?'

'Painting.'

'What you been painting, then?'

'The slogan.'

The copper unclipped his radio and announced his intention to bring in three prisoners.

Lindy, Danny, and Simon took the opportunity to admire their work, offering each other congratulations, covering their anxiety with good humour and laughter.

'I'm well pleased,' Danny said. 'It's about time facts of this kind were more widely publicized, don't you agree, constable?'

The meaty young policeman rolled his shoulders and said, 'Shut up and stand still.'

'It certainly looks okay,' Lindy said. And Simon added, 'Thank God the paint didn't run.'

'I don't understand you... people like you, of your age...' The constable was moving from foot to foot, angry. 'I wouldn't mind if you were football hooligans, kids, but you must be stupid. You're all stupid, ignorant.'

Danny said, 'Yeah, that goes for me anyway, I only got an upper second at university. How about you, Simon?'

'Same, and Lindy. You're right, officer, second class brains, the lot of us. Not ignorant though. I mean, did you know that bit of history?' He indicated the graffito which glistened in the amber street light.

'Bloody shut it!'

A police car arrived and they were squashed into the back. It was a two-door saloon and stank of stale sweat. As it drove off Simon read the slogan. He was frightened and elated at the same time.

1913 – 439 MINERS KILLED – IN ABER VALE
MINE OWNERS GUILTY: FINED £25!

Danny began to argue with the two coppers. The cocktails made his mood volatile, he tied the young man in knots. The policeman turned in his seat, muscles tightening the skin on his

196

face. 'Shut it, cunt!' The older cop, who was driving, said something about the strike and his junior turned about and stared out of the windscreen.

Me face were cut and that were stinging a bit, but that were all, like. Bastards'd given us a right pasting with their truncheons. And booted us. I were numb really, a bit cold and dazed like. They've got an hold they put on your wrist, like. I said they'd have to force me if they wanted my fingerprints, cos I'd done nowt against law. So they forced me. Three of them. Then one twisted my arms up my back and another pulled my head up by the hair. They took a Polaroid of me like that and showed it to me. I said, 'Can I have one for my album, like?' Bastards handcuffed me and knocked me about again.

Don't give 'em an excuse to lay into thee.

At the police station there were traces of blood on the wall. They were told to turn out their pockets. Simon's coveralls produced a rubber bung and an oily rag – the last time he'd worn them was to fix a replacement radiator on the Mini. The desk sergeant also noted a half penny and a 'flat cap with five badges'.

The badges caused puzzled amusement. The C.N.D. badge and one commemorating a peace march in Barrow were clear enough. But a small picture of Emma Goldman produced: *Who's the woman then?* To which he answered, *My brother.* The other two badges were home-made. One featured a confusion of multicoloured geometrical shapes and the slogan *ABSTRACT PEACE*, the other was a reproduction of a Van Gogh self-portrait, slogan: *HERE WE GOGH.*

'What's this supposed to be?'

'I'm a peace artist.' He placed the pronunciation neatly between 'peace' and 'piss.'

They were locked in a dimly lit room. After many requests for the use of a lavatory, Simon was accompanied to a filthy water closet. Then they were taken out one at a time and interviewed by the arresting officers. While in the cold room they had agreed to be as forthcoming as possible, to take this as an opportunity to explain their action and motivation.

Simon gradually relaxed into confrontation. The cops had genuine difficulty in understanding, he made strenuous efforts to explain.

'It seems to me,' he said, 'that you don't know how to cope with someone who refuses to deny anything. You keep trying to get me to tell you what I've already told you. Have I been arrested?'

'Seems that way.' The older man smoothed his grey hair and smiled.

'Well, look, I've never been in this situation before. I'm not sure what to expect. I mean, for all I know you might suddenly turn nasty and beat me up. Then again you might charge me and ask me if I want to contact a solicitor.'

The older man smiled again and said, 'I don't think either of those two courses is very likely. I can't see that we'd gain anything knocking you about or taking the second course of action. What do you think, Colin?'

Colin, who sat to one side of the table over which Simon and the older man faced each other, was busy taking notes. He looked up and said, 'I don't understand why they did it. That's what I want to know. Why did somebody like you do it?'

'I'm older than you, constable. I've learned a lot in the last few years. Maybe I know a bit more than you.'

'Like what?' Colin's face flushed.

'Like, well, let me see – Christ, so many things. Well, for starters, how to solarize a photographic print. The names and work of several Nobel Prize Winners for Literature. The fact that in World War II captured officers had the duty to attempt to escape while enlisted men were duty-bound to work for their captors. That twenty-two million Russians were killed in that war. That when 413 miners were killed and the mine owners were found guilty, those same owners were fined twenty-five pounds. I learned that tonight. Now, did you know all that lot? And if not, why not? Could it be that our educational system is a little bit biased towards a certain interpretation of history?' He paused, wishing he'd put the list together so that it just included bits of labour history that were never taught in schools. Colin chewed his pencil for a moment, the older man looked at him and said nothing. Colin's colour deepened, then he said:

'I think all that were told me in school. I might not remember it... I might have missed it when the teacher said it. Been absent. Anyway, I don't see what it's got to do with damaging property.'

'Well then, let's spend time on three things you just said. I'd like to explain how what I've learned since leaving full-time education is linked to what I did tonight. That's one. Two, we should at least exchange views on the nature of property. And three, I think we might usefully talk about the nature of damage. If I were to come and paint your house, for example, would you feel that I had damaged it, or actually protected it from the weather?'

'That'd depend on the colour.'

'Would it? There you have me. I didn't know that the colour of paint influenced its weather-proofing qualities. I think your colleague here will agree that what you are saying is that, depending on your feelings about the colour, you yourself might be pleased or angry but the door would not actually have suffered damage. As a matter of fact that whole fence was painted a cruddy drab green by Tarmac in the last couple of days. Will you be arresting them for damaging the fence?'

And so it went on. The police sat and listened, repeated their questions, and made notes, Simon went on to explore his political beliefs for them, explain his acts.

Finally he was photographed and fingerprinted.

'I think I have the right to be charged, given access to a solicitor, and refuse to allow you to photograph or fingerprint me. Is that right?'

'I think that you might find yourself here for a long time if you play silly buggers, right, Colin?'

'I don't care, me. He's a bloody lunatic.'

'Do you want to discuss that proposition, constable?'

'Look, just shut it and there'll be no trouble.'

'Am I going to be charged?'

'Are you going to co-operate?'

'I'll co-operate. Am I going to be charged?'

They were neither charged nor given access to a telephone. At half past five in the morning their belongings were returned, Lindy used her cigarette papers and wisp of rolling tobacco and the three of them shared the cigarette as the desk sergeant asked them to sign a document stating that when offered the opportunity of contacting a solicitor they had refused.

'What happens if we don't sign on the grounds that it's a total fabrication?' Danny asked.

'Ah, well, Sir, in that event I think we might find ourselves having a lot more questions to put to you. And, what with the arresting officers going off shift, I should imagine you wouldn't be getting home for quite a while.'

They signed.

Cold, stiff, elated they began the four-mile walk home.

Back in Church Hill they admired their work. In the light of a violet and pink dawn the massive graffito looked stunning. Danny shrugged: 'Shame they kept the paint. We could have added: 'THE CHURCH HILL THREE ARE FREE!'

They agreed to meet at noon for a photo-call.

Several weeks later they were summoned to court, charged with criminal damage. They were advised that they could plead guilty and make no statement in court, or plead not guilty and be free to make a statement. They decided to plead not guilty and, over several bottles, began writing their statements.

There are moments when the senses work together and receive something beyond the boundary of language. So it was as Lindy and Simon watched a fishing cobble leave the safety of Scarborough Harbour.

They sat on a bench seat by the castle, eating sandwiches, sharing strong black coffee from the flask top. Seagulls screamed around them, tossed like paper bags in the high wind.

Far below them sand crept over the road, as if to invade the boarded amusement arcades, cafes and rock shops. They felt a sympathetic swell in their stomachs as the swollen humps of water rubbed against the sea wall like affectionate beasts.

Each assumed the other's attention had settled on the red and blue cobble, its orange-oilskinned crew like figures activated by big, slab pennies pushed into an Edwardian slot machine.

Beyond the harbour mouth, the North Sea was marbled green, blue and ochre. Ragged lines of brilliant white marked where the wind sliced the tops off choppy waves.

Lindy suspended the last bite of a sandwich in her fingerless grey gloves and said, 'Do you think they know what it'll be like out there?'

For a few seconds the boat was steady beyond the harbour wall, then the arrowed ripples, which spread through the oily water of the harbour, ruffled like feathers and the boat bounced, caught on the skin of a giant drum.

'Christ, look at it!' Even as he spoke the boat slid sideways, then churned forward and the sound of its engine reached them.

It was November 5th and they were taking a day's holiday, celebrating the man who entered parliament with honourable intentions. A day away from tense city life, away from a prolonged exchange of letters with the Ministry of Defence. Away from the daily confrontation between police and strikers as defeated workers were escorted at speed through a barrage of abuse and disdain. A day away from the ubiquitous riot-screened police transits. Away from the perverse, potent, heavy breather who rang at all times of day and night. Their phone, like those of other peace activists, had gone berserk. It disconnected itself as they spoke, performed a symphony of new sounds and tones: sarcastic voices restated the dialled number or muttered 'Scrub this one!'

A day started before the post, which often arrived weeks late, in envelopes torn and roughly resealed by sticky labels apologizing for 'mechanical breakdown' in obscure sorting offices.

A day away from the fierce emotional buffeting of collection buckets fed, collection buckets spurned.

A day to forget that the Tory Conference had been bombed, and the Tories had made good of it. A day to forget that they and thousands more had signed a declaration of intention to physically oppose the building of a Cruise Missile base at Molesworth. A day to forget that they were now in open, declared opposition to the State. A day to forget the tabloids' portrayal of them and their Comrades as enemies, maniacs and brutes, best locked up or deported to Moscow from where, the befuddled trash readers were encouraged to believe, every left wing cause was financed and controlled.

A day away from the bias and lies of radio and television. Away from the unthinkable phone bill which resulted from their calls of protest to duty officers at the Television Centre and Broadcasting House. A day of respite which once would have been an *ordinary* day.

A holiday.

When they lost sight of the cobble out on the pitted chrome

of the horizon they drove the Mini over the North Yorkshire Moors and on through Whitby to Port Mulgrave.

Wrapped in scarves, hats pulled down against the pounding wind, they slithered a twisting, muddy path to the sea.

Three weather-beaten men in heavy smocks winched a boat onto the shale beach, offering bleak *Nah-thens!* without stopping their slow, back-breaking work.

The long-disused port had little to offer, a row of dilapidated wood and iron huts, some rusting metal, a steep incline of shale, slugs of mud crawling towards a grey sea. The bay absorbed dwindling afternoon light.

They decided to climb the shale cliffs back to the road. A grey sheepdog ran to them, barking, his feathered tail steering him round rocks and pools.

Simon climbed higher, attracting the dog away from canophobic Lindy who traversed the base of the cliff and climbed through fern and brambles. After a while the dog began to panic; its feet deep in shale. It barked for help, and to bring its flock of two together. Simon, who loved dogs above all creatures, stopped, sweaty, face stinging to the cold wind's lash; even before he had calculated a track to the dog, he began to slide. He shouted and waved to Lindy, whistled for the dog to follow, then, ankle deep in moving shale, he dragged himself on, working for momentum.

Gradually he traversed the cliff and, breathless, waited for Lindy to join him. The dog sat in the shale, throwing irregular barks at them. When Lindy reached Simon, the dog struggled to his feet and ploughed and slid down the incline, tail held high, barking for the joy of it. They watched until he was safe on the beach.

'Nice dog,' Simon said, taking Lindy's offered hand. Lindy humphed at him, it was a conventional exchange.

They had decided not to bring the cameras, but, at the last minute, Lindy slipped the compact Rollei into her pocket. On the cliff top they took profiles of each other, the broken crab's claw of harbour wall tiny below them. Later they would tease each other about the political leanings indicated by their noses, his red, hers blue.

At six they were back in Whitby for fish and chips. In the

absence of a perfect cafe, they settled for a brightly lit palace of lime-green and yellow plastic ('It's like Nigel's kitchen, remember?' And she said, 'Piss off!'). The fish was perfect. They agreed to be less arrogant when judging cafes by appearance.

As they walked back to the car a woman stepped out of a newsagent's and held a package towards them. 'Have you got your fireworks? Last two boxes for a quid.'

From the moorland road they saw silent rockets flowering in the black sky. The bloody glow of fires was topped by swirls of dusty sparks. All those dead soldiers, Lindy thought, but said nothing.

At Fylingdales early warning station they stopped and put on their own small display. Cheap rockets hissed towards the invisible golf balls which housed radar dishes and made this outpost of the U.S.A. a prime nuclear target. Headlights flared as a vehicle approached them from the base. They lit a line of golden rains, volcanoes and Roman candles, then, not wishing to spoil the night by confrontation, drove off. Headlights followed them for a few miles.

Back home they played Mozart and drank Natsurin.

'How long would it take to forget everything, if we just lived like this?' Simon asked. Lindy grinned at him, her face flushed. She was beautiful.

'I suppose, if we drank enough, as long as needs be.'

'That a promise?'

'If I was sure of it,' she said, suddenly serious, 'I'd be tempted.'

Simon filled the glasses and rolled a cigarette in silence. 'This is the year, you know. Molesworth, the miners... Do you think we'll win?'

Lindy scowled at him. 'You, asking that! I thought you were the *don't ask questions that draw energy from finding solutions* half of this partnership. We win or everybody loses.'

'Sometimes I need a rest, that's all.'

'Just had one. Drink your Natsurin.'

'I always mope as the bonfires die down. It's traditional.' He took her hand and smiled. 'Bed?'

'Just a minute.' She topped up both glasses, emptying the fat-bellied jug, taking the last drips straight into her mouth as if from a pouron.

'When we win,' Simon said, 'I mean us, C.N.D., no one will acknowledge what we've done. The weapons will go and the credit will go to Kinnock, maybe even Thatcher. We'll have a celebratory demo and the media will ignore it.

'Given an arms deal they'll say the only thing that held it up was people like us. Drop us in any bleeding country and we'll be subversives. Trouble is, states, governments, leaders, they're not very bright, are they? Lowest common denominator stuff. We've always been around, we invented the wheel, religions, philosophies, but do we ever get thanked in our own time? Do we buggery.'

'Want a medal?'

'Tell you what I want. I want to march through London shouting, "We won, you daft sods, we won!" And every year I want a peace march. When I'm old I want ex-C.N.D.-ers to mix with old soldiers, and we'll wear our medals and badges and lay wreaths at the Cenotaph for everybody, everywhere, who gave their lives for peace.'

'Oh, aye, I can see that, man, as Mary would say.' She drained her glass then held out her hand, 'Bed!'

XXV

He stood by the window in his new uniform of grey pullover, silver-grey slacks and open-necked baby blue shirt. He was watching Jenny move out.

Her belongings were soon in the Transit. He recognized some of them, felt a peculiar affection for a leggy cheese plant: its soil held cigarette stubs. The bed base came out as four shallow rectangles; he realized this as the third appeared, balanced on the head of a squat man wearing a carpenter's apron and smoking a cigar.

His sadness intensified and, as if in an aeroplane which hits an air pocket, he lost his stomach.

She appeared at the door with a carton in her arms, the younger of the two removal men took it from her. She said something and smiled.

The cherry trees were bare, their bowls shiny from recent rain. He wanted to be inside her again, to feel the soft smoothness of her body on his. To tell her he loved her. He never told her he loved her. Whenever he got close to it, she would steer him away. It was uncanny, she never allowed him to be fully with her. It was as if she had access to his thoughts before him and with this advantage she controlled the time they spent together.

On the third night she had produced papers and a small flake of cannabis resin. She was right, three nights was enough, four nights had emptied her, overfilled him.

'I've given you everything I have to offer now.' She sounded depleted, as if she wished she had kept her political intensity to herself. He said, 'I think I still have things for you, Jen.' And she kissed his nose and said, 'I am sorry, Simon. I don't put much value on what you have left.'

It didn't make him angry. It made him intensely sad. He stepped closer to the window and whispered: *I don't put much value on what I have left either, Jenny.*

She was disconcertingly honest. On the second night they woke up and made love very gently, then talked. She said, 'I respect your humour, your intellect, your sincerity. I like making love with you...'

'But?'

'But I find your values shallow and predictable, your insight terribly flawed, your emotional development deplorable.'

'What makes you so perfect? I mean, I ask that seriously.' He smiled, trying to show that what she had said did not hurt him (which it did), that he was not attempting to strike an equalizing blow (which he was).

'You have a complex, funny, attractive system of defence. It works too well. Perhaps you can't see anything unless you are standing on its battlements. You can't see far out, and you can't see far in. I'm not perfect. What makes us different is that I know my flaws and I have some simple, hard won certainties. I try to build my life on them. You have a whole bag of inconsistent certainties and you pick them out as you need them.'

'I'm intellectually dishonest!'

'No. Not as simple as that.'

'I'm a mess!'

'Yes. As simple as that!'

She made him feel he had wasted a lot of time. He was six years older than her, but she knew things he didn't, had things he wanted. On the fourth night, when he talked about these feelings, she said: 'Your problem is political.'

He laughed. 'That's your problem, Jenny, not your solution.'

'There are areas of consciousness you dare not touch. You're like a child afraid of the forest, of the swamp, of the rocky hills where the black caves are. Afraid of the dark... Do you know what I mean?'

'Sounds like a put-down.' He saw her face change and added. 'Sorry. I don't understand. I'd like you to explain.'

'It's difficult. We are attracted to each other because we are similar. You have spent a lot of time building a defence for what's inside you. I've spent a lot of time exploring what's inside me. So far as I can tell, the only forest you are prepared to enter is Vietnam. You go in like a psychotic woodcutter, lashing and smashing in all directions. You do it because that particular area of pain and confusion threatens to fill your mind. But there are other issues you turn a blind eye to, or joke about. Remember the Biafran babies? *A million Biafrans every day, pick up a tin of beans and say.... one for me, one for you...*'

'Sick humour is only funny to people who care –'

'That's my point. It can reduce pain, but it's not productive.'

206

He stared at her, his eyes stuck, his attention on the sensation of vault doors swinging slowly open somewhere inside.

'It doesn't do much to change anything, does it?' She was stroking his shoulder, taking the sting out of her analysis. 'It's a device to make you like those who genuinely don't care out of ignorance or heartlessness, or whatever. But you are not ignorant. You are not heartless. You're a child afraid of too many places. I'm not as witty as you, Simon and I am not so flash, but there's nowhere in my head I'm afraid of, nowhere I can't go. I'm in touch with my pain and confusion. I have political ideals which help me come to terms with it all in a positive way. I don't need jokes about starvation or the subjugation of women.'

'Oh Christ. Oh bloody Christ on the bleeding cross – what are you saying to me?'

'Is that a joke or a prayer?'

He didn't know. He still didn't know.

XXVI

Church Hill C.N.D. Newsletter... November 1984:–

... Remembrance Day is here again. The white poppy, a peace poppy, reminds us of all people, in and out of uniform, who gave their lives for peace. Wear it with a red one and explain why you are doing so.

Bertolt Brecht wrote this for a friend who worked for peace in Germany and was murdered:

> *He who would not give in*
> *Has been done to death*
> *He who was done to death*
> *Would not give in.*
> *The warner's mouth*
> *Is stopped with earth.*
> *The bloody adventure begins*
> *Over the grave of one who loved peace*
> *Slog the battalions.*
> *Was the fight in vain, then?*
> *When he who did not fight alone is done to death*
> *The enemy has not yet won.*

And Siegfried Sassoon wrote this from the trenches:

> *If I were fierce, and bald, and short of breath,*
> *I'd live with scarlet Majors at the Base,*
> *And speed glum heroes up the line to death.*
> *You'd see me with my puffy petulant face,*
> *Guzzling and gulping in the best hotel,*
> *Reading the Roll of Honour. 'Poor young chap,'*
> *I'd say – 'I used to know his father well;*
> *Yes, we've lost heavily in this last scrap.'*
> *And when the war is done and youth stone dead,*
> *I'd toddle safely home and die – in bed.*

Working for peace isn't always as easy and safe as it is for us here and now. People around the world, yesterday and today, have been tortured, killed, imprisoned for our beliefs. We owe it

to them to do as much as we can while we can. And let's honour
them all with red and white poppies. And then let's honour them
with our actions, arguments, and commitments.
   Pints and poems - Cardigan Arms fund raiser for cnd and
the miners.
   Nov 13th 8 till late. Be there or be square!

And now it was happening. Simon swayed and the papers in
his hand shook. The upstairs room, where Party meetings were
held, was packed. People sat on the floor, draped around each
other like an indoor blockade.

It wasn't alcohol, he'd been on the waggon for two weeks.
He swayed from anxiety, from a sense of the perverse
agoraphobia that strikes the one person with space in a crowded
room.

The audience waited, watching over the rims of pint glasses,
through coils of smoke. Pints and Poems! It started as a closing-
time joke.

When in the darkroom, part of his mind ran through lines,
tested rhymes, counted spaces and shapes in which syllables
would sit. And as he watched the images of protest form in the
big developing tray, so the poems had taken shape until only the
night before last he sat down with pad and pencil and let them
flow from him.

Being on the waggon helped, at least he knew why he
swayed, and the brittle, sparky thought processes were his own.

The audience stretched and scratched, he heard questions
and answers, just the shapes and sounds, not the content, he
stopped his mind from chasing that thought. There he was,
reflected in a dusty mirror, looking taller than he expected,
curving to the left, oversized Oxfam safari suit falling in fluted
folds, white scarf in danger of slipping from his neck, untouched
glass of Coke in one hand, shaking papers in the other.

Right! He raised the glass to his own image then stood in
silence. He was worried sick because he followed real poets and
singers; his trivia would drop into a pool of crafted dismay and
pain.

'Thank you very much, you're too too kind. That particular
work, called "My Silent Plea for Understanding in a Cruel
World", has been performed many times and rarely fails to get an

appreciative response.'

A little laughter from Lindy, Katrina, Danny, Dave, and Sarah, all willing the others to join in. There was only one way out: Forward!

'And now Comrades, with or without your permission, a little known gem from Billy Shakespeare, our greatest miner sonnet writer.' He let his voice slide into the Richard III- Olivier send-up. (He'd been using the voice and the bounce for the last two days: *'Is that you pissing in the lav-a-try? Then hurry up you hussy for 'tis my turn to pee…'*)

'Thou art more noxious than the smell of spew,
And flowers die when you step in the room.
If to this nation I could give my view
Then I would weave this pattern on my loom:
By bombs and wars, I see your spirits buoyed,
Greed and corruption issue on your breath,
You have not time for sick or unemployed,
Condemning them to everlasting death.
Financiers and loathsome louts of law
Are wont to pander to your slightest whim,
Each is, like you, a septic running sore
Or privy full of ordure to the brim.
Hail Margaret Thatcher, tyrant as of old,
Your mind is narrow and your heart is cold.'

Some laughed, some clapped, some drank, some practised the long-legged-insect walk necessary to negotiate bodies and reach the bar. The audience as such was diverse, not exactly atomized, but not exactly an organic whole.

'Between the bread is found the slabs of meat,
The boys in blue who are on double time,
And with their truncheons our proud miners beat
And have no will to solve or battle crime.
How often are they overheard to joke
And grunt obscenities as they describe
How they have knocked about some honest bloke
Who had not got the loot to offer bribe.
From every corner of our land they come,

210

From Potters Bar and York and London Met.,
This splendid force would ne'er reject a bum
Who'd smash a skull to please some Tory get.
What is this meat of which the Tories boast?
'Tis served with apple sauce when it is roast.'

They were laughing now, nodding and speaking to each other as he paused. He could sense the birth of a creature in the room.

'As oft at morning, 'ere the searchlights switch,
The humble copper polishes his shield
And pickets murmur gentle in a ditch
Of deeds that must be done on darkened field,
When camera crews are plotting over tea
How best to capture images which lie
And can be shown this night on BBC
Because they do not pose the question Why?
There is a moment's silence and repose
Broke only by the snort and stamp of horse
As pigs and pickets find their thoughts on those
Whose twisted features leer at use of force.
Loathe then the smarmy Leon Brittan
Whose face is scarcely fit for us to spit on.'

He snarled out the lines and rejoiced in the audience's reaction. He'd had in mind a ribald, mocking pastiche, but found himself struggling against the heroic. Even now he could see that the laughter was not flowing freely, that his intention was not fully understood. He decided to drop the last one and end with an open invitation to laugh.

'Well, thank you. And thanks to Billy as well. I'm sure you're all responding to the N.U.M. call to *Switch on at Six*.' He saw a few puzzled looks. 'For those of you who limit yourselves to the capitalist media, use as much electricity as possible at exactly six o'clock each night. This puts strain on the national grid which can only be met by massive coal burning at the power stations. So remember that. What's less well known is this: for no cost at all you can cause a run on the electricity generators. You do this by flushing the lavatory, once again at six. The more you flush the

211

more the sewerage pumps come into play, and the more electricity is used. So here, in a more serious vein, is my last contribution. It's called "Switch on at Six".

Flush the bog for victory
We'll give McGregor hell...

And just one more, for the teachers in our midst.
CLASS STRUGGLE
I wanna be a big tough union man
In a donkey jacket and boots
I'm sick of doing morning assemblies
And wearing C and A suits.

I want to write political slogans
That'll thrill you to your radical soul,
Sommat sharp as a razor
To embroider on your blazer
Like 'Meaningful curricula, not dole'
I want to......

And so on. At last, red-faced, he returned to his crushed seat between Dave and Lindy. People clapped and shouted for more, hands patted his back and legs as he waded through the packed room. 'Brilliant!' Lindy said and took his hand to stop it shaking.

Later, when three guitars led them into 'The Red Flag', the glow of personal satisfaction finally converted to that of communality, solidarity. Performance had made him feel more whole, filled a space which the rightness of protest and the excitement of photography left empty.

XXVII

At last she came back out and watched the two men lock the van doors. She was wearing a heavy wool cloak and high boots. When the van went she took a package from her cloak, walked across the road and slipped it into his letter box. He knew that she knew he was watching her. He knew she wouldn't look up. She returned to her flat and came out a few minutes later, carrying a case and a soft travel bag. At the gate she dropped the bag, looked up to his window, blew a kiss, then raised her hand in a clenched fist salute.

After she'd gone, he stared at the empty street until a numb acceptance heaved, then exploded into anger.

Turning from the window he pulled the electric fire out of its mountings in the tiled fire place. The fire grate was still there, coated with brick dust and soot. He stripped and stuffed his new armour up the chimney.

In the kitchen cupboard he found a stone pot of mustard Hilary had brought. He scooped the brown mustard into his hand and smeared it over his hair and face, wiped his hand on his chest.

He had burned his fingers on the handle of the electric fire. They began to hurt. He noticed the pain as he noticed smoke rising from the armchair. The fire was still turned on; heat from its three glowing bars ate into dusty brocade.

He dialled Furnace's direct line and shouted, 'I'm not going back! I'm not going back!' The phone was dead.

The room stank of smoke. His fingers were blistering. Mustard burned his eyes. For a moment he stood like a statue, watching sparks dance as dust burned on the surface of the chair. *Dead soldiers, squirming in limbo... No heaven. There is no heaven.*

He pushed the fire back onto the hearth and pressed his good hand onto the smouldering chair until the pain dragged all of his consciousness to itself.

When the pain was too much, he took a deep breath and stood up, waving his hands like a child awakened from the joy of snowballing. The mustard was drying on his skin. He pressed his hands onto his chest and looked about him.

Pulling a sheet round him, he ran downstairs.

It was skilfully wrapped in brown paper. He poured himself a glass of water, used some to douse the final smouldering, then sat in the chair and inspected the packet.

A series of quotations were written on it in red ink.

I am an Anarchist! Wherefore I will not rule, and also ruled I will not be.

All government in essence is tyranny.

Law never made a man a whit more just; and by means of their respect for it, even the well-disposed are daily made agents of injustice.

The political arena leaves one no alternative, one must either be a dunce or a rogue.

Mackay... Emerson... Thoreau... Goldman.

The inner wrapping carried another quotation inscribed in green ink:

The problem that confronts us today, and which the nearest future is to solve, is how to be one's self and yet in oneness with others, to feel deeply with all human beings and still retain one's own characteristic qualities... Emma Goldman.

He removed the final wrapping and found a slim cloth-bound notebook. *KNOW THYSELF* and *He not busy being born is busy dying* were written in the same green ink on a rectangle of yellow paper embedded in the shiny black cover.

The notebook was empty, each page a shining void. He flipped through the pages and a wisp of flimsy paper fluttered onto his lap. On this, in green ink, was written:

In all beginnings dwells a magic force for guarding us and helping us to live... Hesse. Love J.

He memorized the Hesse quotation, then screwed the paper into a ball and swallowed it. He remembered a record she played when they were stoned.

'Listen', she said, 'listen carefully!'

You're invisible now, you got no secrets to conceal.

'That's you,' she said. 'No direction home...'

He'd been disturbed at the time. Now certainty flowered in him. He felt whole and strong. He went and looked at himself in the bathroom mirror. His hair was spiky and stiff with dried mustard, his face a smeared image he hardly recognized. He ran a bath then returned to the mirror and began to laugh.

XXVIII

November's pools of street light muddied and December, the month of crazy celebration, established itself. On icy nights they made house-to-house collections on a nearby estate. Questions and rejections came through closed doors. Most depressing were the stone-faced workers who gave their reasons for supporting the State against the Left. Parroting the press and television they proclaimed Scargill a monster, a dictator, the miners anti-democratic. Many of them had seen their jobs go after the clothing workers' disputes a decade earlier. A cold selfishness had replaced pride in work and the warmth of solidarity. 'Don't talk about fucking strike to me. Miners have jobs, they should be grateful.' The suggestions that this was a strike to protect jobs, to maintain communities, to place humanitarian values above greed, meant nothing. 'Look after number one, kid,' they said, clinging to a value system which had made them victims.

There were heartening moments. Sunken cheeks lifted and a ten or fifty pence coin dropped into their hollow collecting box. But everywhere was an acceptance that the battle was lost.

'Poor devils,' an old lady said, searching a purse that showed its rib case through tattered imitation leather. And from a prematurely aged man, 'I'll not see 'em starve.' He had a blanket round his shoulders, one dim bulb shone in a room as cold as the night, kids huddled round an electric fire: 'Look, there's no need...' Lindy's voice trailed off. 'I said, I'll not see them starve. I wish it were more.' He thanked them, for calling.

As they walked through the small beaten-earth front garden Lindy took Simon's gloved hand and squeezed it. Three nights in slanting rain raised less than ten pounds.

'We are talking cultural schizophrenia,' he said, and Lindy, staring through the bedroom window at the bleak, misty valley, nodded in silent agreement.

'If you analyse what's in the media, you find we live in several different realities.' He screwed the tabloid into a ball and hurled it at the television. 'Most of them based on cynical manipulation of fantasy, half-truths and lies.'

Lindy walked across the room, picked up the newspaper and

dropped it in the waste bin.

'It's still us and them,' she said. 'And they have greater unity. At benefits and demos we have solidarity, but it's an illusion. We are part of a huge, international rejection of the Right, but the Right have a mass of unthinking, lobotomized followers. I can't see the point of door collections anymore. It's too depressing, too dispiriting...'

He stood behind her and took her in his arms, pressing his chin onto her shoulder, his cheek into her hair.

Danny was the first to go down with flu. It hit him like a truncheon. He woke early, in a sweat. By lunch time he was prostrate, sodden and suffering pain in his joints. After three days he began to recover. It hit Simon as Danny took his first shaky steps outside the house. The pain was shattering. He took a savage analgesic on the second day and spent his time spread-eagled on the mattress, observing the pain move about his body like a quizzical hornet, hovering, settling, stinging.

'It's as if someone puts a spade into your knee and tries to break the joint, then it shoots up into your spine and has another go... Fascinating really.' He looked white and sickly.

On the third day he shook himself into life and went on the weekly picket. Back in bed four hours later he slept fitfully, experiencing disturbing dreams that slid from his grasp whenever he approached consciousness. It was like sinking into a domestic horror film which ran forever. Each descent into dream found him back in Crouch End experiencing intense fear and a sense of transcendental wretchedness.

After resigning from O.A.R. the impetus of Jenny's cryptic messages petered out. For three months he lived in a daze, lethargy oozed from the sheets each time he woke. And as the heaviness entered his body, the queasy horror of his dreams filled him with self-loathing. He defended himself from himself with flimsy, brittle rationalization. Often the system failed, he stayed in bed for days.

The G.P.O. mended his telephone, then disconnected it for non-payment of bills. This suited him, his voice was good for mumbling to himself and little else. Visits to the local shops made him shiver and perspire. His tongue swelled and filled his mouth so that even *Thanks!* was sometimes beyond his verbal capacity. He stank. His bed stank. His clothes stank.

But all this time he, the real Simon, observed himself from the occipital lobe of the left hemisphere of his brain. From this vantage point a timid, pink, wrinkled, foetal Simon watched the other disintegrate. When the dream hit this vestige of identity it writhed and scratched and screamed and fought free. It never unclenched its left fist, and it never investigated the minute silver object held there – this certainty was the *rightness* of his being during the night with Lindy. A talisman. Often, after the dream, his vestigial identity was left exhausted and sobbing, but it came through, then bided its time. It avoided thought, avoided memories of adult life. It survived.

Finally it grew, gained enough strength to plan its own coup, then struck. The battle lasted for three spectacular weeks; saunas, cold showers, daily swims and runs in the park. It was only then, after he had cleaned everything around him that he began to think and make plans for life.

He took most of his possessions to the local Oxfam shop and from there and elsewhere bought himself a survival kit of clothes, camera, and a quality ball-point pen. He strapped the pen with an elastic band to the notebook Jenny had given him. He bought paperback Hesse, Goldman's *Living my Life* and, for good measure, the works of Castaneda. Then he bought a minivan, settled his bills, left the flat and drove to Nottingham. To settle his account with Nigel, to clear the path ahead.

Now he tried to dispel the memories. The pain of them mingled with the pain in his elbows, knees, ankles, spine.

'It's like being eaten by maggots,' he told Lindy. Feeling better, but still with intermittent pain in his joints.

'Don't be so dramatic,' she said, 'Listen.' She'd just caught the tv news, film from the peace camp at Molesworth, set up to discourage the establishment of yet another United States Air Force base in Britain. Heseltine had staged his pantomime. A military operation to see off a handful of nuns, Quakers and Anarchists. The troops moved in at dawn. First they demolished the Peace Chapel, then trashed the benders and tents. Soon there would be an impregnable razor wire topped fence, to defend the base from those it was said to defend. Heseltine was in attendance, flouncing flak jacket and netting scarf, smiling for the cameras. A latter day war lord. Loving every bit of it. Trying to match the image of Thatcher in a tank, desert wind rippling her scarf and the Union Jack. Loving every bit of it. He was obviously hearing patriotic music. Seeing press pictures. Images on tv. Loving every bit of it. Thinking he'd got one over on Thatcher. Loving every bit of it. Neither he nor she knowing that their emotions were stunted, their vision limited. Loving every bit of it. Not knowing they were stoking fires of idealism. Just loving every bit of it. Regardless of cost. Just lapping up the tawdry glory. Regardless of rational thought or morality. Just loving every bit of it.

Thus spake Simon and Lindy.

'You have to laugh,' she added.

'Through our tears,' he said, using his Dylan voice to reduce the chance of a decline from anger and humour into despair.

They had signed a document stating their intention to stop the fencing of Molesworth. Campaigners from different regions of the country would blockade the base on specified days of the week.

Yorkshire was Friday. The mini was now a wreck, but someone lent them a modern saloon which could cruise at seventy and had a working heater. 'Luxury,' Lindy said. 'Bloody luxury, thank god for the heater eh? Anyway, two paracetamols and I feel great.' They bowled down the A1. The snowfall thickened.

As they approached the base it felt like the opening sequence of One Day in the Life of Ivan Denisovich. Deep snow, miles of linked fence, watch towers at regular intervals. They finally found a way to get within a hundred yards of the fence and stopped the car. The M.O.D. police could be seen in the nearest tower, peering through field glasses. Then two Range Rovers came racing round the road on the inside of the fence and police officers got out, clustered to the fence and stared at them.

'Christ, they think we're going in. Up over the fence and through all that sodding razor wire.' Simon waved at the police who huddled together in conference then spread out along the fence. Lindy took a couple of pictures with the zoom.

'I'll pretend to take lots,' she said and did so.

'Smile, their taking us. Wave.' Simon was inspecting the watch tower through his own binoculars. 'I'll do the walkie-talkie stunt,' he added.

They had made plans during the drive. Simon turned about and took out of his bag an old transistor radio. He was careful to let the watchers see it, before speaking into it, waving his arm a little point to at the camp and then to a clump of trees a few hundred yards away. Lindy grabbed his arm, pointed to the trees, waved furiously. She then took out a torch and flashed it in parallel to the fence in an approximation to Morse code. By now another two Range Rovers had arrived and another was bouncing over rough ground towards the copse.

They drove off, intending to move onto what they had named 'Taking the Piss: Plan B.' But as they regained the road, a Saab plastered with peace stickers drove slowly by, its occupants waving. They waved back and swung in behind the Saab. At one point they paused to leave a message under a stone which showed through the snow. (A part of Plan B, it said, *No man is an Island*... Did anyone ever read it?).

The Saab found a lane that ran right up to the fence and they followed. As they introductions were made and stories exchanged stories, a military helicopter buzzed them. Swooping ever lower, until they could have jumped up and touched its skids. They waved, took photographs and the stood against the fence so that the helicopter couldn't threaten them without risking entanglement in coils of razor wire and the rapidly enlarging cluster of police suffered the same racket and down-draft.

The other campaigners moved on, Simon and Lindy waved them on their way, then waved to the police, did another circuit of the base, waited for the inevitable cluster of uniforms, waved again and began the journey north.

That night they agreed it had been a fun day. They told each other it was a way forward. But would it accomplish anything?

'And how long?' Lindy said, 'How long can we go on like this?'

'Jesus,' he said. 'Bloody Jesus. I've seen the future and it's crying.'

XXIX

Let's leave it there shall we? Let's leave it there. Come clean. You know what happened to the strike. The ground beneath my feet is claggy. Everything is up for grabs. You know that Simon and Lindy find each other. Form a partnership.

It's a prolonged, turbulent transition I'm going through. To understand the meaning of '84-'85 I need to understand the meanings of this morning in March 1989 and the days and nights that have brought me here.

It's a messy business.

Back before the strike I searched for an anarchic universal love and acceptance of the world. Back in '83 Ros and I had been together a couple of years, we bear some resemblance to Lindy and Simon, but they are not us. When Michael Foot was elected to leadership of the Labour Party we signed up, time to grow up, to become participants in the party political struggle. That's how we stumbled into the trap of party politics, parts of me are still caught in it. It's all so logical. Don't criticize the party from outside, get in and work within its democratic structure. Dark forces of reaction run through our culture. Party membership is no indication of fairness, decency, lack of prejudice, openness to progressive values, respect for democracy. The membership card weighs heavy. Ideals crumble, strange alliances form, good humour dissipates; the *language* of politics takes over.

The political arena leaves one no alternative, one must either be a dunce or a rogue...

Enough....

Kids in Thorner, the small West Riding village where I was born and lived for eighteen years, treasured the village detritus. We searched the old rubbish tip, the *Skitty,* for useful items.

I'm working round to snow.

Sledges we had, but all too often snowfall was brief. The ground never hardened and our sledge runners cut through to mud. At times like this we used discarded enamel basins and sheets of corrugated iron (today, in these parts, kids use polythene sacks and plastic carrier bags).

From the track that leads into the Cricket Field to a bog by the beck it's a dizzying fifty yard spin through mud and slush, wet bum and shiny wellies crushed into the butter-yellow basin with its rusting holes and chipped edges. If you hit a mole hill you tumble and roll. But a clear run is breathtaking. Legs tremble as you stand in the squelching bog, lift your basin and begin the short steep climb.

That's how it is for many of us now, in Thatcher's Enterprise Society. How quickly the things we thought were stable advances melt like snow. So many mole hills to tumble families into the mire.

In the early days we didn't think she was serious. We didn't recognize that 'return to Victorian values' for what it really was. I'm in the basin, spinning and lurching, trying to find stability from which to assess my culture, myself. And as we become muddy, bruised, disoriented, the spivs and thugs who herald the old gang's return take back everything that's been won. Equality and decency are trampled.

No need to spell it out: massive cuts in tax, cuts in benefits, poll tax, privatization of this that and the other, religious and political imperialism in the schools, Clause 29... Cardboard city. Vagrancy. Destitution. Build more prisons! Build more prisons! Close the caring institutions (that we criticized, calling for community care, humane understanding)... and build more prisons. Each year the noose comes a little closer.

Wealth is the carrot, fear the stick. In their hundreds of thousands our people turn about, like fields of iron filings when someone swings the magnet. The culture is rich in born-again capitalists, proud of their quick profits on knock-down gas and telephones. Pigs in straw. Is there no pinpoint of anxiety in each of them, a tiny, well-sealed box which contains an exact, shining model of the butcher's knife?

Socialism has its inbuilt contradictions, but where else can we establish the values of progressive ideals: humanitarianism, individual dignity, creativity.

The good ship Enterprise has turned about and heads back to individual greed, leaving a wake of poverty and vulgarity, the unloved and the unloving.

In December 1984 Leeds District Labour Party called for members to attend support pickets at the five pits in our area. We met in a pub car park to the East of Leeds. It was the early dark hours, no-one seemed to know where we were going. No-one knew what would happen. A convoy headed off, a stream of cars and vans and Transits full of Leeds lefties swaddled in overcoats and scarves, gloves and hats.

The police stopped us at a roundabout. We left our vehicles and walked a side road to the pit, Ledston Luck. I know it from childhood when, Saturday afternoons, having delivered the village meat on my bicycle, shopping bags swinging from the handlebars, Uncle Pete leaned on me to sit beside him as he drove his death-trap to Swillington, Garforth and Luck.

A short road with stone terrace either side, half a dozen management *villas* at one end, the pit at the other. That was my introduction to miners. They lived in a company village and frightened me with their physicality and tight community spirit.

How many were we, walking in the dark, close to the leafless thorn hedge, talking quietly? Two hundred? Four hundred? We saw light, a floodlight, then the pit.

Here's Paul using words I heard some time later:

'I'll probably spend rest of my life saying *The thing about strike were...* It was a time of deep emotions. At times you felt like a kid because so much were stripped away. You got new ways of seeing things.

'I was talking to Gary the morning they came from Leeds. I won't say we were in poor spirits. But it'd be a fool who couldn't see that things had taken a turn for the worse. Christmas were near and we hadn't two ha'pennies to rub together. No flood back, but the communities were splitting. Good men you'd stood square with for months were off back. We started day with bitterness in our throats. That morning we'd already had some lads and women from other pits come. Cops had been buggering about more than normal. They were in us pit!

'Another thing I'll end my days saying: I'll never forget... I'll never forget the noise them from Leeds made. It was first time I'd heard ought like it: a few hundred folk walking down the road, whispering in the dark. It sounded like... like wind in beech trees. Then we saw them as they came into floodlights, more and more of them. We'd never expected this many. A crowd. We got a crowd of supporters and suddenly you felt the strength of your movement again. You felt the rightness of what we were doing.

And we knew that come what may... one way or another, we'd win.

'I still believe that... I still know that. It's years ago and it's yesterday and it's still all boiling in me. Pits are going down like nine pins, but what we stood for then was right, and it's still right. One day, no matter what happens between, we'll win.

'When I get pessimistic I remember things that make my heart swell. Hearing them voices and shuffling feet in the dark made my heart swell. It still does.'

In the pit lights we saw the Leeds Left in force, people we recognized from peace marches and demos over the years. And more...

A steward stood on the low brick wall by the gate. He told us what to expect, how we could, if we liked, give the buses *a bit of verbal*. He spoke of the push between pickets and cops. He offended lefty sensibilities by asking for care because there were women in the crowd.

The buses came and went, the push took place, verbals were given. I for one couldn't shout Scab! Who was I to abuse those who buckled after prolonged suffering?

The mucky buses, engines screaming in low gear, police Land Rovers before and aft, hurtled through the gates. Some of the picket moved back up the road to chant the names of those seen entering the bath-house.

Ros was using flash with the Rollei compact. She temporarily blinded a few. Nobody objected. We have a picture from that morning, myself and my son's friend, John, a local journalist/musician; flat caps, scarves, raincoats, behind us the pit with its name in ghostly letters: LEDSTON LUCK.

That was our first visit to the pits. We had collected, organized benefits, performed, marched, but we kept away from the picket lines. Many hadn't, I speak only for Ros and myself. On that first visit we held back like shy strangers at a party. But the miners tracked you down and talked. They said, over and over again: Thanks for coming, our kid. Thanks for coming.

Some of us were hurrying off to schools and offices, factories and building sites. Ros and I came back home, breakfasted, began the lengthy assessment of what had happened, exchanged feelings, thoughts, snatches of overheard conversation; made plans.

After that first picket we made weekly visits to the pits. We became confident of a warm welcome, a place round the fire, a joke, the exchange of news and views. We never went empty handed. We never left without a feeling of gain.

We were amongst those in our branch who pushed for donations to the N.U.M., for benefits, for collections of food, clothing, money. With our neighbours, Pat and Alan, we turned our cul-de-sac into the location for an August street party. The contributors to the characters Paul and David (of the 'Burn McGregor' T-shirt) drove off with a hundred pounds and a car load of food, clothes, bedding. Paul, let us say, (in fact Ken Capstick in this case, later to be President of the NUM) swaying gently in the glow of a wood fire and fairy lights, stood on a stool and made a speech. I remember wondering if these stone walls had echoed to such a speech before. The passion, the good humour, the spirit of it all. Across the waste-land lights came on, people came to doors and windows, no-one called the cops. It was the little stuff of history.

Every other week we signed on, every week our debts grew. It didn't matter. If only we'd done more, if only more had done what we did. If only the TUC… if only the Labour leadership... if only…

Most of the characters are amalgams. But not Mary. One morning I stared into the green screen of my new Amstrad, settled Lindy by the camp fire, drifted into space and up walked Mary, bold as brass.

I take no responsibility for her. She is her own being: the spirit of something. At times it felt as if she would really mess things up, that Simon would fall in love with her – that's why I engineered the hint of a relationship with Gozzer. Truth is, I suppose, *I* was feeling the first movements of love for big Mary with her knobbly features and patina of dirt.

Say this of Mary: she is one of the joys of writing, the independent character who swans along, glances over your shoulder and veers off or takes up residence.

'Away! I'll tell you one thing for nothing, he's an arrogant bastard. I mean, it's people's lives he's playing with you know. Thinks he's B. S. Johnson, Ryszard Kapuscinski and Fyodor

Mikhailovich Dostoyevsky rolled into one. Anyway, you've got to work with what you've got and I've got his nibs, so there you are.

'I'll say this. He was going on about something between me and Simon and having to put the kybosh on it and '– that's why I engineered the hint of a relationship with Gozzer,' He couldn't be wronger, man. I mean, I like Gozzer, who wouldn't, but you don't catch me in the same trap twice.

'Another thing, him and Lindy, or Ros, if you want, as he keeps saying now, smart arse, they didn't have to go getting mixed up in the Labour Party. And then they get so cock-a-hoop about it. I could have told them. It's not a revolutionary party, it's not a progressive party, it's not a democratic party... it's a bloody funeral party.

'Look what it's done to that nice Mr Kinnock in next to no time – given him a head like a skull with reptile's eyes. That's what power does for you. It's S. H. I. T. E. don't care who's got it, where from, how. Give anybody the impression they have the right to lead, the right to tell others what to do, and you've got a bag of shite. Look at married couples for a start. Nine times out of ten there's a dominant one, and nine times out of that ten it's a chap. Nine times out of that ten he's a bag of shite.

'Mind you, it's no use blaming them. No use blaming Thatcher. No use blaming Reagan. No use blaming Heseltine, Kinnock, scabs, pigs. No use blaming Peter Sutcliffe or the bastards who run porn shops, sweatshops, sex shops. No use blaming the teacher who looked down your uniform blouse and touched you up. No use blaming any of them, you might just as well blame the poor buggers who've got leukaemia or diabetes.

'Power's a disease, man, pure and simple. I mean, I look forward to the day when you can get treatment for power like you can for bad eyesight. When decency rules ok. It'll be a long time coming, I know that, but it'll come. At least he knows it as well. It'll come. He saw it in people's eyes in the strike. He knows it's there, waiting to be released. But, by god, we must look after love for a good few years to come.

'And another thing, getting back to his book, he can't sort out how to get Simon and Lindy together. Loading that Simon with anarchic quotes and French mustard! If you believe that you'll believe anything. I'm not saying it's not true mind, I'm just saying it's a bit hard to swallow, like his French Mustard.

225

Anyway, his problem is he doesn't know how they got together. He's making it up, do you see?

'Me, I know how they got together! I shared a bender with Lindy and it's long nights when there's snow about and some bugger might be outside with a petrol can. We laughed and we cried and we drank out of the same mucky cup. I slept with her and we kept each other warm through cuddling. A good cuddle warms you up, outside and in.

'Anyway, as I say, I know how Lindy and Simon met because Lindy told us. He doesn't even know where Lindy comes from. He tried to make her background up one time, but cut it out as soon as he'd written it. He did a lot of cutting out. He cut a bit about me out once, I was bloody fuming, man. He put it back in. Anyway, he reckoned Lindy came from a mining family, that her sister was married to a copper... Shite! I mean, how corny can you get. Her dad was a grocer in Grantham...

'Away, I'm only kidding you. I'll tell you about Lindy, what I know, but I know sweet F.A. about Ros.

'Lindy never went to university and she never did postgraduate studies, (that's another bit he's taken out!). I'm not saying he got her wrong, I mean he's got her on paper well enough, just got a few facts wrong.

'Her dad was a flight sergeant in the R.A.F. so she spent her first few years dragged from one camp to another. Then she went to a private boarding school, but that didn't last. She was getting rough times because she was common. Her mam found out. The other kids had mams and dads in I.C.I and British Cable and Wireless and a lot in the forces, but Lindy and her sister were the only ones with an N.C.O. for a dad.

'Now the sister's story is bizarre, that's all I'll say. I think it's one of those things Lindy still has to come to terms with. I mean, to understand Lindy, like anybody else, you need to know what's inside her that she can't cope with... and that's her Lucinda.

'Anyhow, she's a bright girl and she got a place in a grammar school even though she'd been from pillar to post. Her mam gave up the married quarters and I suppose they had a bit of settled life for a while. But it were not enough. You can't drag a couple of kids through a dozen homes in a dozen years then expect them to settle. Poor buggers didn't really know if they were coming or going. As soon as she could, Lindy went. Off the

rails, you might say.

'Her dad got his papers in one of the big military cuts and he took a hardware shop in the Dales. He had ulcers by then and she says she can't remember him smiling from one year end to the next. On top of that he wanted boys, wouldn't you bloody know. So one minute he's telling her she's his little Lindy and she'll go to university and do all the things he couldn't ever do, next he's telling her to get herself on a short-hand typing course.

'She buggered off, hit the night life in Darlington. I'll say no more. Funny, as a kid she'd seen the Middle East, Malaya, Canada and Germany. Then, when middle class kids were finding themselves in foreign countries, and I was finding myself on a council estate, being knocked about by Little Tommy, Lindy moved through Workington and Wigan and Bangor... Course she ended up in London.

'She's funny about it all though. She was in with an arty crowd, just before they started carrying flowers and wearing kaftans. Me I never noticed for I was keeping the house spotless and making Tommy's tea. Lindy says she spent weeks wearing nothing but a tie-dyed grand-dad shirt and painting black patterns on the Evening Standard. Smashed out of her skull most of the time. Being fucked by all and sundry.

'At one stage she went two years without contacting her mam and dad, and when she did her sister was dead and her dad was down with cancer. So she went home. Then she found middle ground in Nottingham and got herself screwed by Nigel. On and off. That's when she met with Simon, a bit like he says.

Hell's bells, that's put me off my stride! I'm off. I'll be back. Do a bit of tidying for him.'

It's a mystery to me now, the Christmas of '84. I think it might have been the year we had Christmas dinner with Alan and Pat: two vegies, two carnivores and little Joe who was very choosy about what he ate. Joe died early in 1989 after a heart operation – six years old. He had great innocence and joy, Pat and Al weather this tragedy and seek positive expressions of their grief. They are not saints but intelligent, caring people – the stuff of the peace movement, of the Left, of progression.

We took a cardboard carton, covered it with Christmas paper and stuck three words on it: *MINERS... CHILDREN...*

CHRISTMAS. We put the carton outside Grandways, our local supermarket, stood to one side and waited. As ever it was the 'ordinary' who gave: money and groceries.

One Sunday afternoon early in the New Year I went into Leeds Town Hall to deliver a script written at three days' notice, a knockabout assault on the government by Old King Coal. Some of our Councillors formed the cast for a performance that night. When I arrived for a rehearsal the great Victorian pile was empty. I sat at a grand piano, on the stage, where the Leeds Piano Competition takes place. For a few minutes I pretended I could play – simple pleasures! Empty seats, freshly marbled pillars, sanctimonious exhortations to labour in the name of god around the walls.

It was a chaotic evening, some performers never performed. A speaker took his expenses and, by the time he was 'on', two hours later than expected, couldn't make the stairs up to the stage. The Black Diamond Band, a folk group whose leader, John Battle, would become our M.P. and a junior minister, rehearsed all night and never played a note for the audience. At the end of the night a scratch Three Johns/Mekons band played to a handful.

Mine was a stand up comic act: Billy Shakespeare with Emu and his dog Toby, Britain's Leading Miner Writer. Friends laughed!

The night raised over a thousand pounds and, to say there had been no publicity, I guess that wasn't too bad.

A few days later I was a clown in Doug Sandle's Headingley Labour Branch pantomime. An expatriate Polish miner sat beside me as we put on our make-up. 'This good entertainment,' he said, 'not like bloody thing at Town Hall. Damned idiot dress as Shakespeare. Intellectual bloody rubbish.' Perhaps so. Perhaps so. 'It was me,' I said. There was a bubble of hysteria and elation expanding inside me and I couldn't wait to pass on the story. Brian, for that is his name, looked aghast for a moment, white face, pink cheeks, red nose. Me a white faced clown with indigo tear drop and massive drooping red mouth. Then we laughed.

We had three good nights and the audience loved it. During the final-night party Ros and I, drunk, fell into bitter conflict. At three in the morning I stood in the road, snowballing cars and trees and crying freely. It's life.

Need I tell the Christmas stories? Briefly then: a miner dressed as Father Christmas under arrest. A collecting bucket for kids at Christmas, MacGregor walks up, makes as if to throw money in the bucket, then laughs and walks away.

And the oft repeated but delicious snowman story. By the pit gates the pickets make a snowman and plonk a toy police helmet on its head. Good humoured stuff, yes, there was still good humour... Inspector Plod has the humour of a scorpion, tells the lads to remove the helmet, destroy the snowcop. They laugh. Plod becomes angry, issues threats. The lads laugh. Plod loses control, leaps into a nearby police Range Rover and drives into the snowman... which is built round a concrete bollard.

Was it really a police state in those winter months? New laws enacted, medieval laws resuscitated; laws broken by law-makers, civil rights ignored. 'Our press,' the Lefty Press, reported the battles, bloodstained faces on every page. Pictures printed abroad, but not in the UK establishment media. Here's one: night time in a Yorkshire pit village, a young man handcuffed to a lamp post, being truncheoned by two coppers...

February 9th, 1985. A day of action and support. Ros and I get the instructions wrong, meet at the wrong place and find ourselves with another Branch Party. Not knowing which of the five pits our group has gone to, we string along and go to the Prince of Wales on the outskirts of Pontefract.

It's a big pit, much bigger than Ledston Luck where police and pickets press into thorn hedges and grass verges, overgrown and tufted with frost or ice.

Prince of Wales stands back from a main road, by the race track. Police have room to parade. It is dark, the sky just beginning to grey as we arrive. And cold. God it's cold. We are wrapped and wrapped in clothes, I have a heavy fur coat over the lot of it. I've never before shivered in this coat (Got it a jumble sale, I believe it's bear skin – but that's the kind of thing I make up to create an air of security about me).

February 9th then and a sub-zero wind sweeps across Pontefract race course. We stamp our feet, flap our hands. As the sky lightens we see faces take on unnatural shades. Ros's face, it could as well be Lindy, but I am searching non-fictionalized truth. Ros's face then becomes deep purple, others are grey, dark apple red, chalk white.

The police look on, a long black line. Several vans have driven in with dogs. How many were we? Thirty, forty... growing all the time. I walk up the road, hoping to take photographs in the leaden light. I use the Contax without taking off my gloves. I hear a copper say, 'Look at that cunt in't fur coat...' Maybe it wasn't 'Look', maybe it was 'Get'...

Listen, my part in this strike was derisory, pathetic. I did nothing. The few pickets I attended I did so with my head full of silent screaming... always afraid. It was like early days at primary school. We were village kids, five to fourteen. There were days when a brutal madness swept the yard like a savage March wind. Big lads charged round the school. Nowhere to hide. Always someone to veer from his path and deliver a running punch or a slash round bear legs with a nettle or a whippy michaelmas daisy. Gradually, following leaders, the chaos became two groups, hurtling in opposite directions until they finally met head on in a ginnel between a house wall and the lads' lav. The push. And me frightened, knocked about like a twig. The flailing arms and boots, damp corduroy and scabbed knees, the smell of cold sandstone, disinfectant and piss.

When I heard the cops talking about me I hurried to the safety of a bus shelter where the growing picket huddled, seeking protection from the wind that painted exposed skin.

On the pickets I found snippets of memory, squeezed from childhood into my panic. The voices brought my village days back. Carefully pronounced vowels that make bread into a two syllable word. Subtle variations on thee and thou. Childhood all about me: snow on ploughed fields; skeletal trees; crows ragged by flesh-slicing wind; winter smells.

And the faces. Sometimes, as in the bus shelter that morning, someone spoke and I knew the face as well as my own, had always known it, had grown up with it. A hard West Riding face.

He was in his mid-twenties, milky blue face, black hair, black donkey jacket. He clenched and unclenched gloveless fingers, flesh shrunk to the bone and cracked by the cold, I recognized him by his hunched shoulders. My mother would have called him a 'starved rat'. I recognized him by the way he moved his curved body, not walking straight to you, but sidling, looking from the quarter of his eye.

He sidled through my early life then went missing in my teens, I never saw him in London. But he came alongside in 1985. Our exchange would have been commonplace. Obvious that I wasn't a miner. *Where you come from? Thanks for coming. Bloody freezing.*

When I caught up with the exchange he was acting out of character, standing in front of me, looking straight at me.

When I caught up with the exchange he was a hero. An ordinary hero. My Christ, there were so many of them. Ordinary heroes.

And when I caught up with the exchange he was a poet. An ordinary poet. His language given depth by intensity of feelings.

'We not going back. I've lost my house. I've got nothing left. Nowt they can take.' He turned to face the pit, staring beyond the police lines. 'I've seen lads carried out dead. Lads I grew up with. We don't go back till we've won.'

The picket was growing. From the protection of the crush of bodies you saw stooped figures hurried by the wind, pulled towards the pit gates, tears and flotsam and fists of them, black against the mottled snowfields.

Blood has been spilt at these gates, skulls fractured by staves.

Someone shouts, *Yonder!* Thirty or forty men march two abreast, the bin men... joining a day of action. Cheers go up like gulls fighting an icy wind.

More and more are wound into the picket. And the marching bin men, arms folded, arms swinging, arms hugging, arms raised to give the clenched fist salute.

Heroes! Heroes! Ordinary heroes fired by love, decency, solidarity, humanity, courage. Something that burns inside and brightens the eyes in these chilled faces.

What happens to us? Is it just me? Don't we all belong to the same species? I see the police as harsh lines of greed, hate, scarce-concealed self-loathing; thugs smacking leather-gloved fists into open palms. And about me I see the pickets with fire in their eyes.

If only you had seen the dignity of these people. If you had felt the flame of sympathy and recognized the awesome promise of it...

We were ordered and shoved around, then drab green buses caked with mud and salt roared through the pit gates.

There had been blood on the road, but not that day.

We disperse to empty houses or the Welfare. Ros's face was almost black with cold. We dropped into a sunken lane, the wind whipped above us, our faces burning. In the Miners' Welfare she went tomato red. There was back slapping and laughter.

XXX

Back home I ring an N.U.M. steward to check out an activist who spreads unhelpful rumours – the details don't matter. I've known the steward on and off since the seventies. He is another contributor to the fictional Paul. His voice is thick with emotion: it rips through me, gouging a great bloody hole with edges of frayed memory because he sounds like my long dead father. He coughs a lot as he tells me: 'I think we'll be off back next week.'

I sit on the sofa next to Ros and sob uncontrollably for the strike, the country, my wasted life, and a world of injustice and suffering. I weep for my dad who lied about his age and reached France in 1918, in time to be gassed and take a bullet in the arm. He came home with lungs that plagued him for the rest of his life. He died in 1963. Once he told me that he had wanted to be a tap-dancer. So many talents and ambitions trampled by a system that rewards the greedy, inglorious, and unscrupulous.

A few days later I watch the news on TV. Arthur Scargill, tied in a knot of uniformed police, announces the return to work. The chant of 'We're not going back! We're not going back!' is replaced by a howl of anger and pain. The camera finds a face sodden with tears. Ros and I sit transfixed, silent. Even now, as I write, I hear that howl of animal despair. I feel the icy chill of it all about me...

*

'Away, it's me again. Tidying up like I said. Lindy's told us a lot about Simon. Mainly he can be a prat, though I can't see he's as big a prat as she cracked him up to be, some bugger'd have cracked him one. .

'Puts me in a difficult situation really, only I'm not sure what I should tell you and what's sort of confidential, if you know what I mean. And I don't want people just going and thinking I'm his mouthpiece.

'Me, I'm taking a law degree now! Young lecturers make a big fuss of me – I scare them shitless! And I'm seeing Simon and Lindy next week, first time in yonks. They packed up and left. Shook the dust of England from their feet, they said. Anyway, they rent this house in a village near Bordeaux, dirt cheap and about five mile from the sea. I'm dead excited me. Never been

233

abroad before. I'm spending the summer with them. They say they can get me a bit of work - teaching English, Simon said. 'When you've learned it,' Lindy said.

'They've cracked it. I mean, when I was with them they lived on next to nothing. Now they need even less, mild winters and long hot summers!

'Lindy told me this. She says she still doesn't really know if she and Simon met again by chance, after the party. She says Simon's told her often enough, but she doesn't always understand what he means. He was a bit mystical like, or daft. That first meeting with Simon made a big impression on her. It's a bit like he says about Simon when was bleeding: she wanted to put her life in order and live clean. Cut the crap and the compromises. All roads roam to Leeds – an Irishman called Peter told her that one – she says she went there because she'd never been and she heard it had a good music scene. Anyway, a year later, when Simon was snooping round the party, she was up North, working in a health food co-operative. It was big on co-operatives – Leeds.

'That Hilary, the posh one with the liquid refreshment problem, Nigel sent a card to Lindy and told her to tell Simon that Hilary had topped herself. That's a quotation from the card, by the by! 'Tell Sime that raddled Hil has topped herself'.

'He is a shit.

'Seems she were found in that swimming pool you heard about, lot of alcohol in her blood. Then, there would have been, wouldn't there? I asked Lindy if this Nigel'd have acted like Hilary told Simon he'd done. She just said maybe. What do you mean, maybe, I said. And she said, Maybe, I don't know. I don't think about those times much anymore. It's very hazy now. And I don't talk about it, she said.

'Anyway, Simon goes to the party and next morning he asks Nigel where he could find Lindy. Then he took a chair to the bastard's kitchen and messed things up. Then he said something like: "Good. I feel better for that, you fucking heap of dog shit."

'I say 'something like' because, you understand, this is of dubious provenance (I told you: Law Degree!) I mean, Lindy's heard it from both of them and I've heard it from Lindy, now you're hearing it from me. Oh, and I'm a fictitious character made up by a bloke who lives in Leeds 5 with Ros and his dog.

Anyway, Simon told Nigel, I understand, something along these lines, "I'll do a deal. Give me her address and I'll never come to your fucking party and this fucking city again and you just keep out of my fucking life or I'll fucking swing for you."

'It took him a couple of weeks to find her. She was on the look-out for him anyway because Nigel had written and told her all about it.

'Well, they didn't live happily ever after, that's for sure. Stormy times, like. Very stormy. Simon half off his rocker with romantic love, randiness and an identity crisis. Her trying to stick to her new shit-free life and loving him something daft. Nigel ringing and writing and stirring shit. And the pair of them, Simon and Lindy, getting into Scotch and then Natsurin in quite a big way.

They spent some nights roaming Leeds, smashed out of their heads, calling for each other or avoiding each other. The rows... well, when Lindy told me I began to think she might have been better off with my Little Tommy. And they had a few fights.

'Trouble was Simon. By all accounts he was mean-minded. We were sitting round one night talking about things that can blight your life. Simon suddenly says the most painful thing to him was Lindy's constant infidelity. I didn't understand, I mean, as far as I could see they never spent two minutes out of each other's company. And Lindy had never said anything. Anyway, Lindy says nothing and I can't hide my surprise, or my curiosity, I ask when she has time for infidelity. Oh didn't you know, he says, his voice going smarmy and posh and hard at the same time – She was at it all the time before she met me.

'He laughed it off then, but it seems that earlier on he'd taken retrospective jealousy twice round the block and once up his trouser leg. Lindy says that when he fuelled it with Scotch he fell right off his twig. Psychotic, she says. Good job the money ran out and they were onto nettle hock.

'Of course it's no defence in law! I'm doing this university bit for no one but myself, I plan on being a barrister in about six years' time. I'll be in my late forties and with any luck we'll have got shut of the Tories for a bit. But I reckon our lot, the likes of me and Simon and Lindy, if they decide to come back, the likes of Paul and Gaz and Gozzer, the women fighting for equality, the comrades trying to fight corruption in the Party and the unions.

*You know who I mean, I mean the people. The people who get
crapped on from on high. It's not a group, it's a condition, it
breaks out in different degrees of purity: Poland, Hungary, Chile,
Philippines, Orgreave, Greenham, Brixton...*

*'Get back to my point. I reckon being a barrister might be of
some use. That's my way. They went to France. Little house big
garden. That's there way. I don't blame them, I don't criticize
them. I love them. But it's not my way, it's theirs. And it's not one
that's available to everybody... away, to be Candide with you,
when I've done a bit more of my bit, it could be my way.'*

I first met Jean at the Town Hall Benefit. A big woman with
an open, girlish face and short curly hair. I was waiting under the
stage, Emu under one arm and a stuffed dog on wheels at my
heel. Wondering who was getting rapturous applauds.

'Oh, hecky.' She stared at my red fishnet tights. She was in
an electric blue jumpsuit and her face was flushed from the
performance. 'Have you a thing about your legs or summat, love?'
We clicked.

March approached. Economic pressure clamped its fingers
round the miners' throats. We ran more and more benefits,
acutely aware that every hundred quid kept the struggle going,
pushed forward one more day the time when some poor sod's
dignity crumpled and he crossed the line between hero and scab.

Jean and I often performed together, alternating her riveting,
accessible verse with my contributions. Of course the audiences
were wonderful – none better. Later, as the strike settled into the
wake of our lives, we still occasionally performed together, for
progressive causes, or just for pleasure; Jean never fails to bring
the house down. Never fails to make some ribald comment on my
legs.

Auntie Jean, she is, after all, at least a year older than me,
has close ties with Ledston Luck. She has lived all her life within
spitting distance of the old winding gear, seen the new buildings
rise... and now fall. Her ex-husband worked in the pit and so did
her son, Thomas.

It was Jean who said to us, 'When they go back, don't go
with Leeds lot, come with me to Ledston. So it was that while the
Leeds Left as a whole clapped miners back to the beat of a silver
band, Ros and I waited at the buckled blue gates of the Luck with

a handful of families. No band, no crowds, just the quiet country road on a misty March morning.

It was part of our life, the straggled thorn hedges, the trunk of an elm draped in ivy that still looks like a giant dancing bear. On pickets we'd watched men tramp across the fields on paths that had known miners' boots for a hundred years. But now the fields were empty. As nine o'clock approached the twenty-odd of us fell silent.

Then we saw the miners walking from Kippax. It took an age for them to reach the Luck. The clapping began when they were a hundred yards off.

It wasn't a victory, we all knew that. But nor was it a defeat, the miners at this tiny pit returned with heart-swelling dignity. For a moment there were tears, then confusion and laughter.

The pit gates were chained and pad-locked. After a year of bullying, blackmailing and bribing these men to re-enter the pit, they were denied entry. It was never reported in the national media (although I rang several news editors). It was just a little incident at a pit which is now no more.

The miners re-lit the picket fire, then, banner first, broke through the hedge at the side of the gate and re-formed outside the offices. It was a brief, symbolic occupation. They came out again, having made their point.

The pit manager came to the gates, to explain that he would decide when and who could come back. I watched a tall, thin lad, dressed in worn denim. He put his foot on a chair by the fire, rested his elbow on his knee, his chin on this elbow, grinned into the manager's face and said: 'I don't mind, Mr Jagger. I don't want to come back, me.' I never spoke to him, I don't know who he was, but he became Gozzer.

All over the country miners marched back. At some pits sacked miners picketed and the marching men, voices raised in song, turned about – You don't cross picket lines! It was a day of relief, pride, anger, and intense sadness.

At an airport on the other side of the globe a playwright slumps, jetlagged, on the spongey bench. The abrasive prattle of a newscast comes from the screen above his head, it is interrupted by the sound of a brass band and Welsh voices singing 'Here, we go!' He looks up and sees images of the march back to work. He cries. No one takes much notice.

The Government doesn't gloat in public. Too many people have been moved by those final images of the strike. Sophisticated advisers have whispered in the ears of the powerful.

In the pits there is tension, depression, endless victimization.

One by one the pits are closed. Pit villages are sold to the highest bidder. Families and communities are destroyed.

A year later, at the annual miners' gala, I watch a fight. A man with a squashed beer can in his hand steps up to another. Knocks him to the ground. Repeatedly, savagely, smashes the can into the younger man's face. People are trying to pull the aggressor away, he kicks and punches at them, as if he has a dozen limbs. Then he is up and away. I watch him run. He is joined by a tall, wide-shouldered man in smart casual jacket and white shirt. Open mouthed, this older man kisses the fighter on the lips. The fighter draws a magical power from the kiss. They walk from each other, sealed from the press of the crowd by some invisible barrier. I remember the punks at Grosvenor Square who drifted through the melee.

There is so much in life we do not understand...

Leeds Weekly Citizen 19th April 1986.
ERIC LYTHE. SOCIALIST. DIED 13th APRIL 1986.
Eric Lythe was a lifelong socialist, an idiosyncratic
humanitarian, and a vigorous peace campaigner. Eric the Red
we called him, because he had the energy and ideals of a young
socialist, the experience and wisdom of an old one.

Almost as old as the century, he'd seen it all, including D
Day: he was a sergeant in the Military Police, attached to a
Canadian regiment ('Oh, you should have seen them,' he told us.
'They were swigging rum by the bottle and grinding knives. Well,
I didn't get any sleep on that boat – all them big fellers getting
drunk and grinding their knives!') He was a smashing story-teller
and relished an appreciative audience. Who else went to
Normandy with the latest Stanley Gibbons catalogue in his
haversack?

Although we were in the same Branch Labour Party, it was
in the peace movement that we saw Eric at his most politically
active. He was a founder member of Kirkstall C.N.D. and a fine
comrade when it came to marches and demonstrations.

The only time he let his sergeant stripes show was when he
came face to face with the police, even then it was his waspish
humour that was most devastating. Catch sight of a slovenly
copper and Eric was off: 'Eh! Is this the best you can find to do?
Hanging round street corners, and just look at the state of your
shoes.'

And, to an Inspector, this, at the big C.N.D. demo in
Barrow: 'Don't you come smiling and nodding over here. You're
just one of Mrs Thatcher's bully boys and you're not wanted.
Clear off!' It always worked, and Eric, absolutely delighted with
himself, would chuckle it all over again and – 'Did you see his
face? I told that one. They've got to be told though, you see.
That's the thing.'

It was on that demo that Eric, always elegantly dressed (he'd
trained as a tailor and still made many of his own clothes) was
described as being in 'punk attire' by the local paper – he was as
pleased as Punch. We, that is the members of Kirkstall C.N.D.,
instead of having a well ordered die-in, on a roped off section of
road, dashed into traffic and caused five minutes' chaos. Blame

Eric the Red: 'I'm not doing it here. It's damned silly. Come on, we'll get in front of that lot.' And off he went, clutching his shopping bag. There was no time to argue, until the traffic was stopped. Then the argument was Eric vs police and C.N.D. Stewards: 'Oh get off, don't be so daft. I've only just got comfy, you see.'

But he was never really comfy; apart from national and local politics he poured his apparently endless energy into reading, painting, gardening, stamp collecting, tailoring, music (he played violin, flute, mandolin), and, in earlier days, cycling. And yet for all this, and the jumping cracker fizz and bang of his conversation, you could sense a deep sadness. And sometimes it came out, peeped out like a mouse: 'They don't care, you see. People don't care enough.' Then his face would crack into a laugh, and off he'd go on another flight of fact, fantasy or analysis.

During the last months of his life he was troubled by sickness, became reclusive. 'Oh, yes' he agreed, the Tuesday before he died, 'I'll come out with the snowdrops and daffodils!'

He knew all the words to the International when he was eleven and he still knew them seventy years later.

So long, Eric the Red. May you rest in the peace you fought and worked for.

* * *

The sun rolled round and the day rolled on. A day of argument, laughter and easy companionship. Dave took the trilby from Sarah and said: "It don't matter what happens. We've already won this strike. This'll always be our victory, you know what I mean?" And they did...

The End

Lightning Source UK Ltd
Milton Keynes UK
UKOW01f1216160916

283153UK00002B/44/P